MARRIED WITH CHILDREN

Other people look forward to Sunday mornings. Once upon a time, I was the same. On Sunday mornings I would wake up around ten, make percolated (not instant) coffee, take a long, hot shower, then wander down to a café on Oxford Street for brunch—eggs, French toast and banana pancakes— which I would eat while leafing through the newspapers.

This morning, I got up at 5:45 A.M. Why? Because Jonah's an early riser and can't be allowed to roam about unsupervised, even in a house where every power point has a protective plug in it, and every cutlery drawer is fitted with a childproof latch.

As for Emily, she can't go anywhere without her bag. It's a blue plush monkey with a zippered hole in its gut, and she always stuffs it so full of hairclips, doll's clothes, markers, novelty key rings, old Christmas cards and plastic farm animals that it looks permanently pregnant. She has this idea that you can't go anywhere unless you're laden with junk.

But I really don't have a right to complain, considering the baggage *I* always carry around. When you travel with two young children, you can't afford to overlook *any eventuality*. If you forget the water, they'll want a drink. If you pack a sandwich, they'll want an apple. And if you don't include a change of clothes, you're laying yourself open to all kinds of disasters: toilet-training accidents, carsickness, milkshake spillages.

That's why I can't trust Matt to handle any preparations for a family outing. That's why some trips are hardly worth the hassle. And that's why my social life always leaves me so exhausted. Preparing for a picnic is like preparing for a three-day hike . . .

BOOK YOUR PLACE ON OUR WEBSITE AND MAKE THE READING CONNECTION!

We've created a customized website just for our very special readers, where you can get the inside scoop on everything that's going on with Zebra, Pinnacle and Kensington books.

When you come online, you'll have the exciting opportunity to:

- View covers of upcoming books
- Read sample chapters
- Learn about our future publishing schedule (listed by publication month *and author*)
- Find out when your favorite authors will be visiting a city near you
- Search for and order backlist books from our online catalog
- Check out author bios and background information
- Send e-mail to your favorite authors
- Meet the Kensington staff online
- Join us in weekly chats with authors, readers and other guests
- Get writing guidelines
- AND MUCH MORE!

**Visit our website at
http://www.kensingtonbooks.com**

Spinning Around

CATHERINE JINKS

KENSINGTON BOOKS
KENSINGTON PUBLISHING CORP.
http://www.kensingtonbooks.com

KENSINGTON BOOKS are published by

Kensington Publishing Corp.
850 Third Avenue
New York, NY 10022

All Kensington titles, imprints and distributed lines are available at special quantity discounts for bulk purchases for sales promotion, premiums, fund-raising, educational or institutional use.

Special book excerpts or customized printings can also be created to fit specific needs. For details, write or phone the office of the Kensington Special Sales Manager: Kensington Publishing Corp., 850 Third Avenue, New York, NY 10022. Attn. Special Sales Department. Phone: 1-800-221-2647.

Kensington and the K logo Reg. U.S. Pat. & TM Off.

First Kensington Trade Paperback Printing: April 2005
First Mass Market Paperback Printing: October 2006
10 9 8 7 6 5 4 3 2 1

Printed in the United States of America

To Meredith Osborne

Acknowledgments

The author would like to thank Trish Graham, Andrew Hellen, and Phillip Jinks for their help.

Chapter One

Friday

How did I ever get into this mess?

Look at me. Just look at me. I'm a walking disaster area. Check out the hands, for a start—you get hands like this when you have babies. They're in water all day long, what with the nappies and the spills and the bottles that have to be disinfected, so they crack up like dried-out creek beds. Happens practically overnight. With the result that I'm a thirty-eight-year-old law graduate with the hands of a fifty-year-old hop-picker. A fifty-year-old blind hop-picker. Count the Band-Aids. This one's so old, I can't remember why I put it on. I know why I haven't changed it—no time—but I can't remember why it's there. Number two is there because I'm ecologically responsible. I was washing the lid off a tin of stewed pears, in preparation for recycling, and gave myself the kind of gash you'd only reasonably expect to pick up after scaling a barbed-wire fence. (No more civic duty for yours truly. They can wash their own bloody tins.) Number three was Emily's fault: she dropped a glass. I picked up the pieces, put them in the kitchen tidy, forgot about them, and when I was trying to compress the rubbish by giving it a shove, so that I could insert just one more eggshell into it—*yeow!* Of course, it's my fault that our garbage bins are always overflowing. I never seem to have time to empty them.

Number four is a particularly bad crack; it got infected. Number five is a fingernail repair. Half my fingernail was ripped off because I always let them grow too long (no time to cut them), and they get nicks in them, and then the nicks get snagged on woollen jumpers, and the nails get torn way down into the fleshy bits, and there's nothing much you can do about that except wrap a Band-Aid around the damage and wait for the nail to sort itself out. Either it grows or it sheds. Whatever it does, however, you know that the Band-Aid is going to be there for a good, long time. Weeks, usually. I've forgotten what my hands look like without Band-Aids on them. Just as I've forgotten what my clothes look like without stains on them.

This top, for instance. This top dates from my breastfeeding period. You can tell because it buttons down the front, and because it's covered in faint, yellowish marks that are either baby puke or breast milk. (They're the same thing, really.) If I'd tackled those stains early enough, I might have got rid of them with a paste made of powdered laundry detergent, but of course I wasn't up to it, in those days. I was so sleep-deprived that soaking clothes in a bucket of NapiSan was about as far as I could extend myself. Anyway, what would have been the point? Because this stain here is much more recent (chocolate biscuit fingerprints) and this one is too. Don't ask me what it is. A mystery stain. What's watery and greenish and ends up on your shoulder? I don't think I want to know.

Stains on the top. Stains on the shoes. Stains on the skirt, which has an elasticised waistband. Yes—an elasticised waistband. That's how low I've sunk. Or rather, that's how big I've got. I used to be size ten, before I had Emily. I used to wear natural fibers, and iron all my clothes, and shun things like track-pants and elasticised waistbands. I also used to wash my hair more than once a week. How the mighty have fallen!

You may wonder what stops me from washing my hair. Well, nothing really—except the fact that every time I step into the shower, despite all my attempts to bribe and distract, the kids start scream-ing in the kitchen. And I can't shower when they're asleep, because of the noise made by the plumb-ing. It's extraordinary, like the engine room of the *Titanic;* I don't know what it is about the pipes in this place. It's as if they're haunted. I've heard them grumbling and wheezing away at two o'clock in the morning. They're yet another aspect of this house that needs a complete overhaul.

But don't get me started on the house. If you want to talk about mess, here it is—mess central. Just cast your eyes over my domicile, will you? Note the layer of dust from the renovations, and the matching pile of builder's rubble outside the win-dow. Note the sticky patches on the kitchen floor, the fingermarks at knee level, the biscuit crumbs, the cockroach traps, the soggy fragment of chewed Crispbread on top of the video player, the doll's house furniture and plush animals and frayed silk scarves and capless marking pens and bits of ribbon and Tonka trucks and broken Fisher-Price activity centers scattered all over every available surface. Note the big, nasty stain on the couch (blackcurrant juice), and the scribble on the wall. That was Jonah. I used to nag Emily about leaving the caps off her colored markers, but I'm wiser now. After all, Jonah can't do much harm with a dried-out marker, can he?

Last, but not least, take a squint at the refrigerator. I ought to get a biological hazard sign. The inside certainly wouldn't pass a health inspection; you can't pull the crisper drawer out because some kind of sticky brown paste has welded it to the white plastic surface beneath it. As for the outside, it's almost as bad as the inside, though in a different way. All those unsightly, reddish bills stuck up there, glowering at me. The letter from my cousin in England that's six months old and that I still haven't answered. The laughable builder's quotes. The reminder about the day care fete which utterly slipped my mind. The takeaway menus that are never used, these days, because we don't have the money to splurge on Thai food. The back-care health leaflet. (Don't ask.) The Tresillian Parents' Help Line number. The invitation to my twenty-year high school reunion.

I remember the ten-year reunion. At least, I remember *me* at the ten-year reunion. I had twenty thousand dollars in the bank, a great figure, a trendy haircut, an impressive and secure job, fantastic clothes and a phenomenally sexy boyfriend.

Now I'm overweight, in debt, dowdy and unshaven. My hair looks awful. I've got minced hands, a part-time job that I can't enjoy because I feel too guilty about it, and a husband who seems to be cheating on me.

So I repeat: how did I ever get into this mess?

It was Miriam who broke the news, needless to say. Miriam Coutts. She's Senior Manager of the Investigations unit at the Pacific Commercial Bank, and she's always had a nose for suspicious behavior. That's why she does what she does. She started off as a branch teller, but was so successful at stopping frauds over the counter that the bank moved her to its Investigations unit, and had her chasing down credit card scams at the age of twenty-three. That was when I first met her. Since then she's taken over the unit, but she hasn't really changed much. She was always old at heart. Even when we were sharing a shabby terrace house in Paddington, and living on practically nothing, she had a managerial look about her. Very neat. Very organized. A routine for everything, and a file for everything else. That makes her sound deadly, I know, but she isn't. She has a very dry, very sharp sense of humor, and some interesting eccentricities: an addiction to Space Food Sticks, a taste for watching stock-car races, a collection of antique medicine bottles. She's also one of those people who don't age very much, for some reason—perhaps because she has olive skin and a "thin" gene. Even her hair is the same as it always was, shiny and dark and cut in a pageboy style. Only the labels on her clothes are different.

She turned up this evening in a Carla Zampatti suit. She also wore shoes that matched her handbag, which was a kind of sage green. I remember when I used to wear sage-green shoes with my sage-green handbag. Or taupe shoes with my taupe handbag. Back in the Good Old Days, when Matthew admired me for my stylish wardrobe as well as my pert little bottom. (I seem to have lost both.) The last time I used my suede brush was to scrub dog shit off the soles of Emily's white sandals. I bet Miriam still employs her own suede brush to brush suede, and keeps it in a drawer along with the conditioning oil she still uses on her handbags.

Just listen to me, will you? I sound like such a whiny bitch. What does it matter that my shoes no longer match my handbags? I mean, how trivial is that for a goal in life? I have a beautiful family. I have a well-paid job that's an absolute breeze. I shouldn't be jealous of Miriam; she might be wearing "warm hand wash only" garments these days, but her job's beginning to get her down, I can tell. She never used to complain about brainless senior management, or inadequate security measures. She never used to get irritable at the mere mention of her boss. I'm beginning to wonder if she's hit a glass ceiling—or if she's going to bail out, and try something different. I raised the subject, recently, and she flashed me a humorless smile. It wasn't so much the job, she said, it was the bankers. And where else would someone with her credentials find a job, except among bankers? It was an odd thing for her to say, I thought. It didn't sound like her, because she's never had a problem with bankers in the past. It made me realize how far we've drifted apart lately.

It's sad, when you consider how well we used to get on. We were on the same wavelength, once.

She was from the south coast and I was from the North Shore—she had a mother and not much else, whereas I was well endowed with family, extended family, tertiary qualifications and a network of undemanding friends—but we shared a similar outlook nonetheless. For one thing, we were united against the other girl in our house, who was an airhead named Briony Crago. Miriam and I both saw eye to eye on things like wiping down the stove, paying the rent, and not distributing spare keys as freely and generously as promotional literature. Briony, on the other hand, was a great one for hauling strangers home from the pub, or leaving containers of taramasalata out for the cockroaches. It was hard not to regard her vision of the world as slightly skewed, because she would fuss over potpourri sachets for her underwear drawer while there was a sewage leak out near the clothesline. Miriam and I would laugh and grouse about this in equal measure. We would alert each other about sales at Grace Bros, and admire each other's taste in doona covers, foreign films and gourmet ice-cream. We were a team, in many ways. Comfortably equal. We went out together sometimes, and watched videos together sometimes. I suppose, at that point, she was my best friend. (I don't seem to have one, these days.) Certainly I knew her long before I knew Matthew. She was present on the occasion of my first meeting with Matt. She was also present at my hen's night, my wedding, and my only housewarming party.

Trust her to be on hand for the latest milestone event in my life.

She came this evening, at half past five. She always comes over here, because of the formidable logistics involved in my trying to get out of this place with two kids in tow. Having a good old heart-to-heart in a coffee shop, with Jonah squirming to get under the table and Emily spilling milkshake into your lap, is not really an option. Neither is her townhouse, which is full of so many steep little flights of stairs and challenging balconies that you might just as well drop Jonah on his head and be done with it. At least here we've got *Sesame Street* videos and teddy bear biscuits. At least here I can plunk the kids on a rug in front of the TV, with individual portions of chocolate mousse and the bribe that Miriam has brought with her. She's such a wise, well-organized woman that she always brings a few bribes. Usually it's stuff from a two-dollar shop, like a plastic dinosaur and a set of fake fingernails, or a toy car and a miniature gardening set—something like that. The kids love Miriam. They love it when Miriam visits, though she makes very little attempt to communicate with them. Not that I blame her, mind. She usually sees them when they're covered in mashed potato, and getting cranky after a long day. No one's at their best in such circumstances.

"Look at this," I said, as I gloomily surveyed my offspring stuffing themselves with sugar in front of the tube. "Do you know there's a mother from Jonah's playgroup who has three kids and *no television?* No television. I don't see how it's possible."

"Oh, stop it," said Miriam.

"Not only that, but she's a wholefood mother. Bulk lentils from the co-op. It's so depressing."

"I bet she smells funny," was Miriam's reply.

"No."

"Then the kids are monsters."

"Not at all. Really caring and sharing. Really nice."

"They don't wear shoes, then."

"Yes, they do. Sandals, anyway. Mind you, her husband's a creep."

"Ah."

"I mean, you wonder if the wholefood thing is entirely voluntary. On her part, that is. He's got all these theories about the way she should be washing the dishes—that sort of thing." I had to smile as I remembered. "We only went over there once," I went on, "and he sat talking about passive solar designs and composting toilets while she rushed around feeding everyone. God, he was awful. Hairy. Ginger hair."

I should add that I hadn't gone to Mandy's house with Matt, but with a bunch of playgroup mothers. Because it was the middle of the day, we had all been very surprised to find Ginger at home—a bit freaked out, in fact. Especially since Ginger had hijacked the conversation, asking each of us with a patronizing, toothy smile about our domestic arrangements, and preventing us from settling down to a good moan about our kids and our husbands (one of the unexpected benefits of playgroup). We had been forced to do things like praise the bowel-cleansing powers of pumpkins, and condemn the appalling effects of television, while at the same time admitting—weakly—that we didn't have the strength to cut up whole Queensland blues *or* ban television from our homes. God, it was annoying. Especially since Mandy's kitchen was plastered with examples of her kids' astonishing artistic prowess, and heaped with produce from her vegetable garden.

Yes that's right. On top of everything else, she

grows her own vegetables. I mentioned this to Miriam, who seemed unimpressed.

"Mmm," she mumbled. I glanced at her, then, and realized that this wasn't just going to be a catch-up session. She had something specific to say—something about men. Whenever Miriam needs advice, whenever she loses control a little, it's invariably because of a man. In that respect, I was always slightly ahead of her. Sure, I've made some mistakes, but they were never as bad as Miriam's. I never went out with anyone who stole checks from the back of my checkbook, or whose entire collection of literature had been lifted from public libraries, or who was busy stalking a past girlfriend while he was courting me. Miriam seems to be a magnet for people like that, whose failings aren't always immediately apparent. Oh, she's not stupid; she susses them out pretty fast. But she concedes that there must be some flaw in her genetic makeup which drives her to fall for them in the first place—a kind of "bad boy" gene. She's a bit like me, I suppose. We're both good girls who find bad boys attractive, though my bad boys were never as bad as hers, thank God, perhaps because I could afford to pick and choose a bit. Miriam couldn't, as a rule. There were never many men interested in Miriam, I don't know why. Because she wasn't one to flaunt her belly button, or giggle a lot? Because she could often come across as rather formidable? The unhappy fact is, bad boys are usually lazy, despite their glamour—far too lazy to tackle a challenge like Miriam.

Mind you, things have changed recently. She's been with Giles for eighteen months now, and so far it's been all seaside resorts and bagels for breakfast. That's one reason why I haven't seen much of her over the last year. It's the old story of the New Man not having much time for the Old Friend (especially the Old Friend who can't do brunch anywhere except at McDonald's). Besides, I don't like Giles. I've tried, God knows, because Miriam obviously thinks he's *wonderful*, she can't stop talking about how brilliant and stylish he is, and she's right—he is. He's one of those top-notch money market guys, smart as a whip, slicked-back hair, marble Jacuzzi, that sort of thing. With a goatee, just to show everyone that he's not your typical corporate animal. Obviously, Miriam feels that she's met her match at last. But I can't help wondering.

The first time I met him, at a family beach picnic, he spent most of his time talking to other people on his mobile, while the rest of us polished our fillings on chicken sandwiches full of wind-blown sand. I suppose it wasn't his fault that, after this first disastrous effort at socializing, he had me labelled as a complete bonehead. (It's hard to make coherent conversation when you're trying to keep an eye on two kids—neither of whom can swim—in a beachfront setting.) But the second effort wasn't much better. After practically taking out a second mortgage on the house, Matt and I had hired a babysitter for three hours and joined Giles and Miriam for dinner in the city. A Big Deal for us—our first night out in something like fourteen months. Anyway, although it was a pretty flashy restaurant, with pretty fancy food, Giles had found fault with everything from the poor mobile reception to the pedestrian wine list. Not that he wasn't an *amusing* whiner—you couldn't help laughing when he compared his antipasto selection to something cleaned out of a badly maintained aquarium. But the way he talked, you found yourself wondering what he'd be saying about *you*, the minute you turned your back.

He gave you the impression of a person who, though easily bored, was not easily impressed. Perhaps that's why Miriam behaved in a slightly uncharacteristic way when he was around; she's always been dry, but with him she was positively brittle. The two of them kept indulging in these witty, sophisticated exchanges about plastic surgery and tax havens and architect-designed beach houses. It made Matt and me feel like a pair of clodhopping preschoolers.

In other words, quite frankly, I think Giles is a bit of an arsehole.

Or maybe I'm just jealous, now that I'm not even ahead in the relationship stakes. I mean, I used to be the one who pulled the halfway decent men. It's petty, I know. It's unforgivable. It's a measure of the depths to which you can sink when you're sleep-deprived. But I get so depressed when she starts talking about a peaceful stroll through the art gallery, followed by afternoon tea at Watson's Bay. The last time *we* were at Watson's Bay, Jonah dropped his chocolate ice-cream down the front of my white blouse, Emily trod dog poo all over the picnic rug, and Matt caught his hand in the stroller's fold-out mechanism. Par for the course, I'm afraid—though I shouldn't complain, I know. After all, both my kids are healthy. And the trip wasn't a *complete* disaster. It's a nice feeling, when you're sitting in the golden afternoon light, watching your gorgeous husband play with your chortling son, while your beaming daughter runs towards you with a blue-tipped feather in her hand. You learn to enjoy these heavenly Hollywood moments while you can, knowing full well that any moment your daughter's going to trip and fall, your son's going to cry for his mum, and your husband's going to get hit in the face by someone's Frisbee.

Oh dear, there I go again. Moan, moan, moan—it's a psychological tic. And what am I moaning about? The fact that I have a full, rich family life? Other people don't even have that. I feel so embarrassed sometimes, when I listen to some of the single mums at playgroup; it makes me realize how lucky I've been. (How lucky I *am*, please God.) I've got to be more positive—more glass-half-fullish. It's that North Shore perfectionist coming out in me again. I've got to squash the tendency, it's like a weed. And of course it's made worse by the fact that I'm not even consistent. Because when I realized, this evening, that Miriam wanted to talk about Men, part of me (the bad part) was relieved at the possibility that she'd stuffed up yet again, while another part was appalled at the prospect of having to Give Counsel. Giving Counsel was always my role in these situations, but I don't have the energy any more. How can you display a boundless interest in every inflection of a man's voice, every enigmatic phone call he makes and statement he utters, when you know that with each tick of the clock you might be losing a heaven-sent opportunity to give the kitchen floor a quick mop before Jonah finishes his Vegemite sandwich and has to be coaxed into the bath?

If Matt had been available, I could have sympathized at my leisure. But Matt was on his evening shift. What's more, the dinner–bath–bedtime routine was looming. I could see that if Giles proved to have a bloke on the side, or was living under a false name, or had ordered Miriam to shave off all her pubic hair, the kids wouldn't be getting to bed until after eight.

As it happened, however, I needn't have worried. Miriam was short, sharp and to the point.

"I'm sorry about this," she declared, settling down in my grease-spattered kitchen with a frown on her face. There was a pause as she drummed her fingers on the tabletop. She seemed uncharacteristically tense. Almost jittery, in fact.

"I'm really sorry," she continued, "but after a lot of thought I've decided to tell you something that you're not going to like. Something that you're not going to thank me for. I was wondering what I should do, because it's difficult, but I've decided to bite the bullet. It's the best thing, I think, for both of us."

I stared at her in astonishment, my mind racing and my cheeks reddening. I couldn't imagine what it was that she proposed to tell me. Did I have BO? Some kind of annoying mannerism? Was she going to take me to task about my negative attitude, or the weight I'd put on?

"It's about Matt," she said, and her fingers stopped moving. "Maybe I'm out of order here—maybe there's a perfectly reasonable explanation—but I saw him in a restaurant at lunchtime, today, cuddling a girl who can't have been more than twenty-two."

I just gaped at her.

"She was snuggling into his neck, and he was kissing her hair. This was on Oxford Street, by the way—the Indigo Café, you know? I'd been at the courts." Miriam sighed. "I saw them there once before, about three weeks ago, and he was holding her hand, but I thought—I mean, it could have been a secretary with AIDS, or something. I *was* a bit surprised, but I didn't like to overreact. Maybe I'm overreacting now. She had purple hair and pale skin. One of those tattooed bracelets on her upper arm. A kind of orange chiffon singlet slung over a black T-shirt with the sleeves cut off. Three studs in her left ear. I couldn't see what she was wearing on her bottom half—it was behind the table. I couldn't see her face very well, either." Miriam cocked an eyebrow at me. "Sound familiar?" she asked.

I shook my head, speechless. During the brief silence that followed, I could hear Sleeping Beauty singing "Once Upon a Dream" in the next room.

"You might end up hating me for this," Miriam concluded, "but in the end I felt that I couldn't walk away from it. Not with my background. I've had too much to do with guys who've gambled away all their money, and lost their jobs, and started juggling credit cards and signing away their houses and their wives haven't had a clue, though they must have sensed that something was going on. You've got to nip deceit in the bud, or it'll end up just the tip of the iceberg. Believe me. I've seen it. All these fraudulent lending managers who start off with a mistress on the sly and end up draining church bank accounts. It happens."

"But—"

"I know. I know." She lifted a hand. "Matt isn't a thief. But if he turned out to be throwing away all your mortgage money on this . . . um . . . person,

I'd never have forgiven myself if I hadn't told you. That's all."

Tick, tick, tick. The kitchen clock ticked away. I checked the time automatically. Five to six.

"What time did you see him?" I asked. "In the restaurant?" Normally, on a weekday, Matt leaves home around twelve, so that he can work for *Rural Spotlight.* (He does sound mixing for a lot of ABC programs, including *Rural Spotlight,* the news, and that arts one whose name always escapes me.) This means that he'll either grab a bite of lunch at home, before he leaves, or drop into a coffee shop on the way—when we can afford it. That day, he had left a little early. I remembered the excuse that he had given: namely, lunch with his friend Ray. Ray was one of Matt's colleagues who had also become his friend. He was like a younger version of Matt, because they both enjoyed the same kinds of music, bars and television shows. Unfortunately, Ray had recently moved from the on-air mixing desk to postproduction, which offered its staff more sensible hours—so Matt didn't see as much of him any more. Hence the need for lunch appointments. "Matt has to be at work at one," I pointed out. "When did you see him? Exactly?"

"About half past twelve."

"Oh." So that fit. I scratched my arm, avoiding Miriam's eye. "I'll ask Matt," I said, in a surprisingly calm voice. "There must be an explanation."

"Probably."

"I mean—was he really cuddling her?"

"Well, he had an arm around her shoulders, and he was pulling her against him. And her face was buried in his neck."

"And he was kissing her hair."

"A couple of times."

I swallowed. "Are you sure it was Matt?"

"Dead certain," Miriam replied, with a level gaze. I turned away from her. I couldn't think.

"Mu-um!" Emily called from the living room. "I'm finished!"

"Okay."

"I'm finished, Mum!"

"All right. Good girl."

"I'm still hungry!"

"You can have an apple."

"Oo-oh." Whine, whine. "I want something else."

"It's nearly dinner. Just wait."

"But I'm hungry . . ."

"Just *wait*, Emily!" I found myself rubbing my forehead with one finger as I lowered my voice. "He has a cousin in Perth, but she's got multiple sclerosis. He has a bunch of sisters-in-law, but they're older than I am. He has a niece, but she's only twelve. This girl—are you sure she wasn't twelve?"

"I doubt it. I very much doubt it. Unless his niece has been on the streets for a while? Doing drugs?"

"No," I said, and realized that, in any case, Christine would never have allowed Sophie to dye her hair purple. Not in a million years. "But there must be an explanation."

"There probably is."

"I'll ask Matt."

"That's the best thing."

Suddenly my daughter appeared. She came and swung on my chair.

I was grateful for the interruption.

"Jonah made a mess," she informed me.

"Really."

"What are you cooking, Mum?"

"Nothing, right now."

"Can I have chips for dinner?"

"No."

"Please?"

"You're having rice."

"Can you put tomato sauce on it?"

"I'd better go," Miriam announced, rising abruptly. "Unless you want me to stay. Do you? I'll stay if you want."

I looked at her. She wore a grave expression, to match her sober suit. I wondered if I wanted her around. Probably not, I decided. It would be hard enough, feeding the kids while I digested this unwelcome news, without Miriam watching me burn the sausages.

She had never, I recalled, been all that enamoured of Matt. Not disapproving, exactly—just unconvinced.

"I'm really sorry, Helen," she said, studying me intently. "Are you all right?"

"Oh, yes. It's okay."

"I feel awful about this. I didn't want to do it. I just felt I had to. Before—" She stopped suddenly, and swallowed, glancing at Emily. Emily, of course, wasn't interested in the esoteric pronouncements of her elders. She was rearranging the fridge magnets. I could tell, however, that Miriam was trying to assemble cryptic phrases that wouldn't alarm my daughter. "Before things get out of hand," she finished.

"I know." I didn't blame Miriam—I really didn't. She had always been a very loyal friend. "I'm glad you told me. Though I'm sure it's nothing."

"I hope I haven't screwed up here. Well—I hope I have, of course. Made a mistake." She gave a dismal little laugh. "Thanks for not shooting the messenger. Are you sure you don't need anything?"

"Like what?"

"I don't know . . . maybe Sara Lee chocolate ice-cream? I could go and buy some for you."

"Yes!" Emily exclaimed. Even I smiled at that. But I assured Miriam that I required nothing special, not even a cup of strong coffee. Then I said goodbye, and she told me she'd call me. She said she was sorry, and on the front doorstep she gave me a hug, holding me tight. I noticed at once that she was wearing perfume, but I didn't know what kind it was.

I've no idea what any of the new fragrances smell like, these days. I just haven't been keeping up.

So there I was, calmly putting the kids to bed while inside my head it was like that movie *Twister*, with thoughts and emotions careering around, tumbling, colliding and whirling away again. "Big Bear took Little Bear's hand," I read, telling myself all the while that it must be a mistake. "Five little ducks went out one day," I sang, as surges of panic made me break into a sweat. And Jonah was restless, of course, calling me back again and again, disturbing Emily, refusing to lie down. And you can't afford to lose your temper in these circumstances, or it's going to take the Problem Child even longer to settle.

As for Emily, she was so unbearably sweet that I nearly burst into tears. "I want to whisper in your ear," she said, and when I leaned over she confided that she loved me, and daddy too—just like something out of a Disney movie. I needed a glass of wine, after that. (How do they always manage to hit you right where it hurts?)

I knew that it had to be a mistake. I knew that there had to be a reasonable explanation. But even so, deep down inside, a little kernel of doubt was starting to shoot. It had been sitting there in the dark, all these years, and it needed only the smallest gleam of light—the faintest trace of moisture—to encourage it to take root. *Right from the beginning*, you see, I had always had this . . . doubt. This tiny, unquenchable fear. Because the fact is, I had married a wild one.

Now I know it sounds phobic. I know that. But just consider the circumstances. Matt and I, we were a classic case of opposites attracting. Matthew was a tattooed, dope-smoking, shaggy-haired musician from Newcastle. I was a typical North Shore girl from Killara. God knows how many times I've tried to hide this fact—especially from myself—but whenever I used to visit my parents (before they moved), and went to buy brie at the local deli, I would look around at the sleek blonde Anglos, with their small ears and delicate gold jewelry and pastel sportswear, and I would know that I blended in there as I never will here, in Dulwich Hill. Dulwich Hill isn't an Anglo sort of place. You can always get decent baklava in Dulwich Hill, and the butchers stock interesting things like rabbits and sheeps' heads. All of the doctors bulk-bill. If the churches aren't Greek Orthodox, they're holding services in Vietnamese. I'm not saying that I stick out like a shag on a rock, exactly—I'm just saying that this isn't my natural milieu. It's an inescapable fact of life. I'm North Shore from pedicure to perm: my father was a lawyer, until he retired; my mother is, and always has been, a housewife. I went to a private school. I have a law degree from Sydney University. I simply can't pull off a grungy, gothic, feral or flamboyant look. I'm the sort of person, in other words, who looks hugely out of place in a bar in King's Cross.

That's where I was when I first met Matthew—in a bar in King's Cross. I was there by invitation because a friend of mine from school, who also lived in Paddington, was throwing a sort of postmodern hen's night. The idea was that we would go on a traditional hen's-night pub crawl, taking the piss out of the vulgarity of it all while secretly enjoying it at the same time. (The equivalent of having your cake and eating it too.) I should point out, here, that Caroline, the bride-to-be, was never a great friend of mine. We simply knew each other from school, and associated because we lived on the same street. Having studied at the Darlinghurst College of Art, she had become a graphic designer, though she's now living a luxurious life in the most exclusive part of Vaucluse with her (wait for it) *second husband*. Miriam had got to know her too, through me, so we were both invited—probably because Caroline wanted a crowd. I think it was a boost to her ego, having a lot of people following her around; at any rate, there must have been a good twenty women who turned up that night, and traipsed from one end of King's Cross to the other—past staggering junkies and touts and alcoholics—like a pack of sailors on the prowl.

I can't say that I enjoyed the concept very much. I'm not a big drinker, you see; I start to throw up after I've had a couple. As for Miriam, she doesn't drink alcohol at all. Consequently, when the other girls started to get pissed, and joined up with a mob of young lawyers and stockbrokers who were enjoying a buck's night (though not a postmodern one), Miriam and I bowed out. We withdrew from the fray, and went up to the bar. Which is where I got talking to Matthew.

He was working there, at the time. It was one of his many jobs. When I asked him for an orange juice I noticed that he had tattoos on his arms, and a missing tooth, and dismissed him from my thoughts immediately. Not because I was a snob, you understand. It was simply because he obviously *belonged* in a bar in King's Cross, whereas I didn't. North is north and west is west and ne'er the twain shall meet, in other words. I had never sat on a motorbike before, and knew that I wasn't the sort of person who would ever feel comfortable doing so. Therefore, Matthew didn't recommend himself to me at first. It didn't even cross my mind that he'd be remotely interested in someone who didn't do drugs.

But when he brought me my juice and my change, he stopped to talk. He said that he had seen me on the premises before, trying to give some guy the brush-off. That's when I started paying attention, because it was true; I *had* been in there some weeks previously, with a nasty piece of work named Colin. Matt asked me if I had "got rid of" Colin, and upon learning that I had, made approving noises. Colin, he said, had looked just like the bad guy from that movie *Big*. Did I remember him? The corporate wanker with the blond hair? I replied that Matt was exhibiting the most extraordinary grasp of Colin's character, and we then started discussing movies, with particular reference to Tom Hanks and Ron Howard. Of course we kept on getting interrupted—Matt had a job to do, after all—but even so, it soon became apparent to me that Matthew's rather aggressive appearance was totally misleading. Not that he looked like a gorilla, or anything. Don't get me wrong. He has a very nice face (what you can see of it, under the hair and stubble), and his eyes are lovely. But there were the tattoos, and the missing tooth, and the easy familiarity with King's Cross slang . . . well, you know what I mean.

So we talked for a while, until I realized that Miriam was being increasingly left out of the conversation. Then, when she and I began to discuss whether we should walk home or get a cab (like we had a hope in hell of flagging down a cab in King's Cross on a Friday night), Matthew asked me for my number. Naturally, I didn't give it to him. I mean to say, a large, shaggy King's Cross bartender with tattoos? You might as well walk naked down William Street and have done with it. But he insisted on giving me his number, and I took it without the slightest intention of ever using it. After which I went home with Miriam, to find that Briony was busily entertaining a total stranger who looked even larger and shaggier than Matthew.

I can't believe we weren't all murdered in our beds, during Briony's occupation of our house.

Anyway, I didn't call Matt. I figured he probably scattered his telephone number about like grass seed, hoping that a little interest might germinate here and there. (He was a bartender, after all, and a tall, dark, handsome one at that.) But about three weeks later I ran into him on Oxford Street, and we arranged to have coffee together that afternoon. A tentative first step—pretty harmless—nothing too extreme. Yet within a month we'd run through the entire, predictable cycle: dinner, movie, bed, breakfast, endless phone calls, picnics, weekends away, meet the parents, shared parties, expensive birthday presents . . . you know the sort of thing. All because of that cup of coffee.

It was the sugar, you see. When we first ordered coffee together, Matt asked for a cappuccino. He took one sip and then sat behind the steaming cup for about ten minutes while we made awkward conversation, commenting on the parking in Taylor Square, the Greek restaurant up the road, the rents in that part of the world, until I was finally driven to ask, "Aren't you going to drink that?"

"Yeah. Sure." He eyed the cappuccino for a second, picked up a packet of sugar, and dumped its contents into the coffee. As he reached for another packet, I stumbled onto the subject of Briony, who turned out to be a real Godsend. Matt enjoyed hearing about Briony almost as much as I enjoyed talking about her. We discussed Briony's rune-reading. We touched on her eccentric taste in men. Matt was quite sure that he knew one of the shaggy interlopers trundled out for my inspection, every Sunday morning: we tried to work out if it was the same guy—known as "Relic" to his mates—but couldn't be sure. All the while, Matt sat behind his cup of coffee.

Finally I said, "You're *not* going to drink that, are you? What's the matter? Is it too strong?"

Matt gave a shamefaced grin. "It's these bloody *packets*," he complained.

"The what?"

"The packets. Of sugar. They're not like the old canisters—you could use as much sugar as you liked, with them, and no one would know what a wuss you were. With these packets . . ." He gave the crumpled remnants a poke. "You get up, and the waitress knows you've been pouring six sugars into your coffee."

I put on a serious expression.

"Matt," I said gravely, "you can pretend three of them are mine. Your secret's safe with me."

"Nah." He shook his head with exaggerated sorrow. "Nah, I know what you're gunna do. You'll walk away and tell your friends, 'I met this woofter today, he was trying to be hard, but he snuck six sugars into his coffee.' "

"You mustn't let sugar define your self-image, Matt. Napoleon liked cream puffs, you know."

Matt looked surprised. "Really?" he said.

"Oh sure. I wrote an essay on it." But I couldn't keep a straight face any longer. "Shit, I don't know, how should I know? Don't be ridiculous. Woofter, indeed. We don't talk like that, in the public service."

"Zat so?" He was grinning by now. "What do you say, then? 'Masculinely challenged'?"

"We say 'ten-sugar screamer.' "

And that was that. He fell about laughing, and I was hooked. I was landed. Because he was a real find—especially for someone with my background.

You have to understand, he was *so* hip. *So* hot. For one thing, he was a drummer in a band that you could actually *go and see* (on occasion) in clubs and pubs that people actually *went to*. The Breaks, they were called, and they played mostly covers, though the lead guitarist wrote a few songs. Drummers aren't generally the pin-up boys of most bands, so it wasn't as if Matt was exactly beating off the groupies, but still—there must have been any number of groovy young things who had cast an acquisitive eye over him.

And then there were the jobs. Matt had jobs with real street savvy. To start with, there was the bartender job, which allowed him to become acquainted with all kinds of seedy King's Cross personalities: bouncers, spruikers, drug dealers, crooked cops—and the barmaids, of course. Barmaids as hard as nails, as sharp as razors, and sometimes as exotic and bizarre as the cocktails they served, which were all tarted up with suggestive swizzle sticks and glacé pineapple. Matt was a good bartender. He had endless patience, never lost his temper, and was quite skilled; he'd done a cocktail course at the Silver Shaker training college. In fact he had quite a memory for noxious mixtures. I tested him once, out of a book, and the only one he got wrong was Kelly's Comfort. He remembered the Southern Comfort, the Bacardi, the vodka, the milk, the ice and the strawberries, but he left out the grenadine. (And a good thing too, in my opinion.)

Then there was the recording studio job. He worked part-time in a dingy Darlinghurst recording studio—as a sound mixer, or something. I never did find out quite what he did because, when I visited him there, he and his colleagues seemed to spend most of their time stealing each other's cigarettes, arguing about who was going to wash the coffee cups, and laughing about a guy called Clifford. Even so, Matt must have done something of importance, because he got paid, and was even

acknowledged on the odd album cover. It was
through his influence that The Breaks made their
one and only recording: an original dirge called
"Stone" that sank like one. I think it only went on
sale in one store, a funny place out near Central
Station, owned by a friend of the bass guitarist.

Anyway, that was Matt. And I know he sounds
frighteningly cool, but the thing is, he wasn't really.
Not in himself. He was simply doing what he liked.
He wore black jeans and T-shirts all the time, not
to make a statement, but because he couldn't be
bothered washing his clothes much, and had discovered that stains aren't so obvious on black. He
wore his hair long because he couldn't be bothered
cutting it, and favored a trendy stubble because he
couldn't be bothered shaving every day. Any fears
that I might have had about the self-consciousness
of his image were utterly dispelled when I first visited his flat, which he shared with another band
member. It was reassuringly untidy, and completely
lacking in the faintest pretense at style. I swear, the
only thing those boys spent *any* money on was their
sound equipment.

This isn't to say, however, that Matt had a problem with style or cleanliness. On the contrary, he
admired them. He didn't aspire to them—I guess
he didn't feel capable of anything so out of character—but he did admire them. He admired *me*.
He admired the state of my kitchen, the smell of
my sheets and the gloss on my shoes. He called me
"dazzling." My hair was so shiny, it was "dazzling."
My schedules were so tight, they were "dazzling."
He didn't see anything risible about suits, or graduate programs, or the public service. He seemed
proud to take me to lunch in the central business

district, where I looked just like everyone else with my black pantyhose and my briefcase and my hair scooped up under a tortoiseshell slide. He especially admired my beautifully organized Filofax, which was, I have to admit, one of the Seven Wonders of the World. (These days it's all electronic organizers, of course—and even back then the sun was setting on the Glory Days of the Filofax. But I still have a soft spot for my old leather-bound companion, scuffed and scratched though it may be.)

Miriam also had a Filofax—in fact Miriam was just as well organized as I was, if not more so. But for some reason, Matt didn't admire her as much. Perhaps she was a little too crisply starched for him. Perhaps her sense of humor was a little too dry. Or perhaps it was because she was naturally organized, it was in her genes, whereas my organizational skills were simply a way of heading off my tendency to panic at the slightest setback. I have always had an inborn propensity to fall into a dithering heap when confronted with crises of any sort, especially domestic ones. Miriam, on the other hand, took things like leaking pipes and flea infestations in her stride. She wasn't the type to start squealing like a stuck pig when she discovered that the fish was off, just before it was due to be served up to eight people for dinner.

I remember that occasion very well. Matthew was fantastic. Very laid-back, very reassuring, very helpful. While Miriam and I frantically prepared an alternative menu, he entertained the other guests by mixing lewd, absurd and entertaining cocktails with ridiculous names. He had such an easy, relaxed air about him that everyone else relaxed. We didn't sit down at the table until half past nine, but nobody seemed to care. Certainly not Matthew. And though I thought that Miriam had emerged from the episode looking a lot more competent than I had, Matt still seemed to prefer me. He said that I'd been "cute." He gathered me onto his lap, and tucked my loose hair behind my ears, and said that I ought to trip up on my own hemline more often.

It was at such times that I felt I knew him through and through, as if I was looking into a mirror.

But then I would hear about how he'd met some miners in a bar, and gone off with them to the dog races, and had ended up rock-fishing off Clovelly because their car had broken down, and suddenly I would feel as if I didn't know him at all. He could do these things, you see. He had it in him. He had Aboriginal friends, and television actor friends, and biker friends. He had a sprawling, extended family situated around Newcastle and Morrisset and Fassifern, which entertained on its fringes all kinds of ex-con third cousins and religious maniac great-uncles. He had a long string of bizarre experiences and extraordinary jobs under his belt. Sometimes, for instance, he would talk about his spell at a chicken farm, where he had culled cockerels and collected eggs while wearing a red-and-white suit that was supposed to make him look like a chicken, and he would seem as strange to me as a man from Mars. Or he would relate to me the story of his lost tooth, which had been knocked out while he was shooting pigs in Queensland, and it was as if he was talking about another person.

That other person, I should tell you, was the only person my parents saw when they first met him. It was the tattoos, needless to say. I would look at Matt and think: pig shooting is not his first choice of pastime, but he's an easygoing guy with a wide circle of acquaintances and the sort of amiable character that would lead him to take part in a pig-shooting expedition simply because his mates were interested. My parents, on the other hand, would look at the tattoos and think: pig shooting. Drug dealing. Unsafe driving. Dogs in the kitchen. Kids with rat-tails. I could see it on their faces, when I brought Matt to my sister's twenty-first birthday party. I'll admit that he did look somewhat out of place, among the Regency stripes and the Laura Ashley florals. The leather jacket was probably a bad choice. In fact he pretty much presented the appearance of someone whom I had deliberately, in a fit of postadolescent defiance, brought home for the purpose of annoying my parents and up-staging my sister.

My sister and I get along pretty well, most of the time, but there have been some rough patches. Being the youngest sibling, she's more of a party girl than I ever was; my parents always worried about her rebellious streak, which manifested itself in things like her belly button piercing, her decision to go backpacking around the Northern Territory after high school, and her wish to become a fashion buyer. (Rebellious streaks on the North Shore aren't quite what they would be in, say, a Detroit trailer park.) The fashion-buyer fad didn't last long—much to my parents' relief—and by the time she was twenty-one, Danielle was studying business management. As a matter of fact, she's a very sharp girl. She'd have to be, or she wouldn't be working in London, now, organizing sales conferences or whatever it is she does.

At her twenty-first birthday, she was busy flaunting a new boyfriend called Crispin, who was a pleasant surprise for both my parents. Previously, Danielle had spent something like two years having fiery arguments and passionate reconciliations with a troubled med student who flunked university during the course of their relationship. Crispin was a great improvement. He was from a family of wealthy graziers, he was receiving high marks in law, and he was innately placid and well organized. My parents liked him very much. They were also immensely gratified that Danielle, at the time of her twenty-first birthday, seemed to have actively rejected some of her unpredictable friends, and was going through a conservative stage. Her twenty-first was quite a sedate affair. There were linen tablecloths, candelabra, and many North Shore girls with gleaming blonde hair and perfect teeth. The boys, too, were pretty well buffed. Nearly all of them seemed to have mobile phones. When Matt appeared on the doorstep, wearing his scuffed leather jacket and shabby sneakers, he ruined the whole effect.

In his defense let me point out that he *had* shaved, and that his hair was tied back. Also, he was absolutely gorgeous. Danielle saw this at once; she's not stupid. As a result, she became a bit temperamental with the unfortunate Crispin, while my parents fluttered around, smiling and sweating. Poor things—I do sympathize. No sooner had Danielle begun to settle down, thereby lifting a huge weight from their minds, than I had suddenly turned up with a large, hairy, King's Cross bartender. They couldn't help worrying, even though they tried not to show it.

Both my parents have very good manners, you see—so good that Matt never realized just how worried they were. He loped around, smiling his big, larrikin's smile, while my mother introduced him to my extended family, invited him to sample her salmon vol-au-vents, and twittered on about the garden, which is her pride and joy. My father's pride and joy is his library. Matt was transparently awestruck by the flawless state of my mother's lawn, and the extent of my dad's book collection. He expressed reservations about sitting in certain chairs, in case he should break them, and was careful to wipe his feet thoroughly before stepping from the patio onto the pale living-room carpet. He laughed his radio announcer's laugh at every one of my father's jokes, and praised with genuine feeling the excellence of my mother's butterfly cakes. Most impressively of all, he chatted away to my Great-Aunt Ida, balancing a Royal Doulton teacup on his dirty black knee. Ida's a bit deaf, poor woman, but she heard Matt, all right. He told me later that his Nonna was going deaf, so he knew how to pitch his voice for Aunt Ida.

In other words, he did everything right. He even apologized, afterwards, for not cutting his hair. As for the tattoos, he informed me that he had been drunk when the bet was made with his brother's friends . . . He'd won seven hundred dollars all up, having those tattoos done. But it hadn't been a smart thing to do; they didn't usually make a good impression.

"Next time," he promised, "I'll get some new

clothes. And a shirt—a proper one. Maybe some chinos." Like a tourist from another planet, he had taken note of the outfits worn by Danielle's friends. "Maybe you can help me," Matt added. "Maybe you can point me in the right direction, so next time I visit the ancestral home, I won't feel like something the cat dragged in."

He was so sweet. When I heard him wondering aloud if my mother would approve of paisley prints, I realized suddenly that he was The One. There was no doubt about it. Only a man with a truly lovely nature would have breezed through that party, ignoring snubs and finding things to admire. He wasn't a moron; he knew that his appearance had caused some consternation. But with his generosity of spirit, he didn't realize that my parents were hoping desperately that he never *would* turn up again.

They couldn't fool me, though. I knew the signs. When my mother pressed a doggie bag of sponge cake on him before he left, it was a dead giveaway.

I was determined, however, to follow my heart. I was grown up and reasonably intelligent—I knew what was good for me. Matt thought I was wonderful. He was entranced by the fact that I could put up my hair without consulting a mirror. He got a kick out of the way I would cry at practically anything in a movie. (Perhaps he liked comforting me afterwards.) He was flattered by my interest in Italian culture—though, he said, he couldn't help me out much, since the closest thing his family ever got to culture was the old Botticelli calendar hanging in his mother's kitchen.

As for me, I adored every square centimeter of that man. I felt like a groupie. We would have such great laughs, together—that's something I remember very well, the way we heaved with laughter in the most peculiar places. At a municipal waste depot, once, after getting rid of the most disgusting couch in the world, Matt had looked around and declared, in a voice heavily larded with cockney: "Wot a bleedin' dump." In a monumental traffic jam, when somebody had finally got out of their car and stepped behind a tree to piss, I had hummed the first few bars of "Everybody Hurts"; we were already almost hysterical after the endless wait, and that pushed us right over the edge. We had the same sense of humor. We both loved Italian food. We shared identical views when it came to films, books and television—though Matt had a taste for football which I couldn't share, and my admiration for certain musical performers left him cold. But his giggle filled me with rapture, and the sight of my feet in high heels drove him crazy. We had similar memories of kids' TV shows and past fashion fads. Our reactions to things like elections, sashimi and the nocturnal house at Taronga Zoo were so close that I started talking about soul mates—just to annoy him. He's got a fairly low tolerance for New Age lingo.

In the end, I forced my parents to acknowledge him. They didn't have a choice; we took them to lunch, we signed both our names on birthday cards, and I brought him along with me at Christmas. After a while, Mum and Dad came to realize how sweet he was. They came to recognize his good points. He was so lavish in his praise of me, and so frank in his confessions of a straitened childhood, that they couldn't help but be disarmed. Nevertheless, they still thought him unsuitable. Not because of his Italian heritage. Not because he had never gone to university. Not even because he refused to "waste money" on a bridge, to fill the gap in his mouth.

No—my parents simply thought that the difference in our respective backgrounds would be difficult, if not impossible, to reconcile. They didn't believe that our mutual delight in each other's company was a firm enough foundation on which to build a life together. Not that they said as much. They didn't have to; I could read the vibes. Anyway, they felt guilty about their opinions, because Matt was so nice. Only a complete arsehole could have failed to recognize his charm, and my parents aren't arseholes. They're a bit constipated, but they're not arseholes. No matter what I might have thought before the wedding.

In some ways, that wedding went very well. To begin with, Matt had just bagged himself a terrific job with ABC: a sound engineer's job. The pay wasn't exactly stunning, but the benefits were good. What's more, the wedding preparations went off without a hitch. God, it was a beautiful wedding. Mum and Dad didn't stint, bless their hearts, so we were able to afford a seaside resort, with pool. The ceremony took place beside said pool, in front of a kind of classical portico thing that was wrapped around with garlands. I wore a Jean Fox Thai silk gown, and carried Madonna lilies. Danielle and Miriam, my bridesmaids, were dressed in fitted suits, very elegant, with saucy matching hats. There were seventy guests, most of them Matt's family—who seemed a bit taken aback by the delicate portions of lobster and quail served up to them for dinner (though the extensive dessert buffet made up for the nouvelle cuisine mains). A string quartet played until the sun went down, at which point glowing Chinese lanterns were lit, and a friend of Matt's took over the music selection.

I remember dancing with Matt, who looked almost indecently sexy in his tux. His brothers looked terrific too, all kitted out. There were toasts to the married couple's future happiness, and my sister burst into tears as she hugged me, smearing her mascara all over my neck. Even the cake was a triumph, with its feathery sugar flowers and silk ribbon. Poor Mum snapped off a high heel in a pool grating, and Matt's Nonna couldn't make the trip, but on the whole it was a fairytale event.

There was just one bad moment, and that didn't occur at the wedding. That happened the day before. I was frantically counting place cards, nagging florists, and directing pre-nuptial traffic when Mum decided to drop a hint. She murmured something about Matt's level of "commitment," and urged me to "think carefully" because I was about to make a "big decision."

"You mustn't worry about us, dear," she said. "We don't mind how much money we pay—or lose—as long as we can be sure that you're happy."

You can imagine how well that went down with me. I was furious. Of course I didn't tell Matt, but I stewed over it for months. Months and months. I castigated my parents privately, over and over again, for their unbearable North Shore conservatism, their stuffy prejudice, their *boorishness*.

But I've been lying here thinking: what if they were right after all?

* * *

Matt came home at ten tonight. I was propped up in bed with a book, but I hadn't been reading; I'd been thinking. Thinking and thinking. I heard him come around the back (so as not to wake the children), fall over a pile of builder's rubbish, swear horribly, and slam into the kitchen. He usually eats dinner at work, but sometimes he has a plate of ice-cream or a glass of port in front of the TV before coming to bed.

Tonight, though, he was too tired even for that. He looked exhausted. Dark circles under his eyes, grey hairs glinting in his stubble. He staggered into the bedroom and threw himself onto the bed.

"Augh," he moaned, as the mattress bounced gently under his weight.

I didn't say anything, except "Hello." I was watching him, you see, trying to work out if he'd changed. He didn't give the impression of someone nursing a salacious secret. He didn't seem particularly guilty and careworn, either—at least, not more than usual. I should explain that Matt has a bit of a CD addiction. He can't go a week without buying one, though I've pointed out several times that our budget won't stretch to it any more. So now he sometimes buys them surreptitiously, and hides them around the house like empty bottles of gin. I can always tell he's done it, even before I find them; he has a sheepish look that I can pick a mile off. Half the time, all I have to do is lift an eyebrow at him and he'll confess.

So how, I thought, could he be having an affair? How could he possibly keep such a big secret to himself?

"What a fuckin' awful day," he said, rubbing his eyes. "God."

"Busy?"

"Flat out. We had inserts coming in at the last possible moment. What about you?"

"Messy."

"Did the builders show up?"

"No."

"For God's sake."

"You haven't seen that little blue horse of Emily's, have you?" I was going through the motions, my heart pounding, as I summoned up the courage to ask the real question. The important question. "I spent at least half an hour, this morning, looking for the damn thing . . . I don't know. She must have lost it."

Matt took his hands away from his eyes, and blinked at the ceiling.

"What blue horse?" he asked.

"The one with the pink tail. About this big. Sort of squishy."

"Doesn't ring a bell."

"No. Well." It didn't surprise me. "God knows what she's done with it."

"It's probably been given a Mafia burial. It's probably part of that cement slab out back."

"Maybe."

"Or that dog next door ate it." Matt groaned again, rolled over, and sat up. He began to take off his shirt.

Staring at his broad, white back, I said, "So how was lunch?"

"Huh?"

"With Ray? How was it?"

I could feel the pulse in my throat as I waited for

a response. When it finally came, I couldn't believe my ears.

"Okay," Matt said. "It was good."

"So what's the latest?" I'm amazed that I could even talk coherently. It was as if a heavy stone had landed on my gut. "Any new girlfriends I should know about?"

Normally, Matt can't spend half an hour in Ray's company without picking up at least two really good stories. When they worked together, he was always coming home with tales about what Ray had said in a planning meeting, or what Ray had done with a "grab of John Howard actuality." (Don't ask me what the lingo means—I've never been able to sort it out.) Even after Ray's move to postproduction, his infrequent lunchtime meetings with Matt always resulted in something worth passing on. Especially since Ray was always getting involved with the most monstrous women.

Not this time, however.

"No new girlfriends," said Matt.

"No funny stories?"

"Not really." His shoes hit the floor. Thud, thud. "He sent me a funny e-mail though. This afternoon. I've got it in my bag. Hang on while I get it, okay? It's off the Internet."

Was he trying to escape? I don't know. I don't know anything. I'm lying here, and he's asleep beside me, now, and I don't know what to do. I just don't know what to do.

Maybe I'll wake up tomorrow morning, and realize that this has all been nothing but a nightmare.

Please God.

Chapter Two

Saturday

Y ou won't believe this, but I didn't say a word to Matthew about the Girl With Purple Hair today.

Not that I had much of a chance, mind you. He works a full day shift on Saturdays—nine to five, more or less—so he was gone pretty early this morning. I was still shuffling around in my most revolting dressing-gown, mashing banana, while he was gathering up his keys and his wallet, smelling of aftershave. Give him his due, though, he did change Jonah's nappy. *And* wipe the seat of the highchair. He even examined Emily's mozzie bite, with grave attention, before pronouncing it "very nasty" though not life-threatening.

"But it's itchy!" Emily wailed.

"I know. Poor Em."

"I wanna Band-Aid!"

"What's the magic word?"

"Please!"

"Do you want a Wiggles Band-Aid or a Winnie-the-Pooh Band-Aid?"

"Ummm . . ."

"What about Winnie the Pooh?"

"No, Wiggles!"

"This one?"

"No, Dorothy!"

"This one?"

"No, the *other* Dorothy!"

"I don't think there *is* another Dorothy, Em. You're thinking about the dinosaur Band-Aids, sweetie."

"I wanna dinosaur Band-Aid!"

Somehow it didn't seem like the right moment to raise the subject of the Girl With Purple Hair.

It wasn't the right moment this evening, either. Oh lord—why not admit it? I'm scared. I'm scared to ask him. Sure, a simple question might have cleared up the whole problem. But what if it hadn't? What if he had said, "Yes, I've found my soul mate?" What if he had *walked out of the house for good,* like the husband of a girl I know at work? This poor girl, her name's Jenny, and she found out that her husband had been seeing someone else for *three years.* So she confronted him with the evidence (a telephone bill for a mobile that she'd never even known about) and he calmly packed his bags and left. Just like that. And she had an eleven-month-old baby at the time.

You think to yourself: how could that happen? It couldn't happen to me. Jenny must have married a prick. She must be a bit slow, not to have worked it out. Not to have spotted the signs.

But it can happen. It does happen. And I don't *want* it to happen, that's the thing. If it's true—and it probably isn't—but if it's true that Matt's seeing someone else, and I ask him about it, what if I'm opening a huge can of worms? What if he wants a divorce? What if he *asks for a divorce*? I don't know what I'd do. I think I'd have a nervous breakdown. I'm practically having a nervous breakdown just thinking about it—about what it would do to Emily, for a start. She wouldn't understand. Jonah wouldn't understand. Surely Matt would never do something like that to the kids? He might do it to me, but not to them. He must know it would break their hearts. How could he bear it, knowing that Emily was falling asleep every night with tears on her cheeks? *I* couldn't.

And then there's the house. How could we possibly keep the house? Suppose he decided on divorce, and wanted to rent his own place—how could we keep up with the mortgage payments? We couldn't. We'd have to sell this place, and I'd have to move out to . . . I don't know. Punchbowl? Penrith? What's more, I'd have to quit work, because we can only afford childcare two days a week as it is; Matt always looks after the kids on a Tuesday. Unless I was to ask my mother for help, of course. But I'd rather die than ask my mother. I'd never hear the end of it. "I told you so" would be hanging in the air for ever after, and I wouldn't be able to ignore it because I'd be in her debt, God forbid. I'd be a pitiful welfare mother living miles from all my friends, squabbling with Matt about child support payments, agonizing over his new girlfriend, over his new *wife*, over his new *family*— my God, what if he goes off and has more *children*?

But that's silly. I've got to calm down. Because this whole business about the purple-haired girl— it might be perfectly innocent. And if it is, would Matt ever forgive me for suspecting him? Would it

screw up our marriage? I don't want that to happen. I don't want it to happen because I love him,
and I don't want to lose him.

It's true, I'm not angry. I'm frantic—even
though he's been annoying me so much lately. I
know it's unreasonable, but I can't seem to help it.
I've been grinding my teeth over all sorts of things:
his CD addiction, for instance. He's always been
one for impulse buying, and not just CDs—he'll
often come home with toys for the kids, boxes of
Darrell Lea chocolates (he loves Darrell Lea), new
videotapes or strange liqueurs. He's been pining
after a DVD player, recently; I'm so frightened that
he'll go out and buy one. God knows, I'm not
mean. I didn't *mind* when we had separate bank accounts and no mortgage. I didn't mind when I had
lots of my own money. But those days are gone,
and he doesn't seem to realize it. He still seems to
think that he can throw his money around the way
he used to, even though we're on a tight budget. I
don't think he understands about budgets. He
probably thinks they're what people used to have
before credit cards were invented.

And then there's his drum kit. It's so big that it
fills up *vast tracts* of our sunroom (because he
won't put it in the garage, even though he hardly
ever practices, these days). It's impossible to clean,
and it's blocking the linen cupboard, and when he
does play it—about once a month—it's so noisy
that I live in perpetual fear of the neighbors complaining. There are cobwebs on it, for heaven's
sake. And yet when Jonah scribbled on the snare
drum with a marker, Matt threw a monstrous
tantrum, even though he tells me that I "overreact"
when Emily gets into my makeup or jewelry.

As for the housework issue, don't even ask. The fact that he's never been much good didn't matter before—not when we were living in that rented flat in Darlinghurst. I remember we used to do the housework every Saturday morning, with the stereo turned up high, singing along at the tops of our voices. We'd take it in turns to vacuum, wash the kitchen floor and clean the bathroom, and it didn't matter that Matthew was hopeless, because the flat was such a tip to begin with. The bathroom was so moldy that the grouting was past redemption; nothing that either of us did made the slightest difference (and God knows, I nearly poisoned myself spraying mold killer about), so in the end we gave up. Same with the toilet, which had an unsightly brown stain on the porcelain just where the water gushed down from the cistern. When the shower curtain became slimy and black, we threw it away and bought a new one. When the plastic soap dish became too encrusted, we applied the same principle. It didn't matter that the mirror was always streaky after Matthew cleaned it, because it was already a spotty mess, with brownish patches showing where the silver had peeled off, or rotted away.

As for the carpet, it was so disgusting to begin with that vacuuming made almost no impression at all. Neither did steam-cleaning. We had it steam-cleaned when we first moved in, and the only result was an analysis of all the stains that seemed to be indelible. We were informed by the steam-cleaning man that the greyish spot near the wall had been a leaky sewage pipe, that the round, brownish one near the sofa was vomit, and that the orange one beside it was very possibly tandoori chicken. "It's the smell that gives it away," he said

cheerfully, before hastening to assure us that he'd
seen worse—much worse. In one flat he'd cleaned,
the previous tenant had kept several large dogs,
and the carpet had been disfigured, not only by an
ankle-deep mist of fleas, but by countless shit stains.

When we bought this house, however, we were
lucky. The carpet was brand new, and the bathroom was only two years old. It's a lovely bathroom, with brass taps, a wooden toilet seat and a
claw-footed bath. The shower recess has glass
screens, not a curtain; there's a porcelain soap
dish cemented to the wall. Naturally, I've worked
hard to ensure that this room has remained lovely,
polishing the brass and keeping an eye on that
hard-to-reach spot under the bath, where the dust
collects. But has Matthew felt the same sense of responsibility? Has he hell. He never remembers the
spot under the bath unless I remind him. He
seems to think that scrubbing the ring off the bath
and giving the S-bend a quick poke with the toilet
brush constitutes a "good clean." I don't know
how many times I've pointed out that we *paid big
money* for this bathroom—that it's an investment
which shouldn't be allowed to deteriorate. I might
as well be talking to myself, for all the notice he
takes of me.

Sometimes I wonder if it's a case of middle-class
hang-ups versus working-class informality, and become prostrate with guilt. After all, hadn't that always been part of Matthew's attraction for me? His
had been a childhood of noisy, communal sessions
in front of the TV; friendly, beat-up, smoke-kip-
pered lounge-room furniture; football boots on
the kitchen table; five strapping boys being served
by ancient, stoop-shouldered Nonna as the dog

snored underfoot. Weren't Matt's housekeeping deficiencies the natural result of his exotic background? Should I really be giving my pinched, Anglo, middle-class worldview so much priority in our relationship?

At one stage I decided that I'd stop flogging a dead horse, since it was perfectly obvious that Matthew wasn't going to stop vacuuming around things (instead of moving furniture), or start wiping down windowsills without being endlessly nagged about it. I thought to myself: why fight the forces of history? Why not go with the flow, stop struggling, and surrender yourself to your traditional role? But that didn't work either. For one thing, I would have been forced to give up my job, and for another, Matthew couldn't manage the traditional male role any better than he'd been managing the New Age one. He broke our lawn mower the other day. He also cracked a wall putting some pictures up. And though he's not a bad hand with the fuse box (thank God), his understanding of tap washers, car engines and barbecue gas bottles is as rudimentary as mine. In other words, while I've been playing my part, he hasn't been playing his. And even this wouldn't matter so much if it wasn't costing us money. It costs money to fix a lawn mower. It costs money to have a couch recovered, because he let the kids play on it with markers. Couldn't he see what was going to happen? Why doesn't he *think ahead* sometimes?

I don't know—maybe it's biological. I saw a documentary on television the other day that described how men's and women's brains are wired up differently. Apparently it's a *scientific fact* that women are better at multi-tasking than men are.

So why am I blaming Matt, when I should be blaming myself for my unrealistic expectations? Lots of people would ask me what I'm moaning about: Matthew lends a hand, doesn't he? He looks after the kids, and irons his own shirts. He even cooks, on occasion. At least he makes an *attempt* at cleaning, and who's to say his way is the wrong way? Who's to say it matters that there's soap scum on the shower screens? Perhaps it doesn't. Perhaps I'm being a neurotic perfectionist. Sometimes I stop, and think, and realize that I'm turning into my own mother. Once that would have been an appalling thought. I used to say to Matthew: Please, please, if I ever start turning into my mother, you must tell me. You must warn me.

Now, however, it doesn't seem so simple. After all, it was my mother who taught me how to hemstitch, and what to do with bloodstains. Matthew didn't even know how to sew on a button when I met him. I had to show him how to do it. Am I really so anal, just because I insist that he doesn't walk around with half the buttons off his shirt? Perhaps I am. I must be, or why else would he be seeing the Girl With Purple Hair?

When I think of losing him—when I think of how lovely he is, and how mean I've been—I can't bear it. Do you know that he once came home with a cappuccino maker he'd bought for me (an impulse buy) and I was cross with him for wasting our money? How could I have done that? And the drum kit. Why have I been so horrible about the drum kit, when I used to love watching him play so much? The power of his arms, the loose and casual speed of them—I loved that. I loved his half-closed eyes, and his huge smile, and the way he sat on his stool, with his long legs folded up in their dusty black jeans.

One Tuesday, when he was minding the kids, he went out with them and bought some furniture polish. They were going to help him polish the coffee table in the living room, you see, and what's more they did it. But naturally they used too much polish and didn't wipe enough of it off, so the coffee table was sticky and streaky when they had finished. And of course Matthew had neglected to change the kids into their old painting clothes before they started, so their nice little matching Osh Kosh overalls (a gift from Mum) were ruined. And I was furious. Really. When I got home I was furious, even though the whole episode was one of those endearing, klutzy things that made Matthew the sweet-natured guy he always had been. Can you see what I'm saying? Can you see why I'm scared?

I'm afraid to ask Matthew if he's having an affair, because in a funny sort of way I'm also afraid that, if he is, it's because I deserve it.

I decided to look through our old phone bills. Fortunately, we get them itemized for tax reasons because I work at home a lot, so I knew that it would be easy to check whether Matthew had been making any unexplained phone calls. But I couldn't get on to it right away. I had the dishes to wash (no dishwasher, unfortunately), the laundry to do and the kids' breakfasts to make. What's more, I had to tackle all these chores whenever I wasn't changing nappies, making beds and settling quarrels. It's amazing how scatty I've become, since having

Emily. The house is always full of half-completed jobs, because no sooner do I begin to hang up the washing than Jonah demands another piece of cheese. So I cut the cheese, and give it to him, and then the phone rings, and then Emily wants me to put a dress on her doll, and then Jonah does a dump in his nappy, and I have to change it, and next thing you know it's hours later, and the cheese is drying on the kitchen benchtop, and the wet laundry is still sitting in the laundry basket.

It doesn't help that Emily takes her time over breakfast. She grazes, in other words; the meal can be spread over two hours, and I never know whether that's a good thing or a bad thing. On the one hand, nutritionists say that it's natural for small children to graze, rather than eat three solid meals a day, because they have small stomachs. On the other hand, dentists say that grazing leads to tooth decay. All I know is this: it plays havoc with my schedule when Emily demands one piece of apple, followed (ten minutes later) by one piece of orange, then one rice cracker, then one dry Weet-Bix—which will shed its flakes all over the floor—one prune, one apricot bar, one cheese stick . . .

At least she eats, though. Jonah doesn't eat. The lengths I go to, trying to persuade him that his meals should be put in his mouth. The vegetables I've tried to disguise! The boats I've made out of fish fingers and halved cheese slices! He's very creative, though—I'll give him that. What *he* does with his food is far more original than what I do with it. It's been left in some pretty amazing places, I can tell you. And every time he sits down to eat, his highchair tray ends up looking like a work of abstract expressionism.

This morning, he asked for a honey sandwich. And I was delighted, at first. I'd forgotten that when Jonah is given honey, it ends up everywhere. On everything. And then he spilled his drink on Emily's T-shirt, and Emily insisted that she had to change her clothes, and while I was helping her Jonah trod on the farm truck that he loves, and broke it, and cried, and I had to divert him with an old plastic pig of Emily's, which she suddenly wanted to play with . . . well, you get the picture.

But I made it to the shops, at last. I put Jonah in his stroller, and pushed him up to the local supermarket (very slowly, so that Emily could stop every two minutes to check out an ants' nest, a discarded shoe, a dead caterpillar, a bit of graffitti . . .), and bought a few things for dinner, more to keep the children entertained than anything else. I never do much shopping when I don't have the car, because I can't carry more than I can put in the stroller. Anyway, I don't really care for that supermarket. It's a bit crummy. The rice shelves are infested with weevils, and I've seen a squashed cockroach on the floor. What's more, there are always big, sticky spills everywhere; there was one this morning, which Emily trod in. She made a bit of a fuss, because the soles of her shoes started to snap when she walked. But then Mandy came by, and she was distracted. That's the thing about Emily. It doesn't take much to cheer her up—not like Jonah. Jonah broods. He broods because he can't get his stroller harness undone, or because he can't line up five plastic horses precisely in a row. He's frustrated, I think, by the fact that he's still a small child. It's a difficult sort of age when you're a perfectionist.

Anyway, as I said, Mandy came by with two of her three in tow. Mandy is the wholefood mother I was talking about. You know? The one without television? I tell you, she depresses me so much. There she was, looking slim and pretty, with her three-year-old Hamon walking quietly beside her and the baby, Isoline, hanging from her neck in a pouch. (I could never master those pouch things. They always gave me a sore back.) And there was I, overweight and dishevelled, pushing a grizzly Jonah as Emily dawdled along three meters behind me, making patterns on the shiny floor with her sticky feet. Needless to say, Mandy's trolley was full of wholefoods: rolled oats, dried apricots, tofu, bean sprouts, soya milk, tuna in springwater. The fabric roof of my stroller, in contrast, was piled high with chocolate biscuits, pretzels, tinned peaches, cheese crackers, Ovaltine and jelly crystals. Oh— and the chicken nuggets, of course. Don't let's forget the chicken nuggets, which Mandy always says aren't made out of chicken at all.

Then, just to top it off, Mandy started talking about her eldest, Jesse. Apparently he wasn't happy at his current school. It was chaotic, she said, and the teachers were all disillusioned. Rather than have him travel long distances to a Steiner school—one in which a child's individual talents were nurtured and acknowledged, rather than ignored—she was considering the benefits of home schooling. *Home schooling.* This, mind you, from a woman who has two other kids under four, a bloody vegetable garden, and a job making children's clothes that she sells at local markets. (Her children, needless to say, are always beautifully dressed in casual, stylish gear

that she whips up herself out of thick-weave cot-
tons and fake linens in shades of stone, wine,
denim, watermelon and buttercup.)

I just stood there with my mouth hanging
open.

"Well," she said at last, dismissing the subject
with a little smile and a wave of her hand, "I don't
know yet. There's the social aspect I have to consider. Anyway, how are you? You look well."

"I'm fine." Wild horses wouldn't have dragged
the truth out of me. "What about you?"

"Oh, I've been having a terrific time. Remember
that book club I told you about? Well I went to it,
last night, and I took Jesse and Hamon and Isoline,
and it was *wonderful.* Just wonderful." She fixed me
with her mild blue gaze, and smiled her pleasant,
gentle, earth-mother smile. "You ought to come,"
she urged me. "Bring the kids. They'd love it."

Oh sure, I thought. They'd love to loll on my
knee during a discussion of the latest Peter Carey.

"They have their own book club," Mandy continued, "where someone reads to them, and asks
them questions afterwards."

I could just picture it: Jonah trying to wrest the
book from this literary person's hand (being under
the impression that every book on earth is his personal possession—he loves his books with a vengeance), while Emily wanders off to check out the
bone-meal biscuits in the dog's bowl.

Terrific.

"Sounds great," I mumbled, wondering how soon
I could tear myself away without looking rude.
Jonah was starting to grizzle again, while the angelic
Hamon looked on in wonder. He'd probably never

seen anyone grizzling before—certainly not in his own family.

"I'm sorry I missed playgroup yesterday," Mandy went on. "Iso was a bit under the weather."

"Oh dear." Of course my instant reaction was: Christ! Germ alert! And I immediately set about obtaining a run-down of the symptoms. "What was it? Not that tummy bug that Jonah had?"

"No."

"Liam's throat virus?"

"No, no."

"Don't tell me it was something new." I tried to be jovial, though it was no joke, believe me. You have to be alert for the latest illnesses when you're a mother, or you spend your life in a permanent panic. When you know that scarlet fever's going around, you don't run the risk of mistaking it for meningococcal meningitis, and completely losing your mind. Similarly, if you know that it's chicken-pox season, you won't miss any telltale rashes. "Lisa told me about that friend of hers, whose baby got whooping cough—"

"Oh no, it's nothing like that," Mandy reassured me. "Iso was just a bit fretful. So I gave her a massage with essential oils and let her sleep most of the day. She's fine, now."

Just a bit fretful. Shows you, doesn't it? For Mandy, fretfulness is a bloody *disease*, instead of a way of life. Like a bout of bronchitis. As for the baby massage—well, don't talk to me about baby massage. Mandy tried showing me how to massage Jonah, once, but it wasn't a success. He squirmed about in his coating of oil until he managed to wriggle straight off the change-table. Just as well Mandy caught him in time.

"You didn't miss much," I said. "At playgroup. Just as well you weren't there, in fact—Lisa and I were doing the food."

"Oh, now Helen." She laughed fondly. "Don't be so hard on yourself."

"No, really. I mean it." The news was bound to get back to her, so I bravely confessed. "It was all chips and green cordial. Hamon would have starved."

Her expression shifted, slightly. But she was very kind.

"It's hard, isn't it?" she said. "So many children, and some of them so picky. I had a terrible time myself."

Which was a barefaced *lie*, but I didn't argue. When it was Mandy's turn to provide the playgroup morning tea, she had rolled up with home-made bran-and-banana muffins, a choice of three (freshly squeezed) juices, home-baked sourdough bread, a dried fruit platter featuring mango and papaya as well as apple and apricot, carrot sticks from her own garden, and a dip she'd whipped up out of honey, yogurt, wheatmeal, soy flour, pumpkin and all kinds of other things that have escaped my memory, though she must have given me the recipe about four times. Playgroup hasn't been the same, since then. There's always been a bit of competition when it comes to socializing skills and toilet training, but Mandy's Morning Tea was like a gauntlet thrown down. People have taken to turning up with great slabs of carrot cake, pinwheel sandwiches, prune mice, orange jelly baskets, banana bread, muesli crunch biscuits . . . you name it.

I feel like a total failure whenever I shamefacedly break open a packet of party pies, or start sloshing the peanut butter around.

"Anyway, we did some macaroni necklaces," I continued, as Jonah drummed his heels against the footrest of his stroller, making it perfectly clear that his view of the laundry detergents was getting extremely dull. "And Harlan bashed Nicole over the head, and that pedal car lost a wheel. Big crisis. In fact they were all a bit ratty yesterday, so you were well out of it."

Mandy clicked her tongue. But before she could gently raise the subject of sugar-induced hyperactivity, I raised a hand.

"Well, gotta go," I said, "or Jonah will strangle himself in his own harness."

"Yes, of course." Mandy was most sympathetic. "It must be because he's so bright that he needs constant stimulation—"

"Right. Absolutely. Well, bye!" And I took my leave, hurrying away from her serene aura as if it were poison gas. I don't know how she does it, I really don't. How do they do it, these natural-born mothers? I guess it's genetic. I bet Mandy never had any problems with breastfeeding. I bet Mandy was never under the impression that you only have to strap older babies—more mobile babies—into prams. I bet she never suffered the embarrassment, in consequence, of pushing a laden pram up over a high curb and seeing her newborn slide out of the bottom, feet-first, into a gutter.

What's more, I bet that if she had done such a thing, her first instinct would not have been to look around nervously, lest someone had witnessed her potentially fatal mistake.

It has to be said, I'm not much of a mum.

Though it also has to be said that I was quite proud of the way I managed to make breakfast, wash up, wipe down, do laundry, change nappies and dress small bodies this morning while in a state of shock so severe that I actually went to bring in the garbage bin, even though the garbage is usually collected on Wednesdays. But I'm afraid that I screwed it all up when I came home from the shops, opened a cupboard door, and saw that I had forgotten to buy dishwashing liquid. Then I burst into tears like a little kid, and had to be comforted by Emily.

"Don't cry, Mummy," she said. "It doesn't matter." I despise parents who do that sort of thing to their children. I despise parents who behave like five-year-olds, and expect their kids to mother them. And yet there I was, crouched on the kitchen floor, doing what I most despise.

Emily is such a gorgeous little girl. She doesn't deserve the sort of terrible things that go hand in hand with a divorce.

Should I just shut up and ignore my suspicions?

I finally managed to cast my eye over the phone bills after I got Jonah to sleep at one o'clock. He generally sleeps for about two hours in the middle of the day, unless the builders are here. When they are here I gnaw my fingernails and flinch at every hammer-blow, every squeal of the electric drill, every roar of bricks being tipped out of a wheelbarrow. Sometimes these noises wake Jonah; sometimes they don't. I can never pick what he's going to do. He has nerves like violin strings, that boy.

Today, however, I didn't have to worry about builders, and Jonah went down pretty well. He had my old Rubik's-cube key ring to amuse him as he drifted off. Not that he was trying to solve it, or anything, don't get me wrong. He may be bright, but he's not *Mensa* material. (At least, I don't think he is.) He's just one of those children that you can boast about—you know what I mean. "Jonah loves his little books." "Jonah adores his Rubik's cube." "Jonah is infatuated with his Meccano set." There's a downside to this as well, needless to say, because he doesn't eat, he's a lousy sleeper, and he's moody as hell, but at least he's a genius. That's been Matt's and my little joke, throughout all the sleepless nights and endless grizzling. "At least he's a genius," we'll say to each other, because it was something a friend once said to us about his kid, in all serious-ness. "He's a genius," this bloke announced, straight-faced, after we had complimented him on the child's highly developed language skills. I was also told by a well-meaning female friend that moody children who don't sleep are often highly intelligent. It's the reward, apparently, for all the suffering that goes with an infant who already finds the world a bit of a bore.

Jonah, I'm sure, is often bored rigid; hence the screaming fits when he tries to draw a horse, and can't. Or when he tries to reach a shelf, and can't. His fine motor skills obviously haven't caught up with his ambitions, which seem to be a bit unreal-istic, poor kid—you can't help sympathizing when he fails to stack ten pieces of macaroni on top of each other, end to end. How can you explain to a child who isn't yet two that some things just aren't possible? Not that Jonah's slow, when it comes to language. I was changing his nappy the other day when he suddenly announced wistfully, as he gazed out the window: "I like the pink flowers against the blue sky." It was creepy, I can tell you. Sometimes I wonder if he's channelling some grown-up dead person: a bridge builder, perhaps. A Chairman of the Board. If he *does* have a channelling gene, though, it's definitely not from my side of the family. I know exactly where it comes from, and that's Matthew's Nonna. Matthew's Nonna claims to be in contact with several deceased members of her family, praying to them constantly and always remembering their birthdays. There are little altars set up all over Matt's family home, studded with photographs and statues and old pennants and trophies and bronzed baby shoes. You get used to them, after a while. (Jonah loves them, actually.) Matthew says he used to get worried about bumping into the ghost of his uncle Fabbio on the stairs, when he was a kid—or having to share a bath with his dead grandfather—but he's over that now. In fact the channelling gene must have skipped a generation, because he never remembers the birthdays of his living relatives, let alone his dead ones.

Anyway, Jonah fell asleep, and I deposited Emily in front of a *Barney* video with chocolate milk and a muesli bar. We call this time of day the quiet time; it's when Emily has to amuse herself, without running around, while Mummy has a stab at doing some work for an hour. Today I didn't do any work. Today I sat down and trawled through the phone bills for any numbers that might not correspond to the numbers in the family address book.

I found six.

One of them was the number of a discount CD store. One belonged to the chemist up the street; I remembered phoning it after five o'clock several weeks before, when I desperately needed rehydrating iceblocks (Jonah had gastro), and wanted to find out if it was open late. One was answered by a machine with a male voice: "Hello, you have reached Paul, Marcus and Joe, we can't come to the phone right now, so please leave your name and number and we'll get back to you. In the meantime, party hard!" One was the number for the local railway station—a timetable query, no doubt.

That left two more. But I didn't have time to call them, because Emily started getting restless, and I had to break out the sultanas, the self-raising flour and the margarine, and make some scones with her. She likes cooking, does Emily. I suppose I should be encouraging her to play football as well, but I can't be bothered, somehow. I can't seem to dredge up the energy.

At one point I left my daughter happily slopping dough around, and in a fit of despondency called the nearest estate agent—the one who sold us this house. I asked the secretary who answered the phone if she could send me some information on flats to rent in the area, though I was careful not to tell her that I wanted to get an idea of what it might cost to split up with Matthew. Because we wouldn't want to move, not if we could possibly help it. Not with kids so happily settled at the local day care center. Not with everything so handy. Oh God, I thought, as a sense of panic began to rise in me again, oh God, what if it really happens? What if this is *for real*?

Then Jonah woke up, and it was time to go to Lisa's place.

Lisa lives two streets away from us. She's another playgroup mother, only a very different one from

Mandy. In fact she's not very nice about Mandy. "Oh, don't for Chrissake let *her* get you down," Lisa once boomed, adjusting her generous bosom through the folds of her capacious sweatshirt. ("These days my tits are down there in my purse, hunting for the car keys," she'll say philosophically.) "The thing about girls like *her* is, it's all front. Did she tell you what she used to do for a living? Before she married that dickhead with the overbite? Wait for it. She was a plastic surgeon's receptionist."

"No!"

"I swear to God. She had her nose done."

"That's not true."

"It is. She told me."

"Really?"

"I'd been telling her that I was thinking of getting perkier tits." A braying laugh. "Like I could afford a new *bra*, these days. Anyway, she gave me this big lecture about it all—she wouldn't know a joke if it came labelled, in a package—and told me about her nose. Apparently she has chronic sinus problems. She takes ten garlic pills a *day*."

"God, poor thing. When did she tell you?"

"Oh, ages ago. I asked her if she ended up suing the plastic surgeon, and she looked at me like I was mad." Another laugh. "So you see, her life isn't perfect, no matter how hard she tries to persuade you it is." Lisa then went on to expound one of her favorite theories: the fact that a good portion of new mothers who won't admit to any feelings of rage, despair, frustration or fatigue—who turn a beatific face to the world and assure it that everything's fine, wonderful, no problems, a breeze—end up drowning their babies in the bathtub. "A mother's got to vent," she often declares, before launching into a vicious attack on her father-in-law, her next-door neighbor, the local council or the Taxation Office. She also believes that a mother has to "let go"; that is, abandon certain standards that are only attainable when you don't have children.

Her own house is a perfect demonstration of this theory. She has "let go" with a vengeance, and only cleans up once a week. Because she has two rambunctious boys and one dog, this means that the floors are always littered with toys and clothes, the barren garden-beds with toys and gardening equipment, the raised surfaces with broken toys, broken crockery, and confiscated tools (or poisons), and the back steps with old shoes and chewed-up tennis balls. The only things that she won't leave around are dirty plates, cups, bowls or utensils, because her cockroach problem is even worse than my ant problem.

"If those roaches get any bigger," she remarked on one occasion, "we're going to have to start charging rent."

Her house is an old one, like mine; it's a little bigger and a little darker. She earns a bit of cash doing phone polls, these days, though she used to be a psychiatric nurse, and has lots of terrific stories about her time on the wards. According to her, there are countless lunatics around Sydney leading apparently normal lives—like her next-door neighbor, for instance. She says that her next-door neighbor is a borderline schizophrenic. She says that her husband's boss is a sociopath, and that the woman across the road, who keeps complaining about the positioning of Lisa's garbage bin, has an obsessive-compulsive disorder. According to Lisa, it's easier to

understand the world if you realize that most of
the people in it are nuts.

"I'd say that you were a bit bipolar," she diagnosed, upon our second meeting, "but that's okay,
because so am I. My advice is: keep drinking coffee
and stay off the Merchant Ivory films."

She's good company, is Lisa. It's no coincidence
that she knows most of her neighbors, and is
friendly with a lot of them (the ones, she says, who
only exhibit slight neuroses or personality disor-
ders; they can be interesting and fun). She's a so-
ciable sort of person, unlike me. I don't know any
of my neighbors, except to wave to. I don't even
know their names. It's my North Shore upbringing, I suppose. People who are raised on large,
leafy blocks flanked by the residences of reticent
bank managers, and who are driven everywhere as
children, and forbidden to play on roads, or wander far from home, don't develop the kind of skills
that you need to casually drop in on a friend down
the street. Lisa is different. She grew up in a noisy,
beach-suburb house with a banging screen door
and cousins over the back fence and neighbors sitting around on plastic porch furniture lighting
cigarettes and telling their kids to take the dog
with them, and be back by five.

As a result, Lisa will talk to anyone, freely and
fearlessly. And if they turn out to be tiresome nut-
ters, then she detaches herself with cheerful non-
chalance, not really caring what they think of her
in consequence. I admire her so much.

She's a nice person, too. Whenever her husband
has to work on a Saturday, she invites me around
as a gesture of solidarity, and we sit drinking coffee
while the kids play together. Her boys, as I've said,

are a bit of a handful, but Emily can take it because she's such a resilient, good-natured kid,
just like her father. If she falls down and hurts herself, she just gets up again. Jonah's different. I can't
imagine how he's going to survive school, because
he's terribly sensitive, with a tenacious memory.
Whenever we go to Lisa's house, Emily always dashes
out to play tricycle races with Brice and Liam while
Jonah sits inside, arranging Matchbox cars into
complicated patterns.

I feel so sorry for the poor darling. My heart dis-
solves whenever I see him frowning fiercely over a
tricky Lego attachment. But what can I do? Maybe
I should give him a computer for his next birthday,
and be done with it.

When Lisa answered the front door today, kicking aside her dog as she did so, piercing screams
from the back of the house made Jonah clutch at
my neck, almost choking me. Lisa rolled her eyes
("They're being electric eels, or something") and invited us all in. Emily disappeared immediately; I
hardly saw her again for an hour. Jonah stayed
with me while I sampled Lisa's freshly unwrapped
chocolate muffins (she cooks curries, not cakes),
pressing his brown, silky head against my jaw. He
wouldn't go to Lisa. He wouldn't loosen his grip on
my neck. I had to carry him out to the garden
when I went to look at the new lattice that Simon,
Lisa's husband, had put up. It was framed, and
firmly rooted in the ground against a side fence.
Lisa intends to train a passionfruit vine up over it.

"It'll be another barrier between me and that
psycho next door," she said, in a loud voice. "And
it should be all right, because it gets the sun in the
mornings. What do you think? It's nice, isn't it?"

"Very," I agreed.

"I think I might get Simon to do the whole fence. We'll paint it all white and it'll show that we haven't given up entirely." She pointed to the bald patch in the middle of her backyard, where Liam, Brice and Emily were kicking up dust. "Simon has a fit every time he looks at that lawn," she explained, "but I tell him: 'What are you moaning about? Your head's in a worse state, and *I* still like it.' "

Simon, in fact, is a paunchy, balding, sun-whipped bloke who looks years older than his age, which is around forty-four, I think. He used to be a surfer, but you could never tell it now. Sometimes, when I'm sighing over the fact that he can put up lattice, spray weeds and fix chairs, I remind myself that he's also one of the most physically unattractive men of my acquaintance, all belly and boiled skin, whereas Matt is tall and dark and handsome, and will open his mouth in mixed company.

I reminded myself of this fact again today, before it suddenly struck me, like a bucket of cold water in the face, that I might no longer be justified in laying claim to Matt's rakish good looks and lazy charm.

"What's up?" said Lisa. "Are you okay?"

"Yeah."

"You haven't got a cramp, or something?"

"No. I'm fine."

"That's one thing you can say about kids. At least they put an end to period pains. Did you find that? After you had Emily?"

"Yes."

"I used to get *killer* cramps, I'd be doubled over, right from when I was a kid. And back then I was so embarrassed about it. I told someone I had appendicitis once, would you believe? Now I'd just say that my *uterus* is going into *spasm*, you got a problem with that?"

As she rattled on, I wondered if I should tell her. I wondered how she would respond: by dismissing my fears as laughable, or by stridently condemning Matt as a "typical bloody male; someone ought to bring out a line of chastity jocks"? In the end, I couldn't bring myself to utter the words, though for all I knew she might have had her own problems with Simon (despite his unappealing gut). What's more, she possessed all the qualifications of an excellent confidante and counsellor: the psychiatric training, the quick wit, the sympathetic manner, the trustworthy moral code.

But I couldn't bring myself to do it. It was too shaming—too revealing.

Besides, I thought, with a spark of hope, who's to say that I'm not mistaken? I mean, I haven't even checked those last two phone numbers yet.

I finally did it this evening, after Matt arrived home. He was late again—an hour late—and blamed it on farewell drinks for somebody-or-other. Even so, he was back in time to put Jonah to bed, and then Emily. If he hadn't been, we would have Had Words. The kids are always keen to have Daddy put them to bed on the weekends, because Mummy does it the rest of the week (except Tuesdays). They also prefer Daddy's putting-to-bed technique because he plays the bouncing game—something he inherited from his own father—and doesn't have such a fetish about teeth cleaning. Not that I mind. Let's face it, I'd rather have Matt put *me* to bed. His voice is so rough and warm, it's like a woolly blanket.

While Matt was reading books and singing songs, I had a shower. I emerged from the steamy bathroom to find my husband chopping vegetables for dinner, and instead of melting with gratitude became instantly suspicious. Only guilt would have driven him into the kitchen without prompting, I decided.

Was it guilt for being late, or guilt for being late because the Girl With Purple Hair had detained him?

"It's chilli, right?" he asked.

"That's right."

"Feelin' better?"

"A bit." I mean, it wasn't as if I'd had a long, scented bubble bath, or anything. "What's this? A menu?"

"It was in the letterbox. New Thai place. No mail today?"

"It's Saturday, Matt."

"Oops! That's right. I forgot. Bugger it—I thought my tax refund might have arrived. I should have got it by now."

Matt's an optimist; he always looks forward to getting mail. I don't. The mail always seems to be bills, these days.

I looked at him standing there, stooped over the cutting board with his back to me. He was wearing a thin, grey cotton jumper, very old and loose, that swayed slightly with every rhythmic shift of his muscles. The back of his neck was showing as he bent it, a pale line between the grey wool and the black hair. I couldn't believe that he was there, looking so normal. I could have reached out my hand and touched him—and why did that seem so strange? Was it because, in my mind, he had already fled? Or was it because I expected him to be different in some way from the man I had married?

I turned quickly, and went into our bedroom. It's the darkest room in the house, but at least it's a good size. There isn't much in it: just the bed (which pretty much emptied our bank account), a clothes rack, a shoe rack, and a beat-up, old-fashioned wardrobe that's much too small (hence the clothes rack). On my side of the bed there's also a stool, with a piece of white linen draped over it. That's where I put my books and my tissues and the telephone.

I closed the door, picked up the receiver, and dialed the first of the two remaining numbers on my list.

A woman answered on the third ring.

"Hello?" she said. She had a high, breathless voice.

I cleared my throat.

"Hello," I replied hoarsely. "Who's this?"

"Megan."

"Megan Stewart?"

"No. Megan Molesdale."

"Oh. I'm sorry. Wrong number."

I put the receiver down, and sat there on the bed. Megan Molesdale? Who the hell was Megan Molesdale? I'd never heard the name before in my life.

"What's up?" said Matt, from behind me. I nearly jumped out of my skin.

"Oh!" I gasped. "Oh . . ."

"What's the matter?"

"Nothing. You scared me."

"Who were you talking to?"

"No one. Wrong number." As Matt's eyes widened, I quickly backtracked. "I mean—Lisa gave me the wrong number. I called the wrong number."

"Oh." He raised an eyebrow as he slowly scratched the back of his neck. "Well . . . okay. Do you know where the tomato paste is?"

Selective blindness. Does he really not see the jar sitting at the front of the shelf, or is it just a pretense, because he can't be bothered even looking? Perhaps it's that brain-wiring problem again.

"I'll show you. It should be there." On my way to the kitchen, I was slightly unsteady on my feet. But I made it, and did my usual trick with the magic materializing jar of tomato paste.

Megan Molesdale?

Another sleepless night lies ahead.

Chapter Three

Sunday

Other people look forward to Sunday mornings. Once upon a time, I was the same. On Sunday mornings I would wake up around ten, make percolated (not instant) coffee, take a long, hot shower, then wander down to a café on Oxford Street for brunch—eggs, French toast and banana pancakes—which I would eat while leafing through the newspapers.

This morning, I got up at 5:45 a.m. Why? Because Jonah's an early riser, and can't be allowed to roam about unsupervised, even in a house where every power point has a protective plug in it and every cutlery drawer is fitted with a childproof latch. He's such a determined little thing when it comes to latches—and such a Houdini, when it comes to squeezing through holes—that you can't help admiring him for it, even while you're peeling his fingers off the handle of a bread knife. "I want to make a carrot," he pointed out to me this morning, in injured and perfectly articulated tones, when I refused to allow him access to the vegetable peeler. I told him that he could do it later, when he was Emily's age. (By then, I thought, he probably *would* be making carrots—out of thin air. Using a patented matter generator of some kind.) After which he explained that he wanted to make a carrot *into a kangaroo*, and I wondered, with alarm, if he was suddenly going to start sculpting things out of root vegetables.

Sometimes, I swear, he intimidates me.

In case you're wondering, I'm *always* the one who gets up early, in this house. It's not exactly that my husband and I came to an agreement; it's just that I'm a light sleeper, and Matt isn't. Matt can sleep through the noise that Jonah makes, pounding flat-footed over our wooden floors, whereas I can't. Everything wakes me, these days. Coughs. Cats. Hot-water pipes. It's something to do with being a mother. Something to do with the shake-up that your body clock suffers during those first few months of four-hour feeds.

So I got up with Jonah, and warmed his milk, and changed his nappy, and checked the phone bills again before Matt had a chance to crawl out from under the covers. Six calls to Megan Molesdale. A quick glance at the Coustos & Sons Pharmacy calendar ("Serving the Community since 1974") confirmed my suspicions. The calls to Megan Molesdale, all six of them, had been made on three consecutive Tuesdays, between the hours of nine and five-thirty. When I was at work, in other words, and Matt was at home, looking after the kids.

Yet another telling blow.

As I cut Jonah's apple slices into butterfly shapes, I flicked through the *White Pages*. Molesdale, M.

Only one listed in the book. There was her number—identical to the one on our phone bill—and there was her address. Some place in Randwick.

Then Emily woke up, and put an end to my surreptitious investigations. She was in a chatty mood, spouting questions like a telephone pollster. Why wasn't I wearing my slippers? Why weren't my feet cold? Why didn't Jonah like crumpets? Would Daddy be waking up soon? What were we going to do, today?

"We're going to Kerry and Paul's house for lunch," I replied.

"Who?"

"You know. You know Kerry and Paul. They have two big girls, don't you remember? Don't you remember Gemma and Zoe?"

"Gemma?"

"And Zoe. They have that little white dog. And the orange cat with the bell around its neck."

"Oh!" My daughter's memory is highly selective. "And the swimming pool?"

"That's the one."

"And they have a *big* doll's house!"

"That's it."

"Yay!" She flung her arms around my thighs. "Is Daddy coming?"

"Of course."

"Yay!"

She dashed into her bedroom to pack a bag. Emily can't go anywhere without her bag. It's a blue plush monkey with a zippered hole in its gut, and she always stuffs it so full of hairclips, doll's clothes, markers, novelty key rings, old Christmas cards and plastic farm animals that it looks permanently pregnant. She has this idea in her head that

you can't go anywhere unless you're laden with
junk. As a result, we never visit anyone's house without leaving something vital behind: a stamp, perhaps, or a stuffed rabbit, or the lid of a miniature
teapot. Something, at any rate, that's absolutely vital
to her general well-being, as we always discover
when we're pulling into our garage. Fortunately,
my daughter's displays of misery are loud but
brief, like summer storms. And she can usually be
silenced with something as straightforward as a
muesli bar.

But I don't really have a right to complain, considering the baggage that *I* always drag around. It's
obvious that Emily gets her packhorse mentality
from me. When you travel with two young children, you can't afford to overlook *any eventuality.*
If you forget the water, they'll want a drink. If you
pack a sandwich, they'll want an apple. Spare disposable nappies are a must, of course, as are wet
wipes, nappy bags, tissues, Band-Aids, and a change
of clothes for each child. If you don't include a
change of clothes, you're laying yourself open to
all kinds of disasters: toilet-training accidents, carsickness, milkshake spillages—even complete im-
mersion in a stagnant duckpond.

That's why I can't trust Matt to handle preparations for a family outing. He never remembers to
make Emily go to the toilet before she gets in the
car. He always forgets Jonah's bottle, or Emily's
hat. There's invariably something that we come
away without, if it's left to him. I know, I know.
Don't remind me. I sound like the proverbial ball-
and-chain off on a ranting feminist diatribe, but
it's true. Most men can't seem to organize these
things. Honestly. I've talked about it again and

again at playgroup, and I always hear the same story from every mother there. Sometimes it gets quite surreal, like the husband who loaded up his car with everything except the baby. Or the husband who took his kids on a weekend trip to the north coast without packing underpants or sunscreen.

Mind you, I've never met a man who's the primary carer, so it might not be a gender thing after all. Matt's very firm on that point. He also thinks I'm a bit—well, hyper is probably the word. And I suppose that I do go overboard on occasion, dragging raincoats around everywhere. Providing a choice of beverages (milk, water or juice). Always adding yet one more emergency nappy, just in case.

But what can you do? It's conditioning. After that first year, with all the bottle disinfecting equipment, and nursing pads, and spare dummies, and teething gel, and extra bibs, of *course* I'm going to feel uneasy if a bag seems too light. Automatically, you register an absence. Something forgotten.

That's why some trips are hardly worth the hassle. That's why my social life always leaves me so exhausted. Preparing for a picnic is like preparing for a three-day hike.

I was thinking about this as I hovered over the toaster. If picnics had become like three-day hikes, and the laundry like a full-time job, and evenings like tactical training exercises, then what time had I been able to spare for Matthew, lately? None, of course. Perhaps he had been feeling neglected. Perhaps he had sensed a yawning chasm opening up between us. Our points of connection had been reduced to domestic practicalities. (And don't even talk to me about sex.) When had we last gone out to dinner—by ourselves? Walked along the beach—unburdened by plastic buckets? Visited a second-hand book shop—for more than ten minutes? I'll tell you when. When my parents were still living on the North Shore. Three years ago, they retired to the southern highlands, and that was that.

I've never had much help from Matt's side of the family, you see. It's partly because they all live so far away, and partly because Jonah happens to be my mother-in-law's eleventh grandchild. We went to Newcastle for the festive season one year, and it was like a mosh pit around the Christmas tree: eleven children under the age of ten, ripping into presents as they elbowed each other out of the way. Poor Marcella has her hands well and truly full, up there; I wouldn't expect her to be popping down here every second weekend. And she always remembers birthdays. Plus she's always gorgeous when we *do* get to see her. She's one of those lovely Italian grandmothers, very physical, always kissing and squeezing and tickling and sucking little pink toes. Even Jonah responds to his granny. Most of the time he's very cautious with people, nervous of loud voices, suspicious of proffered arms, but he loves Marcella. He loves Matt's Nonna, too, though poor Nonna doesn't move around much any more, what with her arthritis. Still, she loves spoiling the kids. She's one of the few people who've ever seen Jonah's dimples, besides Matt and me.

Anyway, that's my problem. No accessible grandparents. I don't need a marriage counsellor to tell me that my husband and I would benefit from some quality time together. That we have to rediscover the shared joys, as well as the shared responsibilities, of the matrimonial state. But who's going to put Jonah to bed in the meantime? A qualified babysitter, at $12.50 an hour? Even if we could find one around here, a two-hour meal would come to $25 *before we had even ordered drinks.*

It occurred to me (as I buttered toast) that despite all the deprivations associated with life as a working mother, I hadn't been feeling so neglected that I'd gone off and found myself a nice building contractor to sleep with. I wouldn't have felt justified in doing so, though it wasn't as if Matthew had been very attentive to my needs lately. Not that I've had many needs that I've been conscious of, except the need for a decent night's sleep, and the need for someone to fix that damn cupboard door in the kitchen, but you know what I mean: the sort of needs that people talk about in therapy sessions and modern literature. The need to feel appreciated. Unique. Spiritually nourished. All that sort of stuff. Okay, so I might not have been providing enough in the way of affirmation, but you could say the same thing about him. And did I blame him for it? No, I did not! All I did was blame him for sensible things, like leaving his shaving soap out where Jonah could get at it.

I was thinking all this when Matthew stumbled into the kitchen. Again, it's not his fault that I'm wide awake the second I open my eyes, while he's semi-comatose for a good half hour after rising. You can't blame him for that. It's genetic. You might as well blame him for his hairy chest or his big ears.

Even so, I do wish sometimes that I got to put my feet up in the morning.

"We'll have to take something," I said to him, and he stared at me with bleary eyes.

"Ughn?" he said.

"We'll have to take something to the Irwins. A cake, or something. Wine? Have we got any wine?"

"Dunno." Matt wiped a hand over his bristly face. Then he went to have a shower.

It's impossible to converse with him until he has his morning shower.

By the time Matt emerged, Jonah was getting really antsy. The poor kid had been up since 5:45, and it was already half past eight. So there was a lot of noise and discussion among the dirty dishes (those drains, by the way, are beginning to stink again—should I go straight out and buy Drano or try some vinegar first?), and finally it was agreed that Matt should take Jonah and Emily to the park until the local bottle shop opened, while I cleaned the house, packed the travelling supplies, and made myself presentable. I stressed that we would have to leave for Tamarama by eleven o'clock at the latest. Then I waved them off and shut the front door, savoring the silence that they left behind.

I love having the house to myself. God, it's fantastic. Just me and The Silence, which I picture as a kind of large cat, blinking and fluffy, very still and exuding calm. The kids always scare it right out of the house. But when I'm here alone, even when I'm vacuuming, it's not far away. As soon as I switch off the vacuum cleaner, it's in the room again, as dense as smoke.

I never appreciated it before, not the way I do now. The Silence. The Stillness. I went around picking up toys, Rice Bubbles, dirty socks and old newspapers, enjoying each creak of the floorboards—because you don't notice them creaking normally during the day (too much noise), and at night each creak is like a pistol-shot, making you flinch as you try to creep past the kids' room on your way to the toilet. Unfortunately, however, the vacuuming had to be done, so I was unable to wallow for more than a few minutes. There's always some big, dirty job scheduled for when the kids are out of the house; you never get to sit back and bask in the peace. If it's not the vacuuming (which scares Jonah—he thinks that the vacuum cleaner's going to eat him) it's something involving water or paint. You can't afford to let Emily and Jonah get anywhere near water or paint. Not inside the house, you can't.

While I vacuumed, I had the leisure to think about sex. So far I'd been able to avoid picturing Matt with his dick inside another woman, but there's something about vacuum cleaners, and the way you push that long shaft about . . . well, you get my drift. I couldn't help myself. I thought about this alleged purple-haired girl, in bed, under Matthew, and I was cast adrift. I didn't know how I felt. Afraid? Angry? Disgusted? All three of the above? Miriam had said that the purple-haired girl looked like a junkie. Was she, in fact, just that? Was Matthew bonking a junkie? Surely, *surely*, he couldn't be so stupid? And even if she wasn't a junkie, even if he wore condoms, how could that possibly be clean or safe?

But in a funny sort of way, it wasn't the physical thing that I minded so much. I didn't really believe that sex with her could be anywhere near as good as the variety he got at home—not unless he was willing to sacrifice quality for quantity. Granted, we didn't do it much. Granted, we were both a bit deprived in that area. Nevertheless, as the kids got older, our pace was bound to pick up; couldn't he see that? Wasn't it glaringly obvious that our kind of compatibility couldn't be found on every street corner? We'd always been a natural fit, and years of shared experience had refined and improved our techniques. I mean, I knew the guy—at least in this regard. I knew what he liked. So why the hell was he going elsewhere?

I told myself that there was every chance he hadn't gone elsewhere. I reminded myself that I hadn't established his infidelity beyond all doubt. But if he had gone elsewhere, then the sex—the physical side of it—surely wasn't the reason. I couldn't believe that it was. Matt wasn't one of those men who would screw a sheep or a prostitute or a mate's girlfriend in pure desperation, just because he had to get his rocks off at least once a day. His testosterone levels weren't off the chart. He was a normal guy, I was sure of it. Unless he had been nursing a deeply buried desire to have someone pee on him, or something?

No. Not a chance.

No, if Matt was having an affair, it was because he wanted something besides sex. Adoration, perhaps. Unknown Territory. The freedom to yell during orgasm, without worrying that Jonah might wake up.

A navel stud, maybe?

It made me so furious, the notion that Matt might be wanting fancy underwear or foot massages *as well as* kids, dinner, a clean house, an extra income, a laundry service and my fabulous muffin recipe. But before I could build up a really savage head of steam, I found myself beginning to worry about all the things that I wasn't providing. The list was far too long. His last birthday had completely slipped my mind. (Though I had apologized profusely, the damage was done.) I would often greet him, not with a kiss and an inquiry about his day, but with a complaint about the builders, or about the fact that he hadn't filled the car up with petrol. I had stopped buying the shower gel he liked, because it was too expensive. And of course there were all those other things: movies, restaurants, brunch, sex, unstinting admiration . . .

Then I caught sight of myself in a mirror, as I wiped down the shower stall, and something clicked. The hair. The droop. The unplucked eyebrows.

By the time Matt returned with Emily and Jonah, I had put on lipstick, mascara, eyeshadow, earrings, perfume, pantyhose, my Italian slingbacks and my Lisa Ho cream chiffon dress.

Matt stared at me in a startled fashion.

"You look nice," he said, sounding surprised. I didn't know whether to be flattered or resentful. I didn't really have time to be either, because Jonah launched himself at me, his face besmeared with ice-cream, and I had to duck behind a chair.

That's the trouble with dressing up to go out. These days, I'm always torn between wanting to look nice and not wanting to get any of my remaining good clothes (that still fit me) irretrievably soiled by small, grubby fingers. The Lisa Ho dress, up till now, has fallen into the category of "wedding receptions without kids" or even "if I ever appear on TV/meet Ralph Fiennes/get invited to a Royal garden party." But you have to be realistic, don't you? You have to bite the bullet and take a few risks, if you want to keep your husband.

That's what I told myself, anyway.

"Ice-cream?" I said. "At this hour?" And Matt instantly went on the defensive.

"There was a Mr. Whippy," he explained. "Jonah hurt himself."

"What did you do to your face, Mummy?" Emily asked. But I ignored her.

"Will you wipe him down, Matt? Please? I'm wearing my good dress."

"Yeah. Sure," said Matt. "Maybe I should change. Do you reckon?"

"Better make it quick. We're already late."

So Matt took off his T-shirt and put on a shirt. He's come a long way since I first met him; he'll wear colors now, and tops that button down the front. The result is that he's looking better than ever (despite a certain coarsening of the skin and a very slight—almost undetectable—thinning of the hair) while I'm rapidly coming apart. The hands. The stretch marks. The cellulite.

What if I haven't held together enough for Matt? What if that's the trouble? Could it really be that banal?

Looking at him as he slapped on his sunglasses, I asked myself: suppose he went bald? Would I still love him then?

Actually, I almost wish he would go bald. At least if he was bald, my cellulite wouldn't matter so much.

The trip to Tamarama was accomplished without excessive drama. As usual, there was tension over who got to play what music, with Matt and Emily competing stubbornly for control of the CD player. Having been forced to shelve all songs featuring certain four-letter words and references to guns, butts, sex, whores, drugs and pussies (I'd hate to tell you what Emily started singing in the car one day, on the subject of pussies), Matt's decided that he should be given at least some opportunity to play those songs which haven't been consigned to the headphones only basket. It's a matter of principle, with him. Emily, on the other hand, has her own taste in music. She likes the Wiggles, Sesame Street, Christmas carols and certain Disney favorites, over and over again.

Personally, I'd willingly endure "Santa Claus is Coming to Town" twenty-seven times in a row if it meant that I didn't have to play one round of "What animal am I thinking of?" but Matt feels differently. It's a battle of wills, every time he starts the engine. I don't know why he bothers. How can anyone enjoy Counting Crows while Emily is whining and groaning and asking questions in the background? What's the point? And Matt's choice of music seems so inappropriate, somehow. Fatboy Slim. Pearl Jam. Sloane. This isn't music for people with booster seats and wet wipes in the car. This is music for raging young dudes in combi vans, or slick eastern-suburbs types in linen and Ray-Bans and red convertibles. All I feel, when I listen to Matt's music, is deprived.

Maybe that's how he's been feeling, too. Maybe therein lies the problem.

Fortunately, it was a beautiful day. A real beach day. The sky was blue, the air was fresh, and the sea was sparkling. Even Jonah seemed quite satisfied with life, singing along to the Wiggles with cheerful concentration. As for me, I was so beguiled by the cozy family atmosphere that I began to unwind a bit. The knot in my stomach started to unravel. I shoved on a pair of sunglasses, wound down the window and enjoyed that indefinable atmosphere that Sydney always lays on, when the weekend weather's fine—a kind of laid-back carnival atmosphere, it is—until Emily suddenly threw up. Emily always throws up. She pukes at the drop of a hat: when she's overtired, when she's overexcited, when she eats too much, when she eats too little, when she eats grapes or doughnuts or avocado, when she's been swimming, when she gets her shots, when she's got a cough or a cold, when it's been too long since breakfast . . . all the time. She has a very strong gag reflex. That's what the doctors told me, after she'd been through a battery of tests because I'd started to worry, and was beginning to wonder if maybe she had something really wrong with her. I mean, when she hadn't outgrown this rampant spewing by the age of two, I started to get concerned. Though it turned out just to be Emily. Emily's stomach. She'd get carsick on her tricycle, given the chance.

That's why we have plastic sick bags and old towels strategically placed around the back seat of the car. She's old enough now to anticipate trouble, though not necessarily to aim as well as we'd like her to. Poor darling, you could hardly expect it. So I had to change her skirt and her socks, and dispose of the sick bag, and wash her face, and give her a drink, and as a result we were late getting to Tamarama, what with the beach traffic and everything.

Not that it mattered much, because lunch wasn't served until half past two. This meant that I had to make a pest of myself cutting up an apple and slicing cheese and buttering biscuits for Emily, or she would have thrown up again. (Too many corn chips on an empty stomach does it to her every time.) I hate that. I hate looking like a neurotic mum, asking if there's anything besides Coke or mineral water or lemon squash or tomato juice or soya milk or green cordial—some Ribena, perhaps? It's not even as if Emily has a respectable *allergy*, for God's sake. Just a stomach like a live volcano.

And Kerry, I could tell, hated having me clutter up her kitchen benchtops with jars of Vegemite and strawberry fruit straps and Jonah's special little tubs of (butterless) popcorn and chopped-up dried apple (he's terribly picky about his food) while she was trying to mix salad dressing. She mixes her own salad dressing. She even has her own yogurt maker. But don't get me started on Kerry.

It's a shame, because I always want to go to the Irwins'. They live in the most fantastic house, exactly eight minutes' walk from the beach. They have a cat, a dog, and a pool. They also have two children, one five and one seven—so in addition to everything else, they have an unlimited supply of scooters, Barbie dolls, wooden puzzles, Lego bricks, *Madeline* DVDs, computer games, and everything else you need for a leisurely, stress-free lunch on the patio. Plus the two kids are great—especially Zoe. She looks after Jonah as if she were born to it. Reads to him and everything.

The upshot of all this is that we can never get over there fast enough. Whenever I think of that glassy box cantilevered over that tumbling slope, I think of airy blue vistas and strawberry daiquiris and sandy bathrooms and children's laughter and rockpools and barbecued octopus. And then I arrive, and it all starts to go sour in my head.

I've known Paul since university. He is, and always has been, the funniest guy in the world—so sharp, and at the same time so good-natured. A sweetheart, in other words. Maybe a little nervy and high-strung, but nothing you'd need medication for. We didn't go out together (he didn't turn me on, if truth be told), but we were always good friends, even though he was brilliant and I wasn't. Well—brilliant in his chosen field, that is. He's a big-time corporate lawyer now, making stacks of money, but you'd never guess it. Though his sandy hair is thinning on top, and he wears polo shirts and yachting shoes and a big, chunky Rolex, he doesn't behave like your average bigshot. He's one of those people who's always delighted to see you, who thinks that your jokes are funnier than his own, who has a big, toothy grin and a joyous laugh, who tells a terrific story (but rarely at someone else's expense), and who specializes in taking the piss out of himself. You know the sort of thing. The way Paul talks, you'd think that he bluffed his way into his job, and now spends his time screwing up PowerPoint presentations and doing pratfalls at board meetings. But he doesn't, of course. He's just modest. Modest and eager to entertain.

You might be thinking: what's your problem then, Helen? If Paul's so terrific, if his house is so terrific, if his kids are so terrific, then why the long face? Why are you off on one of your rants again, you miserable, long-faced party pooper?

The answer is: Kerry. Kerry and my own flawed nature. Kerry and I don't hit it off, because she's one of those eastern suburbs girls who always struck me as being incredibly blinkered and dense. She's tall and blonde and willowy, with a long face and porcelain skin; she hardly ever speaks, and her face is inscrutable; she has a high, pretty voice, an impeccable wardrobe and expensive tastes. And that, as far as I can see, is all there is to her. It seems extraordinary, when Paul is so funny and smart and (let's face it) rich, but I honestly can't see what else she has to offer. Because if she's not stupid, she's doing a bloody good imitation. What I mean is—she's a trained florist, right? With some kind of florist's certificate? So I ask her things like: "Are native flowers selling better than they were ten years ago?" or "Do you have to ask a bride if she's allergic to anything, before you make up her bouquet?" and she looks at me as if I'm mad. Honestly. That's the precise expression on her face: a sort of blank-eyed alarm. As if I'd told her that I was planning to donate my womb to the Smith Family.

She behaves, in other words, as if I'm eccentric, as if my kids are underprivileged, and as if we were all living in a fibro housing commission place out in Mount Druitt, or somewhere else equally lacking in cachet. Dulwich Hill just isn't part of her vocabulary. To her, it's out west. What's more, if we ever finish our renovations and invite her over, it won't change her opinion. She'll cast her vacant gaze over the leadlight windows, the tessellated tiles and the ornate ceilings, and she'll fail to be impressed, because the house is on a quarter-acre block half an hour from the nearest headland, French provincial antique dealer or merchant banker.

That's one reason why I end up feeling very

prickly and competitive when I visit the Irwins. I become grudging and petty-minded; I think to myself, That pool's not so big, but it fills up the whole backyard, or, Imagine how dismal it must be in here on a grey, blustery afternoon, with all this slate floor and minimalist furniture. Kerry's taste is very formal, and much more modern than mine. She likes unusual color combinations and spiky flower arrangements and vast tracts of polished blond wood. I'm different. I like old things. That's why we bought the house in Dulwich Hill, which is a double-brick Federation place with a slate roof and wooden floors, a lemon tree in the backyard and a detached laundry. I was pregnant with Jonah, at the time, and we had to find something fast because we couldn't stay in our rented flat in Darlinghurst, with its cramped proportions and moldy bathroom—I was going mad in that place. So we bought our new house as soon as we'd saved up enough money for a sizeable deposit, not realizing what we'd got ourselves into.

Old houses are full of secrets. Not good old secrets, like caches of love letters under the floorboards, or marble mantelpieces concealed behind a sheet of plasterboard—I'm talking about bad old secrets. Our house only had two bedrooms, but we thought that we'd add another when Jonah was eighteen months old and I went back to work. We wanted another bedroom, a larger kitchen, and a laundry with a roof that didn't leak. Little did we know that, on pulling up some of our old linoleum, we would find not only layers of delightful antique newspapers, but termite damage and sewage leaks as well. Pipes had to be dug up, boards had to be replaced, and by the time all that was done our builder was running late; our job was beginning to impinge on another one. So then our builder started to juggle them both, and you can guess what happened. Nothing. Nothing at all, for long stretches of time.

I was such an innocent when I bought our house. I had no idea what it means to own your own real estate. Sure, I knew about mortgages, but I didn't understand about pest inspections, gutter cleaning, electric hot water systems, council rates, plumbing problems, sewage leaks or termite damage. I never imagined that it would all be so *expensive*. God, it's expensive—especially if neither you nor your husband can change a tap washer, or replace a hinge. And it was all made doubly expensive by the fact that I went a bit mad when Jonah was a baby. What I mean is, I became obsessed with interior design magazines.

You know the type of thing I'm talking about. Those thick, glossy doorstops full of ads for upholstery fabrics and tapware and six-burner cook tops. There's usually a "special" feature on beautiful bathrooms (or kitchens), an article on a designer's inner-city cottage—utterly transformed into a four-storey mansion with guest room and Tuscan courtyard—and another one on a converted coach-house in the southern highlands of New South Wales. Well, I don't need to tell you. You've probably seen about a million of them—or two million, if you're anything like me. I was fixated on our house when Jonah was a baby. I thought about almost nothing else, because it was our first house, because I was stuck in it all day every day, looking at the woodgrain laminex in the kitchen, and because thinking about limestone benchtops or concealed range-hoods took my mind off the awfulness of Jonah. God, he was awful. I know I shouldn't be saying it (most people are really shocked, when a mother comes out and says that her child's being a pain) but some babies are sent to try you. Lisa reckons that when she was pregnant with Liam, and as sick as a dog, the only things that saved her sanity were grisly thriller videos like _Seven_ and _The Silence of the Lambs_, from which she could derive the satisfying knowledge that, while things were bad for her, they could be infinitely worse.

During _my_ time of trial, I relied on homemaker magazines. My brief moments of respite—when I was sitting on the toilet, say, or waiting at the Early Childhood Clinic, pushing Jonah back and forth in his pram—were always spent poring over paint catalogues or photographs of window treatments. Raptly, I would marvel at the names of the colors. (Whoever thought of minced onion as a name? Or reef cocktail? Or medici sunset?) Enviously, I would study shots of somebody's renovated 1830s farmhouse, wondering how there could be so many people in the world with money for Georgian book-cupboards and silk tapestries. It was the only time in my life when I've ever been able to talk to Kerry about anything; we could discuss German dishwashers and hardwood inlays and be more or less on the same wavelength, because I had vaulting ambitions, at that stage, owing to my constant reading of _Interiors_ and _Country Style_.

Since then, I've calmed down a bit—just as Jonah has. I've abandoned my visions of parquet floors and Miele appliances, and settled for something more basic. With the result that I'm back to square one with Kerry, reduced to comments about

the weather, or the state of the traffic. It's terrible.
I suppose I could solve the problem to some degree by complimenting her generously on her
clothes, dinnerware, paintings, view, jewelry or entertainment system, but I just can't do it. I'm too
mean-spirited. Not like Matt, who has a better nature than I do. He's always quite happy to admire
Paul's Plasma-screen TV and concealed speakers
with unselfconscious delight, because he doesn't
have an envious or judgemental bone in his body.
I bet he never once even thought to compare our
Persian rug with the Irwins' Persian rug at lunch
today, whereas I was constantly making compari-
sons. For example: This house might be bigger
than ours, but it's too stitched up—you can't relax
in it. This dining suite may be expensive but it's
going to go out of style pretty quickly—ours will
never go out of style, because it's antique. Our
bath is nicer than this one. My eyes are bigger than
Kerry's. My husband is better looking than any
other man in this room.

There were two other men and three other
women, besides Kerry and Paul. They were all
pretty nice. One of the blokes seemed to think a
bit too much of himself (he was some kind of chief
executive officer) and the other one hardly uttered a word, but the women were friendly. The
CEO's wife had this whole routine worked out,
based on the fact that she and her husband had recently—owing to his phenomenal success—found
themselves mixing with people whose tastes and
incomes were beyond anything she'd ever had to
deal with before. So she'd rattle her bracelets and
giggle about how she'd been faking an intimate familiarity with restaurants she'd never heard of;

how she'd been complaining about the *Sydney Morning Herald* to one of the Fairfaxes, without realizing it; how she had made a big, big mistake when she'd started denigrating miniature dogs at a party in Rose Bay. I mean, she was only saying all this because she wanted to make a point about her social horizons, but it was very nicely done. And she knew enough to giggle at everyone else's stories, too.

The other women were genuinely pleasant. Bettina was thin and dark, with huge, luminous, pale green eyes and one of those lovely soft voices that you normally associate with yoga teachers or massage therapists. Even if she had said something rude, it wouldn't have come off that way—and of course she didn't. Every word she uttered was reassuring, sympathetic or grateful. Looking at her, you just knew that she used a lot of essential oils and had a cat called Thalia.

Candice was a lot sharper, but in an amusing way. She made wry observations about being attacked by a modern sculpture, and doing battle with a childproof latch. She talked about the thief she'd surprised climbing through her bathroom window; he'd said "Sorry, love" before making his getaway, as if he was turning down an invitation to a cup of tea. ("I almost said 'Sorry' myself, when I burst in on him," she admitted. "Force of habit, I suppose.") She had big brown eyes behind owlish glasses, and was dressed so drably that I couldn't help feeling relieved. In fact I was astonished that Kerry had even let her through the door, until I discovered that, despite the scuffed sandals and Indian cotton skirt, Candice was the daughter of a literary agent and a wealthy politician (I forget their names) and was running her own successful furniture restoration business when she wasn't looking after her teenaged boys.

That made me a bit glum, I can tell you. Three teenaged boys *and* a successful business! Fortunately, she wasn't a wholefood mother—"I usually go for the easiest option," she confessed to me—but even so it was intimidating. Particularly when the youngest son turned out to be a total delight. Declan, his name was. Fresh-faced, alert, a talented guitarist, thirteen years old and *polite*, my God, I couldn't believe it. Smiled. Answered questions. Responded with genuine interest (instead of total incomprehension) when Matt confessed to having been a drummer in a band. Poor Declan, he was really making an effort; it wasn't his fault that he was a bit hazy on dates, and made the mistake of asking if Matt had worked with—uh—AC/DC? Or the guy who wrote "Eagle Rock"?

Naturally, we all laughed at that, and Declan looked bewildered.

"Bit before my time, those blokes," Matt said gently.

"Oh."

"Bit outta my league, and all."

"They're experts in the art of making you feel ancient," said Candice, once her son had finally managed to extricate himself from adult company. "They do it all the time."

"Oh, isn't it awful, though?" the CEO's wife yelped. "Suddenly I'm middle-aged! I don't know how it happened! I find myself saying the *exact same things* my mother used to say to me!"

"Well, it's inevitable," Paul said comfortably. "You can't help it. You just have to resign yourself—one day, you'll be playing golf every weekend. It's happening already. I've got myself a set of clubs and everything. Soon I'll be subscribing to the *Readers Digest*, and watching *Gardening Australia*."

"Hey," I protested with a laugh. "Don't knock *Gardening Australia*. It's a great show. I *always* watch it."

"Mulch," Matt added. "It's always about mulch. What *is* mulch, anyway, some kind of fertilizer?"

"Mulch, my friend, is the answer to all of your problems," Paul rejoined, reaching for the wine. "People never stop talking about mulch these days, have you noticed? *Every single barbecue* I've attended in the last six months, I've ended up discussing mulch."

"That's a dig at me," Candice interposed. "Just because I showed him my mulcher, last time he visited. Paul, I'm proud of my mulcher."

"This woman puts mulch on her kids. I just know it. Their beds are full of pine bark, you mark my words."

"And what if they are? Has it done them any harm? I don't think so."

"Christ, are we talking about mulch *again*?" lamented the CEO, in mock despair, and Matt laughed.

"It's true," he said, "we're middle-aged. My dad always talks about mulch—mulch and his grapevines. I must be turning into my dad."

But he wasn't, of course. For one thing, he wouldn't know the difference between a grapevine and a tiger lily. For another, he didn't look the least bit middle-aged—not like the rest of the men at that lunch. They were all going bald, and spreading out. They were all wearing polo shirts and mobile phones. Despite the odd glint of grey, and a bit of slack skin here and there, Matt seemed as vital as he had ever been. Perhaps it was something to do with his hair, which sprang from his head in thick, vigorous waves. Perhaps it was the fact that his jeans had a hole in them.

I sat contemplating him while Candice said something about tut-tutting over the skimpy kids' fashions, these days. Then Matt said something about *Rolling Stone*. Then reference was made to the phenomenon of middle-aged men divorcing their wives for young, blonde trophies, at which point I decided that I'd rather not discuss that particular subject, in the circumstances, and went to find Jonah.

I wanted him to take a nap. He had been surprisingly good, since we arrived—thanks to Zoe. She'd dressed him up as a pirate, and he liked that. She'd pulled out her old Duplo, and he'd liked that too. He was at his most gorgeous, all sweet smiles and round, brown eyes and earnest, puckered brow, explaining at length, in his deep, serious voice, that dogs and beavers could be friends. Zoe thought he was lovely. You could see it in her face. She takes after her dad, because it's possible to see what she's thinking from her expression. Gemma, on the other hand, is prim and secretive, like her mum.

But that's all right, because Emily gets along with just about everybody. Nasty comments simply bounce off her, leaving her sunny good humor intact. Whatever anyone else wants to do is fine with her; it makes me tremble a bit, when I see how like Matthew she is. She's exactly the same sort of person—the sort of person who'd go pig shooting in

Queensland because her mates suggested it. She's
going to be a nightmare teenager. Not sullen or
moody, but suggestible. It'll be all tongue-studs
and Ecstasy, I know it will. Unless I come down
hard, the way my parents would have. But should
I? After all, Matt was the same, and look how he
turned out.

An adulterer, maybe, but an irresistible one.

Emily was playing with Gemma's doll's house
when I came to do battle with Jonah. She was
crouched on the floor of Gemma's bedroom, her
knees up around her ears, carefully dressing a Barbie
doll under Gemma's close supervision. Jonah was
pushing buttons on an old toy cash register. He
wasn't cooperative.

"No," he said, when he heard the word bedtime.

"Come on, Jonah, please. Be a good boy."

"No!"

"Don't you want to sleep in Zoe's bed? Hmm?"

"Oh yes, Jonah!" Zoe's eager eyes sparked as
comprehension dawned. "Yes, don't you want to
sleep in my bed? Where I sleep?"

He looked at her suspiciously. His expression
became mulish.

"Come and see Zoe's bed, Jonah," I said in brisk
tones. "Come on. Come and see."

"It's got a big, fluffy toy cat on it!" Zoe continued. That sold him. He allowed himself to be led
into Zoe's room, where I had closed the cedar
shutters (must have cost a fortune) and turned
down the broderie anglaise bedclothes. He's a
stubborn little soul, is Jonah. Touchy and sensitive,
but with a steely streak that Emily doesn't have.
You can tell that—despite all the emotional knocks

he might experience along the way—he's going to end up doing, very successfully, exactly what he wants to do, and that no one's going to distract him from his purpose.

Like playing with the cash register, for instance.

"No—no more cash register for now," I told him. "You can have a nap in Zoe's bed, with Zoe's cat, and *then* you can play."

"No," he said, sticking out his bottom lip.

"You can have some milk. Warm milk. Do you want some warm milk?"

"Okay."

"Then into bed, please."

He shook his head.

"What if I read you a story, Jonah?" Zoe suggested. "If you get into bed, I'll read you a story."

"Oh, boy! That sounds good. Do you want a story, Jonah?"

"Yes."

"Then get into bed, please."

It went on and on like this, interspersed by a couple of eruptions. You might wonder why I bothered. You might think that I was being unnecessarily rigid about my schedule. After all, it was the weekend. Why not kick back and let the kids fall into a natural rhythm, doing their own thing while the adults murmured together over their Thai salad, and the sun arched across the sky?

Well, let me tell you why. Because if Jonah doesn't take a nap in the middle of the day, we all suffer for it. He whines, he screams, he cries at every little setback. He becomes overtired. And if that happens, then it's hard to get him to sleep at night, too. As I said, he has nerves like violin strings. He's even had night terrors, on occasion, and that's the scariest thing I've ever seen. I'd do *anything* to keep those at bay.

The trouble is, it's very difficult to get him to sleep in a strange house. He won't be left alone, for a start. He has to be patted, and sung to, and sometimes even joined in bed. I can spend up to an hour trying to settle him when we're out, and even then he'll only sleep for forty-five minutes. With the result that he wakes up grumpy and clingy, demanding attention. And I never really enjoy the rest of our visit.

He's always been a bad sleeper. Emily was such a good baby: she smiled a lot, she stopped crying when you picked her up and went to sleep after you fed her, she was sleeping through the night at six months and never reverted thereafter. Jonah, on the other hand, was a nightmare. Before I had Jonah, I didn't know what it was all about—not really. Women in my mothers' group would talk about feeding problems and sleeping problems and I would think: There's no way on earth I would ever take my baby to bed/leave her to cry for fifteen minutes/feed her formula before the age of two months. I just didn't understand. I didn't understand that when you get desperate enough, you'll do anything. Literally anything.

But there was nothing I could do—that was the problem. While my presence used to comfort Emily, it didn't comfort Jonah. Neither did food, burping, clean nappies, dummies, or being rhythmically jounced up and down or pushed back and forth. "He's not very comfortable in the world, is he?" my Early Childhood nurse once said, and she was right—he wasn't. Or perhaps he was just bored, poor darling; who wouldn't be bored, lying in a bassinette all day, unable to ask for a thicker blanket? Anyway, whatever the problem was, I couldn't believe that there wasn't a solution somewhere. Fatalism isn't part of the western way of life, after all. If there's a problem, we have to fix it. The trouble was that I couldn't fix it. No matter what I did, no matter what tests he endured for gastric reflux (negative) or lactose intolerance (negative), I couldn't make my child happy.

It did wonders for my confidence, I can tell you.

In the end, I went to the Tresillian long-stay facility. My Early Childhood nurse referred me to a Tresillian nurse, who came around and asked searching questions about my state of mind. I kept assuring her that I was all right, really—because I knew that, compared to the women in my mothers' group who had chronic mastitis, twins, unsympathetic (even abusive) husbands and dreadful gynecological complications, I *was* all right. She wouldn't believe me, though. She kept questioning and commenting until at last I burst into tears, and admitted that there was no joy in my life, none at all, and she booked me in for a week at Tresillian.

Then I got there and wondered what on earth I'd been complaining about. There were mothers whose babies wouldn't eat, mothers with huge families and bad back injuries who hadn't slept for more than ten minutes at a time for a whole year, mothers who couldn't take care of themselves, let alone their babies. And there was I, in a lather just because Jonah kept waking me up every hour at night and cried a lot during the day. I felt as if I was there under false pretenses. But because I was desperate, I didn't care much what everyone thought of me. I'd stopped caring about anything except a good night's sleep.

Perhaps that's when things started to go downhill with Matt?

It's a wonderful institution, is Tresillian. Trained mothercare nurses give advice on feeding, settling, bathing. They help shell-shocked mothers teach their babies how to eat and how to sleep, especially how to sleep. You'd think that these would be natural human functions, but they're not. Some babies need to be taught. Some mothers need to be taught. I met a mother there with four kids, and the fourth was the first she'd had trouble with. Like me, she hadn't believed in leaving a child to cry even for two minutes. That was before the birth of her fourth child. Afterwards, she'd realized that sometimes you just have to do whatever it takes—or lose your mind.

One thing Jonah taught me was not to judge other parents, except in pretty extreme circumstances. For all you know, they're doing the best they can. And one thing that Tresillian taught Jonah was how to sleep for most of the night. He's not perfect—he's not like Emily, for instance—but he's a lot better than he used to be.

As a matter of fact, there ought to be places like Tresillian for wayward husbands, as well as wakeful babies. Places that will teach them how to change tap washers, make kids' lunches, and remain faithful to their wives.

If only.

On our way home, Matt and I had a long conversation. Jonah and Emily were contentedly eat-

ing the emergency jelly snakes that I'd packed
away in the glove compartment. (I'd had to break
them out when we became firmly wedged in a traffic jam leading away from the beach.) A CD from
Matt's collection was filling the car with plaintive
music. The light was golden; the shadows were
long. Matt seemed utterly relaxed, his right hand
draped over the top of the steering wheel. He said:
"What was Kerry complaining about, out by the
pool?"

"Pardon?"

"I saw you with her. You and Penelope. You had
that look on your face."

"Oh." What look? "Well, she was saying she'd
had a hard day yesterday. And when I asked her
why, she told me that she'd spent five hours trying
to find the right curtain fabric for that boat they've
got a share in."

Matt snorted.

"Which is pretty much on par with moaning
about how your nanny doesn't load the dishwasher properly," I continued. "God, she's a joke."

"But you're not laughin'."

"Well . . ." I looked around at the sun glinting
off spoilers and bumper bars. "Maybe I'll laugh
when we've cleared this mess." I was worried about
what might happen, once we'd run out of jelly
snakes.

"It'll be okay," said Matt. "As soon as we get past
these lights."

"We should have left earlier."

"I guess. Well, we would have, wouldn't we if
Emily hadn't lost that damn—I mean, that duck of
hers."

"Ix-nay on the uck-day," I replied, with an anxious look in the rear-vision mirror. But Emily hadn't heard. She seemed to have forgotten about the lost wooden duck.

"It'll turn up," said Matt.

"I hope so." I had a nasty feeling that it might have been left on the beach. "You're sunburned, did you know that? On the back of your neck."

"Yeah? Feels like it."

"Didn't you put sunscreen on?"

"Yeah. I musta missed a bit."

"You should always go under the collar. Just a few inches."

"I know."

And so it went on. A typical, rambling, domestic conversation, as dull and well-worn as the old vinyl on our kitchen floor. And yet I remember every word, simply *because* it was so normal. It seems amazing to me that you can keep going through the motions when you're falling apart inside. It seems amazing that Matt can smile, and relax, and talk about traffic lights, and fall asleep as soon as he hits the sheets at night, when he may very well be having an affair.

I've been lying there thinking about Megan Molesdale. Where did he meet her? At work, perhaps? If I was to ring ABC, and ask for Megan Molesdale, would they put me through? And what would I say to her if they did? I couldn't possibly ask her if she was having an affair with my husband. If I ask her, and it's not true, then I'll become the laughing-stock of ABC.

But I've got to do something. At least I can find out if she works with Matt. Maybe I can even visit her house. Check it out a bit. Establish whether she is, or is not, the Girl With Purple Hair. Smash her window with a rock that's got a note tied to it: "*Stay away from my husband.*"

No, no. On second thought, you can get arrested for that sort of thing. Besides, I might be making a mistake. It might be a perfectly innocent association. Something work related. Something to do with concert tickets, or an REM fan club. Something completely above board.

And even if it isn't—do I really want to make waves? Wouldn't it be better just to let him have his fling, and hope that he'll get it all out of his system? Because it can't have been happening for very long. Not to judge from the phone records—not for more than a month, I reckon, and I can handle that. At least—well, I *can't* handle that, but you know what I mean. It would be different if it had been going on for years and years and years. That kind of vast betrayal, woven into the very fabric of a marriage, is very different from a three-week fling.

That's what I tell myself, anyway. Though it suddenly occurs to me: even if it's already over, how can I possibly trust him ever again? Especially if he thinks that I don't know—if he thinks he's got away with it. Having done it once, what's to stop him from doing it whenever he wants to?

On the other hand, if I tell him I know—well, that leaves me with two options. Either I forgive him, and leave him with the impression that he can walk all over me, or I throw him out. And what's throwing him out going to achieve? Nothing that I want to deal with.

Oh God, oh God. And I'm not even sure that I've

got it right. What am I going to do? What on earth am I going to do?

I've no idea, but it has to be something. Whatever it is, I have to do *something*. If I don't, I'll go mad.

Chapter Four

Monday

I was dreading today. I didn't know how I was supposed to work while I was secretly going crazy. But it turned out to be all right, in the end.

This morning was a madhouse, as usual, with Matt staggering around like the living dead while I struggled to change Jonah's nappy and iron my white jacquard blouse without burning the toast. Just as well Matt doesn't have to leave until twelve on the days when he has a late shift; if we were both trying to get away at the same time . . . well, the mind boggles. As it is, he's normally just beginning to wake up when I'm ready to make tracks, so there's a fairly smooth changeover.

He takes the kids to day care before driving off to ABC.

"Don't forget their fruit," I reminded him, shrugging on my purple jacket as I advanced sideways down the hall.

"I won't."

"And the hats. Jonah's hat is on the clothes-horse—don't forget it. Ow!" I nearly fell over

Barbie's kitchen sink. "Emily! What did I say about cleaning up your toys?"

No reply. She was watching the television.

"Have we paid for this week?" asked Matt, nursing a cup of coffee against his chest.

"No. You can take care of it. Oh—and Jonah's nappy supply needs topping up. I've put them out—they're on the kitchen table. You can't miss 'em." I was going through my mental checklist (keys—yes; handkerchief—yes; purse—yes; briefcase—yes) when Matt suddenly said: "Are you all right, Helen?"

I was poised on the threshold, my eyes on my watch, and for a second the words didn't penetrate. Then I blinked, and looked up at him.

He was watching me from behind a great swatch of black hair, so I couldn't see his eyes properly. But it sounded like a serious question. I swallowed, cleared my throat, and replied: "Is there any reason why I shouldn't be?"

As soon as he frowned, however, I lost courage. I couldn't do it. My knees trembled. My heart took off. Not now, I thought—I'll miss my train.

"What do you mean?" he said.

"Nothing. Nothing."

"Helen—"

"I've got to go. I'll be late. See ya."

It's a thirteen-minute brisk walk from our house to the railway station, but I almost always have to run when I hit the final stretch. Fortunately, I don't wear high-heeled shoes. I'd hate to have to clatter down those station stairs at top speed in a pair of stilettos. Even in court shoes it's a bit of a challenge, especially when you're also wearing pantyhose and a knee-length skirt. God knows what

I look like from the train: all wild eyes, bouncing boobs and jangling earrings. And while I *could* blame the kids for this last-minute loss of dignity, I won't, because half the time it's not their fault. Half the time I'm late because I was walking too slowly, savoring the lovely morning light, the fresh smells, the fascinating glimpses of other people's gardens and porch furniture. I love that walk. Some people might not think much of it, because all the streets around here are fairly built-up and suburban, but I think it's wonderful. There's a beautiful plumbago climbing over an iron fence; a letterbox shaped like a rocketship; a front path inlaid with tessellated tiles; a mysterious boarding house with a dark, cavernous entry hall and sheets in the windows; a corner shop with a little old man permanently parked on a deckchair near the entrance; a cat basking in a concrete yard; a juliet balcony; a weatherworn statue of a cherub; a climbing rose; a King Charles spaniel. Even the station is a poignant and touching place, with its advertisement for the local library (translated into six different languages) and its struggling beds of pansies and petunias. I love it. I love every bit of it.

And lest I sound too flaky for words, let me assure you that I wasn't always like this. It's having kids that's done the damage. Once upon a time, I wasn't conscious of the sheer glory of getting out of the house on my own. Once upon a time I used to hate commuter trains. Now I enjoy them. I enjoy being part of an anonymous crowd of suits—it's such a relief. You don't have to worry about the stroller getting stuck behind a pole, or your kids climbing on the seats, or your son's juice bottle falling onto the floor and rolling down the stairs.

All you have to worry about is you. You certainly don't have to worry about your fellow passengers, because nothing that you do (barring an especially pungent fart) is going to annoy them in the least. You're not about to squeal, vomit, cry, kick or complain. You're not going to cause their hearts to sink when you get on board, because you're one of them. A commuter.

That's what I tell myself: that I'm one of them. Certainly I look like one of them. But as a matter of fact, I don't really feel like one of them—not any more. When I get off the train, and emerge into the smog-filled canyons of the central business district, I feel like a spy. It's because there isn't a child to be seen. Not one stroller, not one baby pouch, not one harassed-looking woman in a stained T-shirt and flapping sandals, pushing the younger kid while calling the older to heel. Sure, there are harassed-looking people in the city, but they seem to be harassed in a focused way. And they're all so neat. Their bags are so neat—neat and black. You don't see them toting floppy, bulging things covered in bright yellow flowers.

I suppose the whole scene feels so foreign because I've only been back at work for four months. I suppose there'll come a time when I won't feel wildly out of place walking through sliding glass doors into a towering foyer made of stainless steel and polished granite. After all, look how adrift I felt when I first turned up, after four years in the maternal wilderness. God, I was terrified. I couldn't believe that I'd ever get back into the swing of it all—the meetings, the deadlines, the assessments, the huge crowds bolting down caesar salad in subterranean food courts to the tune of beeping mobiles. I was concerned that I might have lost my skills, forgotten my law, discarded all the furniture in my head except the kind directly related to child-rearing. What's more, I'd never job-shared before, and was worried about that. How would I manage it? Would I be able to trust my partner to finish what I had started? I remembered how difficult it had been to work while I was pregnant with Emily; how tired I always was, how my brain had turned to mush. It still seemed pretty mushy four years later, whenever I tried to write a simple shopping list. Was mush-brain perhaps a permanent condition of motherhood?

I fretted myself sick about my possible deficiencies, and all for nothing. Because it's a breeze. Really. Compared to looking after two kids, it's a walk in the park. Once upon a time I would become quite stressed when six different things landed on my desk in the space of ten minutes. Now I take it in my stride, because after all, the people who put them there aren't tugging at my skirt, bashing their files on the desk or threatening to wee all over the carpet. When three different calls come in at once, I can put two of them on hold; I don't have to carry out three different conversations at the same time. Even better, there isn't anyone drawing on my reports, messing with my correction fluid, rifling through my files or cutting up my memo pads while I'm working.

Nowadays, I'm in the habit of working very, very quickly. I'm used to grabbing a spare ten minutes here, a spare half hour there, to complete tax returns, write letters, or balance chequebooks. I'm not used to having hours and hours of uninterrupted time to do *anything*. Hence my ingrained sense of urgency. Hence the fact that I've got out of the habit of coffee breaks, long telephone conversations and all the other devices used by some people to fritter away their time at work. In fact I'm so damned efficient, these days, that I astound myself.

And my people management skills—God, how they've improved! You don't realize how much kids change the way you handle disputes. With kids, you're always anticipating problems, heading off tantrums before they occur. If they do occur, because you've failed to plan ahead, then you learn how to reduce their impact. You don't give in (if you can possibly help it), but you don't exactly stand firm, either. Instead you distract. The fine art of distraction. It works just as well with adults as it does with kids—as I learned within three weeks of returning to the workforce.

It only dawned on me recently that I was doing so well. After three months of confusion I paused for a moment, checked my caseload schedule, and was amazed. Not that I can take all the credit, mind you. I'm job-sharing with a woman called Amelia, and she's pretty efficient herself (though very untidy). But I have to say that things are under control, at work—something that I could hardly believe, when it was first brought to my attention. Because the rest of my life is such a mess, you see. I was beginning to feel that I had completely lost my grip. And I'm not much of a mother, so I was delighted to find myself good at *something*. I'd forgotten that I could be good at something. Though my house is a tip, and my hair is a joke, and my kids are TV addicts, at least I can conciliate a pregnancy discrimination complaint like nobody's business.

Of course, some of my work has to be done at home, and that doesn't exactly ease the domestic pressures. Motherhood has definitely become more difficult since I started earning again. There's more to juggle, even less time to do it in, and there's also the guilt factor. I feel guilty, not because I'm going to work (which is an absolute necessity, given the size of our mortgage) but because I enjoy going to work. What I mean is, I enjoy the feeling it gives me. Sometimes I feel like an escaped prisoner, for God's sake, and that's not something to be proud of, is it? My office shouldn't be my refuge—my family should be my refuge. *That's* where I should be feeling empowered and safe and thoroughly comfortable. But what with the renovations, and my frantic attempts to finish reports at the kitchen table, and Jonah's recent bout of gastro, and now this business of the Girl With Purple Hair . . .

I wonder if Matt's been feeling the same? I wonder if that girl is actually a refuge for him?

Oh dear, oh dear.

The Equal Opportunity and Human Rights Board is located on the twenty-first floor of a tower on Castlereagh Street. When you walk out of the lift, you find yourself opposite a sign made of polished brass and steel, mounted on a wall covered in something that looks like blue felt. Then you pass through a pair of glass doors and you're surrounded by acres of expensive wool carpet (industrial grade), seamless stretches of Tasmanian ash, fuchsia-colored feature walls, chrome planters, recessed lighting, pastel prints and stacks and stacks of impenetrable government literature. The reception desk is as long as a landing strip, is topped with polished granite, and is manned (or personned—no sexist language here) by Jean Spence, who takes no prisoners. This woman has to deal, almost daily, with incursions by schizophrenic walk-ins claiming that their human rights have been violated. One of them once tried to prove that radio waves were being beamed into his penis, and Jean didn't bat an eyelid. Formidable is the word that best describes her.

So there it is. What with Jean, and the granite, and the hushed atmosphere of the foyer, and the annual reports weighing down the Tasmanian ash coffee table, the office of the Equal Opportunity and Human Rights Board isn't exactly a welcoming environment. In fact I worry about its impact on the complainants sometimes. It's hard enough for them to walk in off the street with their nervous inquiries about what constitutes sexual harassment; an office like the executive floor of an international corporate law firm must make it even harder. If you ask me, our old address was much less intimidating. It had that authentic, down-at-heel, health-center ambience, all coffee-stained sofa cushions and cork boards covered in public service posters.

I believe it's been argued that our new office has had the effect of elevating the status of discrimination complaints in the overall scheme of things. Unless you look important, you won't be perceived as important—or so the argument goes. But I wonder.

I mean, you'd think we could at least provide a few copies of *Who Weekly* and a coffee machine, or something.

There's a big, glossy wall behind Jean's desk, and behind the wall lies a network of carefully graded cubicles. First come the Enquiries Officers, who don't have access to any windows. On either side of their space, the Assistant Complaints Officers are squeezed into slots with windows, but no doors. Then come the Policy Officers and Complaints Officers, who have proper offices with doors, windows, paintings and credenzas. The Chief Conciliator has even scored a couch—as has the Senior Adviser. They have corner offices, but they can't compete with the Commissioner. The Commissioner's office is so big, it takes up practically a quarter of the entire floor space. It features two couches, a concealed bar fridge, a TV in a cupboard, a glass sculpture, a Chinese silk rug, a personal fax machine and drop-dead views. We call it "the Hangar." The Commissioner rates this penthouse of an office because she's so important in the scheme of things—like a justice of the High Court, or something. When she's around, you can always tell; there's a certain tension in the air. People get jumpy (especially when they're on personal phone calls). As you go about your job, you notice an increase in the number of VIPs wandering about the place, waiting to speak to the Commissioner.

Because I'm a Complaints Officer, I don't rate a couch. Even if I did, I couldn't fit one into my office, which I have to share with Amelia; two desks in that space don't leave room for much else, except a couple of filing cabinets. Not that Amelia helps matters, the way she accumulates crap. I don't know what it is with her. She just can't seem to contain herself. Post-it notes proliferate. Coffee cups accumulate. The files pile up like dirty dishes, spilling off the edge of her desk and onto mine.

Once upon a time, I would have resented this. It would have rankled to the point of an official complaint. Now, however, I'm so used to cleaning up other people's mess that I take it in my stride—especially since Amelia is in every other way unexceptionable. She's fast, she's thorough, she's patient and she's bright. What does it matter if her desk looks like a dumpster? As long as she can find her way around it well enough to do her job, I don't see why I should make waves.

As a matter of fact, she's not beyond redemption. This morning, for instance, wasn't too bad at all: there was a strange red jumper draped over my chair, two dirty coffee cups sitting on my monitor, and a pile of Amelia's lime-green complaint files clogging up my desk space. I moved the case files, rinsed the coffee cups, carefully folded the jumper and placed it on top of Amelia's filing cabinet. Then I picked up the phone and called Miriam at work.

Unfortunately, she wasn't in. I'd suddenly reached the point where I needed to discuss the issue of adultery with some rational, informed adult—I needed comfort, clarification and advice, not necessarily in that order—but Miriam wasn't in. I had to leave a message. It was such a blow that I did what I probably shouldn't have done: I rang ABC and asked for Megan Molesdale.

Only to discover that no one of that name worked for the Australian Broadcasting Corporation.

So that was that. Having exhausted all avenues, I had to turn my thoughts to work-related subjects. And after the first wrenching struggle, I found that it was quite a relief to abandon my own fucked-up life in order to assess the fucked-up lives of other people. Like Lisa's slasher movies, the endless number of discrimination case studies reminded me that many people were far worse off than I would ever be.

As I said, I'm a Complaints Officer with the Equal Opportunity and Human Rights Board. It's my job to investigate (and conciliate) complaints of sex discrimination, racial discrimination, and discrimination based on disability. Mostly, however, I handle cases of sexual harassment and pregnancy discrimination in the workplace. It's become my specialty; I don't know why. Time and time again, I'll open up a complaint file assigned to me and discover the initial intake form, the complainant's letter, and a dog-eared nudie pin-up or an e-mail printout featuring the words cock, tits or blow job—evidence of what some poor souls have to put up with at work. You can't help but sympathize, though you're not supposed to. You're supposed to be objective. The aim of the job is to help the two parties involved in a complaint negotiate a satisfactory settlement, without having to resort to public hearings or other legal processes.

A satisfactory settlement, by the way, normally involves one or more of the following: money, reinstatement, disciplinary action, counselling, the provision of a reference or statement of service, and an apology. If the complainant is lucky, this settlement will be the outcome of a few telephone

calls or a conciliation conference. Otherwise I
have to write a referral report, and the whole thing
gets shunted off to the courts and tribunals.

At the moment I'm juggling about twenty complaints. They're all at different stages, so I spent
the morning notifying respondents, telephoning
complainants, and organizing conferences. I also
had to book a car for the night, because tomorrow
morning I'm scheduled to interview witnesses way
out in Penrith, at 8:45 a.m. The respondent in this
particular case (a certain Mr. L.) won't admit to
anything, and there are no memos or other docu-
ments that might kick-start the conciliation process.
What's more, at least one of the witnesses is practically illiterate; it would be impossible to get a written
declaration from him even if he wanted to give one.
Consequently, I'm going to have to drive all the
way out to this Large Service Company (no names;
confidentiality assured) and see what I can discover.

Thus far, we've got Mr. L. snapping a bra strap
(unsubstantiated), Mr. L. referring to the complainant's mobile telephone as her dildo (witnessed
by a female co-worker), Mr. L. making comments
about the complainant's buttocks (reported to the
same female co-worker by the complainant shortly
after one of the alleged incidents took place), Mr.
L. discussing the complainant's favored sexual posi-
tions and personal habits with the illiterate male
witness in earshot of the complainant (promis-
ing), and Mr. L. planting a sex toy in the complainant's desk drawer (disposed of in a garbage
bin, allegedly, though Mr. L. did subsequently
ask, in a female co-worker's hearing, whether the
complainant's sex life had improved lately for any
reason).

The complainant, Ms F., is a divorced forty-three-year-old mother of two. Mr. L. is thirty-nine, and also married. I haven't interviewed him yet, though I have spoken to her over the phone, poor thing. She has a Portuguese background and a thick accent, and can't seem to believe what's been happening to her. It is, I have to admit, a slightly unusual case; normally the respondent is older than the complainant, and the scenario is therefore of a more traditional nature. Nevertheless, it's a complaint that merits investigation, especially in view of the fact that Mr. L. responded to my notification with a very curt denial. They always do, I've found. Usually there's some sort of elaboration (i.e. "She's a slut," "I'm a family man," "My brother's a policeman—why would I lie?," "It's sour grapes because she can't get a root," "She's vindictive because I disciplined her" or even "Why would I harass a dog like that?") but Mr. L. didn't provide any kind of explanation at all. Just a short, sharp denial. He didn't even list the names of any witnesses who might be able to refute Ms F.'s claims—either because there aren't any or because he won't cooperate with the Board.

Either way, it's not going to be easy.

After booking the car, I transcribed my interview with the witness I'd interviewed the previous week, in a classic sexual harassment case involving a fifty-four-year-old shop owner and his twenty-year-old employee. ("*I enphatically* [sic] *deny that I ever asked Miss B—'Would you like a fuck?'* " the shop owner declared in his outraged letter of response to my notification. "*If Miss B—'s memory was not totally at fault, and her motives questionable, she would recall that my exact words were* 'I suppose a fuck's out of the question?' ") Then, having sent my record of the interview off to the witness for checking, I went to have lunch with my friend Veronica.

My lunches with Veronica happen about once a month. Since she's pretty much the only person I do lunch with any more, I was experiencing a slight lift of the spirits as I wended my way to the elevator. Upon reaching it, however, I saw that the Commissioner was also off to lunch—and that had a dampening effect. She always manages to deflate me.

"Hello, Helen."

"Hi, Diane."

A pause. The damned lift seemed to have stalled on the mezzanine level. Diane's companion—a nondescript bureaucrat who was probably very important indeed—glanced at his watch. I racked my brain desperately for something to say that wasn't related either to crotch-grabbing or to the question of whether someone should be buying soy milk for the tearoom. Something a bit insightful, in other words. But it was Diane who finally broke the strained silence.

"That memo you gave me," she said. "About the gay man?"

"Oh yes." It had been in reference to the third sexual harassment complaint from the same government department in six months. "I thought it was worth looking into . . ."

"I agree." Diane spoke firmly. "That's why I think we should speak to the minister, you and I. Set up a meeting."

"Oh, okay."

Bing! The lift arrived. Naturally, I stepped back

to allow my boss on first. Everybody does. She's
that kind of person: tall, imposing, and very well
groomed. Not a hair out of place—literally. In fact
she sometimes reminds me of that Lady Penelope
puppet in the *Thunderbirds*, because she has the
same helmet of heavily lacquered hair (not to
mention a slightly peculiar bottom lip). I'm told
that when she was first appointed, she hired a style
consultant who gave her a complete makeover. If
so, that consultant was worth every cent. Diane's
clothes are always spot-on, and her lipstick is to die
for. I once asked her about the most *ravishing* per-
simmonish kind of shade, only to discover that it
had cost her somewhere in the region of eighty
bucks. Well, lipstick *is* very important. It's an inte-
gral part of femocratic power dressing.

In the lift, I had to stand breathing in Diane's
perfume and pretending that I was fascinated by
the indicator panel. Fortunately, some other people soon piled in, and they were very chatty. They
talked amongst themselves about someone called
Robert, who couldn't spell "appropriate" and took
credit for everyone else's work, until we arrived on
the ground floor. Then at last I was able to make
my escape and seek out Veronica.

Veronica works for the Family Court, in an administrative position. She does a lot of filing. I first
met her when I was living in Paddington with
Miriam and Briony; she was one of Briony's many
and varied acquaintances, having briefly worked
with Briony as a travel agent. In those days, Veronica
was a little more wild than she is now. She wasn't
above the odd one-night stand or hit of cocaine.
She got pissed quite regularly, and suffered the inevitable consequences. (Huge and dramatic bust-ups

with loser boyfriends, splurged rent money, monumental hangovers, a smashed car, crying jags, lost shoes.) But though she exhibited a lack of control in certain areas of her life, she was never fired after just five days on the job. Only Briony, it was generally agreed, could have achieved that kind of record. And she did it by starting work at a travel agency while she was in the middle of a massive romantic crisis.

"Basically," Veronica said, when I first met her, "she spent a solid five days on the phone to her bloke—what's his name? Justin?—having long, involved discussions about their relationship. She didn't do a *stroke* of work." Veronica sounded almost admiring. "I only wish I had the guts," she concluded.

"Yep. Well—that sounds like Briony," I sighed.

"Actually, she did get off the phone once or twice, when she wanted to talk to me. She gave me the full run-down. Blow by blow. It's amazing— she's got total recall. She remembers every single thing he ever said to her. Is she always like that?"

"Always."

In fact, Briony not only remembered every word ever uttered by every boyfriend she'd ever had— she also enjoyed analyzing the tone, pace and syntax of her conversations with the opposite sex. She would carefully weigh each sentence, picking out a concealed insult here, an equivocal choice of adjective there. It was her favorite pastime. We'd all found ourselves roped into long sessions over a glass of wine (in the evening) or a cup of tea (in the morning); it was like doing a lit. crit. tutorial, only lit. crit. tutorials don't usually finish up with a quick reading of the runes, which Briony kept in a little suede bag under her pillow.

She was a real ditzy one, was Briony. She seemed to have no sense of risk. I've already mentioned the big, shaggy guys she'd bring home, but that wasn't the half of it. At one stage she'd moved in with a gay guy under the (mistaken) impression that he was in love with her, and that she'd changed his orientation forever. She'd been caught trying to smuggle a Rolex, a necklace and a camera into South Korea, after meeting a dubious Taiwanese guy in a Hong Kong youth hostel. (She was simply expelled from the country, her possessions confiscated, but it was still a dicey venture.) She had a tendency to spend her money on French cotton underwear when the rent was looming, and to run up huge credit card bills buying smoked salmon for seaside picnics or tarot consultations when her love life was problematic.

I used to shake my head over Briony. I used to get together with Veronica and Miriam, and we would shriek about her latest excesses. Slowly, however, things have changed. Shortly after Matt and I began to live together, Briony took to hanging around the yacht club at Rushcutters Bay. There she met an extremely rich American, who took her off to the U.S. with him on his million-dollar yacht. From then on news of her was scant but enticing. She was living with the American in Carmel, California. The American had dropped her, but she'd landed a job minding houses for some other rich people in Beverly Hills. She was going out with a Paramount script editor. The script editor had dropped her but an entertainment lawyer had taken up with her, and had installed her in his mansion. She was working in a high-class fashion store, where she'd met Demi Moore and Cameron Diaz.

Veronica has been the source of all these tidbits, because Briony keeps in contact with a friend of Ronnie's, called Samantha. That's one of the main reasons why Veronica and I get together once a month or so—to chew over the latest instalment in the Briony saga. Today was no different. We met in one of those subterranean coffee shops around Martin Place, where they serve things like microwaved chicken crepes and vegetarian focaccia. After ordering a ham and cheese croissant, Ronnie opened the conversation with a Briony update, informing me that Briony was now in Europe.

"Europe!" I exclaimed. "Where in Europe?"

"Florence," said Veronica. "She met an Argentinian artist on a trip to New York, and now she's living with him in Florence. In a tiny little flat near some famous church—I can't remember the name of it."

"Oh, my God."

"And she's working as an artist's model."

"Oh, my God."

"Apparently she spends all her time in cafés with his artist friends, or staying at dealers' villas in the Tuscan hills. Can you imagine?"

"I can, actually."

"Yeah. Me, too."

"She always had a thing about pre-Raphaelite clothes. You know—gauzy."

"Yeah. And that French cotton underwear. And all the cherubs on her photo frames."

"Yeah." There was a pause. I had suddenly been plunged into the most profound gloom; the thought of Briony flitting past the Duomo on her way to work, or draped over a hunky Argentinian artist in some smoky little café smelling of espresso and scampi, was almost too much to bear. For years I had regarded Briony as a disaster waiting to happen—as messy, impractical, dense, flaky and cursed with a terrible taste in men. For years I had derived some comfort from the belief that, because she had her priorities all wrong, she would end up stranded, like some sort of middle-aged castaway, without a career, without any savings, without a house, without children. Yet her terrible taste in men had led her straight to wealth and glamour; her lack of priorities had landed her in the most romantic of lives—a somewhat rootless existence, it was true, but inexpressibly cultured and dazzling.

I don't need this, was my first reaction. I can do without this, right now.

"She always liked that Florentine writing paper you get in David Jones, remember?" Ronnie went on. "She went out to buy something at the Food Hall once—something for a party—and came back with that bloody paper. You told me about it."

"She's got the right hair," I observed. "That Botticelli hair. I couldn't pull it off, myself, I don't have the right sort of hair."

"You reckon?" Ronnie was twitching for a cigarette, I could tell. "But look at my hair. Caroline Tuckett always said I had Titian hair, and what good's it done me? I mean, did Titian ever paint any pictures of Family Court administrative assistants? I don't think so."

"Yeah, but that color isn't exactly yours, is it? I mean, come on."

"Anyway, it's a bit of a shock. I had to have a Bex

and a good lie down when I heard. What I'd give to earn my keep sitting around all day with my clothes off. It's not fair."

Nevertheless, despite the unfairness of it, Veronica seemed strangely upbeat. There was an odd little gleam in her eye. She seemed jumpier than usual. Normally, she cultivates a kind of disillusioned drawl, which combines successfully with her tough-girl haircut, nicotine-stained fingers and long, sprawling legs to create the impression that she couldn't give a shit. Today, however, there was something different about her.

"Are you all right?" I asked, after she had uncharacteristically knocked over the vase of wooden tulips in the center of the table. "You seem a bit . . . I dunno . . ."

As I trailed off, a sheepish smile spread across her face. She lowered her eyes, rubbed her nose, and said: "Phil and I got engaged."

"No!"

"Yeah." The smile turned into a grin. "Yeah, we did it."

"But where's the ring?" I demanded. "You've got to have a ring, Ronnie, my God!"

"Phil's mum's given me his grandmother's ring. But it didn't fit me, so we're getting it altered."

"Well I'll be damned." It was big news. *Big* news. Ronnie and Phil had been living together for six years. Phil was a rangy redhead who worked for the National Parks and Wildlife Service; he was the silent rock against which Ronnie sometimes sharpened her wit. I'd always been well disposed towards him, but could never quite understand the dynamics of their relationship. Ronnie seemed so trenchant, on occasion, and Phil seemed so dull. I'd often wondered if theirs was a partnership based more on convenience than anything else.

Yet here they were, taking action. Moving forward. Getting hitched.

"That's great, Ronnie." I don't know how convincing I sounded; I was still reeling inside. "Have you set the date?"

"Well . . . we were thinking the middle of next year."

"Really?"

"He's got cousins coming down from England then, so . . . you know."

"Right."

"It won't be too big, but we'll have to make a bit of an effort or his mother'll never forgive us."

"Sure." Phil was his mother's only child. A daughter had died in a car accident. "Well—I hope you've at least got room for me, or shouldn't I ask?"

"Oh, I think we can squeeze you in. If you don't tease up your hair too much."

"You should invite Briony."

"Yeah." Veronica laughed. "See if she turns up with the Argentinian."

"Oh, she won't do that. Not a chance. But you wouldn't want her to. Just send her a really posh invitation, with, like, the Right Honourable Lord Cedric and Lady Malmsey invite you to the wedding of their son, Philip Edward George William, and Miss Veronica Eklund, to be held at St Mary's Cathedral—"

"—with dinner and dancing afterwards at the Sydney Opera House, right."

"And a note scribbled in one corner. *I know you probably won't be able to make it, but maybe we'll see you in April, on our six-month European honeymoon. Phil has some family vineyards he wants to visit in Bordeaux."*

We laughed together. Inside, though, I wasn't laughing. All I could think about was my own wedding, and how fantastic it had been: a perfect wedding. So how had I ended up where I was, in such a mess? Why had Ronnie decided to get married just as my own marriage seemed to be faltering? What kind of insidious timing was this, for God's sake?

I remember how, when Jonah was at his very worst and I was floundering about in an hysterical mist of fatigue, everyone around me seemed to be falling pregnant. I used to plaster a fake smile on my face as I congratulated my pregnant cousin, my pregnant neighbor, my pregnant sister-in-law, my pregnant former boss, biting my tongue and hoping that my dismay didn't show. I mean, who was I to cast a pall over their happiness? Who was I to start ranting about sleepless nights and postnatal depression?

So I pumped Ronnie for information about Phil's proposal ("If we want to buy a house together, we might as well get married" was what he had said), and her wedding dress ("a plain silk sheath and a wreath of flowers"), and her stance on garters ("Not in a million years") and I said absolutely nothing about my troubles with Matt. I managed to rein myself in until I reached my office, after lunch.

Then I closed the door and rang Miriam at work. This time, she was there.

"Hi," I said, when she answered the phone. "It's me."

"Helen?"

"Yeah."

"Oh God, Helen, I'm sorry." She sounded contrite—almost flustered. "I only just got back to my desk. I was going to return your call—"

"It's all right."

"Things are really insane here."

"Things are really insane here, too." I didn't know where to begin, so put off the moment at first. "Did you know that Ronnie's getting married? To Phil?"

"You're kidding me."

"I'm not. They're engaged. I had lunch with her today, and she told me. Oh—she also told me that Briony's in Florence now, shacked up with some Argentinian artist. Spending weekends in Tuscan villas. Typical, eh?"

"Typical," said Miriam. Her tone was slightly distracted, as if she was casting her eye over a computer printout. "Amazing."

"Miriam?"

"What?" Her voice sharpened, suddenly. "What's wrong?"

"Have you ever heard of someone called Megan Molesdale?"

"Who?"

"Megan Molesdale."

A pause. "No," Miriam replied at last. "Who is she?"

"I don't know. Matt's been calling her. From our home phone."

Another pause. At last Miriam said: "You haven't asked him yet, have you?"

"No," I admitted.

"Why not?"

I tried to explain, in the process sorting out and

classifying my muddled emotions. I was scared. I felt guilty. I didn't want to scuttle the ship over a slight suspicion. I didn't want to give Matt an excuse to walk out . . .

"You think he'd *do* that?" Miriam demanded.

"I don't know." Hesitantly. "What do you think?"

Miriam sighed. She seemed to be thinking. "Look, don't ask me," she said at last. "You're the one who's married to him."

I was horrified. "You mean you think he *might*?" I squeaked.

"Helen, I don't know. I'm sorry."

"But you really think he's capable of that kind of deceit? We're talking about *Matt* here!"

"Helen, I don't know the guy. I mean, think about it. How well do I know him?" She sighed again. "All I know is that it's amazing what can happen. It's amazing what people will do." She gave a weird kind of snort. "Always expect the unexpected," she added dryly. "That's my motto."

I thought: that's your motto because you've spent your whole life dealing with con men. But I didn't say it aloud.

"Well—I can't do anything about it right now," I bleated, shaken to the core. "Not at work."

"No."

"How are you doing, anyway? How's *your* job going?"

"Oh . . . pressured." Again, that funny, dry note. "A bit full-on."

"Do you fancy a vent? Do you want to try and do a coffee, for once? On neutral ground. I could probably manage."

This time the pause was so long, I began to wonder if she'd put me on hold—though I could still hear background noises. When she finally spoke, her voice was tight and clipped, as if she was upset about something.

"Look, uh—let me get back to you. I don't know, things are a bit . . . I'm so sorry about this, Helen, I wish I could be more help, really."

"It's all right—"

"Maybe I shouldn't have dumped this on you. Maybe I should have left well alone."

"No, no. You were trying to do the right thing."

"Was I? Maybe. I don't know any more. I'm out of my mind here."

"Really? Why?"

"Oh, stuff. Work stuff. I'm sorry—I've got to go. I feel bad, but I've just got to."

"It's okay . . ."

"I'll call you. I will. I promise."

Click.

I was left a bit shell-shocked, I have to admit. And I began to wonder: was Miriam having trouble with Giles, too? Could she have jumped to conclusions about Matt, for that very reason?

Rather than clearing my head, the whole conversation had left me more confused than ever.

This afternoon, on my way to pick up the kids from day care, I took a rather long detour through Randwick. I could do it because I had booked an overnight car; normally, I have to take a train to Marrickville, walk to the day care center, then catch a bus home, all of which takes time. You might be wondering why, in that case, Matt gets to take the car to work. If you're anything like some of my more feminist co-workers, you might be up in arms already. But the fact is, Matt has his own private parking spot, and I don't. Nor am I in a position to rent a spot in the city for $250 a week (or whatever it is nowadays). So Matt gets the car, and I get public transport.

C'est la vie, I guess.

Because I had a car, I found myself with time to spare this afternoon. Not a lot of time—just enough to swing past Megan Molesdale's address before I raced off to pick up the kids in Marrickville. I didn't know when I'd have another opportunity to do this. I also didn't know what I was hoping to accomplish, except to satisfy my overwhelming curiosity. Maybe I was hoping to spot the Girl With Purple Hair. At any rate, and entirely against my better judgement, I fought the traffic all the way to Randwick, where I located Megan Molesdale's house squashed in amongst a line of terraces near Alison Road.

It was a shabby little house. You don't often see shabby houses in the eastern suburbs any more, but this looked like a rental accommodation; it probably hadn't been painted since the seventies, because there was a lot of mission brown all over its doors and windows and iron lace. Nevertheless, it didn't look totally uncared-for. Proper curtains had been hung. An elaborate wrought-iron bellpull had been installed over a hand-painted tile that featured the house number and a lot of baroque curlicues. A set of pottery wind chimes was suspended from beneath the boards of the first-floor verandah. There were more ceramic things in the tiny front yard: two glazed female figures on the gateposts, a kind of birdbath thing inlaid with bits of broken china, several large flowerpots covered in vivid designs. Studying them from across the road, I wondered if the occupant was a potter or a sculptor.

Or an art student, perhaps? An art student with purple hair?

I considered getting out of the car, walking up to the mission-brown front door, and tugging at the wrought-iron bellpull. What would happen then? Would she answer the door herself? I hadn't the faintest idea what I would say to her if she did. As a matter of fact, I had a sneaking suspicion that I might vomit all over her garishly painted toenails, because I felt cold and sick at the very thought of such a confrontation.

Nevertheless, I did get out of the car. I did cross the road, and push open an iron gate so rusty that it shrieked like a slaughtered pig. It gave me a terrible fright; my hands were shaking when I tugged at the bellpull, which clanked in a wheezy sort of way. My heart was in my mouth. My mind was a blank.

I waited and waited.

The wind chimes clinked. In the distance, car horns yelped angrily. I gave the bellpull one more tug, and rattled the security door, which was made of black iron bars like something out of a maximum-security prison. Then I moved over to the living room window, and peered in.

Grubby white lace impeded my view. There seemed to be a table of some kind with a stack of paper on it. A little glazed bowl half full of congealed candle-wax sat on the windowsill.

I returned to my car slowly, more relieved than disappointed. I also felt that I could have done with a stiff drink. Unfortunately, however, I had to ne-

gotiate the peak-hour traffic, and decided to forgo
even a quick stop at the local pub, which looked
fairly civilized. (Lots of canvas umbrellas, not many
yellow tiles.) This was probably a wise choice, because as I was sitting at one of the interminable
traffic lights on Cleveland Street, something suddenly clicked in my head.

Megan.

After that, I was desperate to get home. I practically broke into a sweat just thinking about the
photo albums stuffed into our linen cupboard.
But I had to inch my way up Cleveland Street,
down City Road, along King Street, until I finally
popped out of the crush on Enmore Road and
roared off to the day care center, arriving only seven
minutes late. Then there was the slow process of
collecting bags, finding hats and toys, signing out,
adjusting the seatbelts in the car, which of course
didn't contain anything remotely resembling a
booster seat, and explaining to the kids that they
should keep their heads down. The rest of the trip
was a nail-biter; I was afraid that I might get arrested for not strapping Jonah into an appropriate
restraint. (But it was only a ten-minute ride, for
God's sake—what was I supposed to do?) On arriving home, I had to rush about getting dinner
ready, settling quarrels, washing hands and running baths. Jonah had to be fed. Emily's latest graze
had to be treated and dressed. They both had to
be helped into their pyjamas, after which there was
story time, the toilet (for Emily), a bottle of milk
(for Jonah), tooth-brushing, nursery-rhyme singing,
several calls back into the bedroom . . .

It wasn't until half past eight that they were finally asleep, and I had a chance to tackle the photo albums.

The photo albums are pretty much my domain. Until Jonah was born, the family's photographic record was totally under control; I'd labelled every shot and slipped it into a protective pocket. (All our latest photos are sitting about in Kodak envelopes, of course, but I can't do *everything*.) My own life is chronicled in nine thick albums, dating from my fourth year at high school. Matt's is less exhaustively covered. In fact he's lost most of the photos that ever came his way before he met me, with the exception of those collected and preserved by one of his former girlfriends, Nadia. Nadia was a neurotic girl who took countless brooding, black-and-white photographs which she arranged with great style and sensibility in albums that she constructed herself out of handmade paper and old-fashioned corner mounts. She also used old concert and airline tickets, pressed flowers, postcards, feathers, color polaroids and scribbled phone messages to construct these memory books, one of which she gave to Matt as a birthday present. I'm always gobsmacked when I look at it. For one thing, the girl must have had as much spare time as those Victorian women who used to embroider elaborate designs on their doilies, slippers and underwear. For another, you get the impression, as you leaf through the rough, maroon and charcoal-colored pages, that Matt spent two years of his life contemplating the Oneness of Being in isolated mountain weekenders, or Pyrenean farmhouses, or disintegrating country sheds. Whenever I tease him about this, he replies, in plaintive tones, that he never even went as far as Bathurst, during those two years, and it isn't his fault that Nadia had him picked as a closet folk poet, or something. "Half of those shots she took while I was asleep," he wails.

But this was the album I wanted. This was the album that I emptied the linen closet for, discovering it at last under a pile of my grandmother's crocheted table napkins. I hauled it out, opened it up, and flicked hurriedly through the out-of-focus (atmospheric) landscape shots, the fragment of dried cabbage-palm leaf, the Manly ferry tickets, the portraits of Matt—all dark shadows and glinting eyes—the photographs of river pebbles, of an empty café chair, of a rake leaning against a weatherboard wall, until I came to a typical, rather dingy color snap taken in somebody's living room. Nadia had tried to tart it up with highlights drawn onto hairlines and T-shirts and sofa cushions with some kind of glitter-glue pen. She had even drawn a couple of sparkling purple auras around herself and Matt, and had framed the shot with strips of Christmas tinsel. But for all her effort, the photograph was still a muddy happy-snap, with acres of white wall and people's eyes reflecting an eerie red light.

Beside it was written, in purple glitter-glue: *Gary's housewarming—Matt and Nadia, Gary Comino, Eva Wobilt, Megan Molesdale, Dillon Draper, Mark Verney.*

The date, I worked out, must have been all of seventeen years ago.

Seventeen years ago, Megan Molesdale was a skinny girl with dark, spiky hair cut short, big lips covered in plum-colored lipstick, lots of teeth, and a taste for exotic earrings. Even then, she looked to be in her early twenties.

There's no way on earth that she could now pass for anything under forty.

I went and poured myself a gin and tonic. It was obvious that I'd been barking up the wrong tree. Megan Molesdale was an old friend of Matt's—one of the crew he mixed with when he was fresh out of Newcastle. Mark Verney was in Matt's first band. Nadia had introduced them both to a host of artistic girls who liked Balinese puppets and French cinema and African music and Lebanese food. Megan, I was sure, had been one of those girls. If she was a potter now, she could have been an artistic girl back then. In fact, I was quite sure that I remembered Matt mentioning a potter among them. A girl who wanted to build a kiln in her backyard, and who applied to the Australia Council for a grant to study pottery-making in Java, or somewhere like that.

She wasn't, I felt sure, the Girl With Purple Hair. Though it seemed odd that Matt hadn't mentioned her. Why not tell me that his old mate Megan had suddenly surfaced, after all these years? Unless Megan was *living* with the purple-haired girl? Unless that's how Matt had met her?

It was certainly possible.

But there was another possibility. As I made a half-hearted meal of leftover lamb stew and buttered toast, I chewed over the alternatives, and suddenly remembered that other call. The answering-machine call. "Hello, you have reached Paul, Marcus and Joe, we can't come to the phone right now, so please leave your name and number and we'll get back to you. In the meantime, party hard!"

What on earth had led me to assume that there was an "e" on the end of "Jo"?

I put off the Dread Moment for as long as possi-

ble. I washed the dishes, sorted the laundry, put
on my pajamas and picked up a hamperful of toys
before I finally summoned up the courage to hunt
down that number again. I was almost hoping for
another message from the answering machine. Instead, after two rings, someone picked up the phone.
Someone male.

"Yeah?" he said. There was music playing in the
background.

"Ah—oh. Hello."

"Hang on. *Will you turn that down, for fuck's sake?*
Yeah?"

"Is Joe there?"

"Jo? Yeah, hang on. I'll just get her."

Her! So it was a her! "Wait!" I said. But he'd already put the receiver down. I didn't know what to
do—I was petrified. If I had been able to move, I
probably would have hung up, instinctively. As it
was, by the time I regained full use of my limbs, I
was already debating the question in my head.
Should I hang up or not? If she came to the
phone, what would I say? Then I heard the sound
of footsteps, far away in that unknown house.

"Hello?" It was the same voice. "Listen, she's not
here. I thought she was."

"Oh . . ."

"Can I take a message? Hang on, I'll get a pen.
Where's the bloody pen, Marcus, I left it right here!"

"No—wait—it's all right." My brain was beginning to work again. "Just—can you tell me her second name? I have to post something."

"Cleary."

"Cleary?"

"Do you want the address too?"

"Oh—well, perhaps I'd better check that I've got it right."

He gave me the address—a street in Surry Hills. He was quite polite, really, though he sounded as rough as guts. Certainly he wasn't the person who had recorded the answering-machine message.

I thanked him, and hung up. Jo Cleary of Surry Hills.

A Surry Hills girl would have ready access to Oxford Street. A Surry Hills girl would have no reason not to dye her hair purple.

I sat there for a while with my head in my hands. That fuckwit, I thought. That miserable fuckwit. Then it occurred to me that this still wasn't proof; I still couldn't be sure. Even if I sat outside that house in Surry Hills for a week, and established beyond question that it was occupied by a girl with purple hair, what would that really prove? What I needed was to *know*, for sure, before I could make a decision. You can't make an informed decision about anything unless . . . well, unless you're properly informed. Right? I mean, if you're going to win any arguments, you have to see to it that your ammunition is all lined up in front of you first. You can't afford to be winded by an unexpected blow. That's what I've learned at work, anyway—always be prepared.

I rang Miriam again, but she wasn't at home. There were about eight messages on her answering machine. I left another one (where could she have got to?) and considered the possibility of a private detective. It seems insane, but people must use them, mustn't they? I know Miriam does. She hires them all the time, when the bank's in trouble. At least she must know how much they cost.

All I need is someone to follow Jo Cleary for a day or two, and see whether she meets up with Matt. It wouldn't be too difficult, or expensive. I'd do it myself, if I had the time. If I didn't have to worry about Emily and Jonah.

Private detectives. They're so sleazy. But what am I supposed to do? And if I hire a detective, and he comes back with good news, then there's no harm done, is there? And if he comes back with bad news, then at least I'll know where I stand. I'll be able to say: this is the situation. This is *exactly* how I feel. (It's the not knowing that makes me so confused.) This is my decision, and these are your options, Matt. It's your call, now.

On the other hand, what sort of a person hires a private detective? A pathetic human being, that's who. A hopeless case. A person who needs therapy.

Perhaps I do need therapy. I think I'm really going mad, here.

Chapter Five

Tuesday

Matt came home late last night. It must have been about ten-thirty, and he woke me up. But I didn't say anything.

Why didn't I say anything?

I can't believe that I'm behaving like this. Maybe it's because I've got a cold. I went to bed with a headache last night and woke up with a mild sore throat. For someone with two kids, waking up with a dead horse's head would be preferable to waking up with a cold, because at least horses' heads aren't contagious. Colds in this family last an average of six weeks as they spread from person to person. What's more, if Matt and I get one at the same time, then we're really stuffed. (Have you ever tried looking after two snotty, whiny kids while your own head is bursting and your chest is full of cement?) Nobody ever gets any sleep, thanks to the coughing, and when Jonah's not coughing all night Emily's puking all night, because a gutful of swallowed mucus always sets her off.

I don't even want to think about it. Why did this have to happen *now*? I can't cope with this now. I'm tired enough as it is. I'm miserable enough as it is. I don't need a sinus infection to make things worse.

Anyway, that's one reason why I didn't say anything—because I wasn't feeling strong enough for a confrontation. It was going to be hard enough, driving all the way to Penrith. Driving all the way to Penrith after a night spent trying to salvage a marriage would have been impossible. Besides, I still didn't have any proof. In my woozy state, I clung to the decision that I'd made last night: proof first, ask questions later. I had to talk to Miriam before I talked to Matt.

To tell you the truth, I didn't feel like talking to him at all, this morning. I left a set of written instructions on the kitchen table before I went, reminding him to put out the garbage bin, pay the phone bill, buy some more milk, use the rest of the spaghetti in the fridge, ask the builders (if they came) to fix the drain cover that they broke, and turn on the washing machine. Since he was still in a zombie-like state at the time of my departure, I had every excuse to communicate in writing. But perhaps I shouldn't have done it. Perhaps it looked a bit . . . well, you know. Like a memo to a junior employee, or something. Though in my defense let me say that I *did* add a row of little crosses under my name.

Oh, dear. Another bad decision, no doubt.

What with the peak-hour traffic and my slow reflexes, it took me nearly an hour to reach Penrith, even though I used the Motorway. Then I got lost, and had to consult my street directory. Finally, however, I found the Large Service Company that I was looking for, in a three-storeyed building on one of the main streets. I suppose I won't be sailing too close to the wind if I reveal that it's a specialist cleaning company? Probably not. Anyway, I won't get too specific as regards the floor number, or the size of its staff. I'll just say that the offices were a little shabby, fitted out with a grey, diamond-patterned carpet that must have been twenty years old, and a mismatched assortment of desks and chairs which had also seen better days.

I have to add, by the way, that the whole place could have done with a good clean.

I was greeted by the receptionist, who happened to be one of my witnesses. She looked about sixteen—a sandy blonde with strangely vivid lipstick, who didn't so much as blink an eyelid when she heard my name. She put a call through to her supervisor and branch manager, the notorious Mr. L., informing him that I had arrived. Then she went back to her typing.

Mr. L. came as quite a shock to me. From his letter, I had inferred that he would be a glowering, graceless person who would throw every possible obstacle in my way. It can often be surprising when you first lay eyes on a respondent in a sexual harassment case: many of them are grey-haired and dignified, or dry and bespectacled, or just plain harmless looking.

Nevertheless, after talking to them for a while, you'll often get a sense of something that's slightly out of kilter. The grey-haired doctor's eyes might be cold with rage and contempt. The bespectacled warehouse manager might talk with a barely concealed sneer. The harmless-looking sales representative might resort to an off-color joke. Nothing concrete, you understand—nothing you could take to court. But you suddenly find that you can picture the respondent committing those acts of which he (or she) has been accused. What I mean is, you actually start to entertain the idea that a complaint might have some substance. Because it's very difficult, sometimes, to visualize a balding, fifty-three-year-old marketing manager in a grey suit and rimless spectacles squeezing a publicity officer's tits and uttering honk-honk noises. It requires a leap of imagination that some people can't make.

As I said, we have to be objective. And it's hard not to question the veracity of a complainant who accuses her co-worker of ejaculating into her coffee. An accusation like that tends to raise as many doubts about the complainant's emotional stability as it does about the respondent's. All the same, it's a fact that we hardly ever get any complaints that are frivolous, vexatious or misconceived. The whole conciliation process is far too long and onerous for anyone to endure if they just want to make trouble. So by the time it gets to me, a complaint has to be treated seriously, even if it does involve a wind-up walking penis or a really pathetic memo about crotchless underwear.

But I was talking about Mr. L. To my surprise, Mr. L. came out of his office with a welcoming smile on his face. He was a man of slim build and middle height, with mild grey eyes, lots of curly brown hair (slightly touched with grey), and a soft, pleasant voice. He wore a wedding ring on his left hand, which felt dry and warm when I shook it.

"So you managed to find the place," he said, after we'd introduced ourselves. "Would you like a coffee, or something? Tea?"

"No, thanks," I replied. It was awkward that I had to go through Mr. L. to speak to my witnesses, who were all under his supervision. But he didn't seem to find it in the least bit unnerving. On the contrary, he appeared to be quite relaxed. He asked me if I wanted to use his office or the tea-room for my interviews; the rest of the premises were open-plan, he said, and not very private. I elected to use the tearoom. As well as a sink, a fridge and a microwave oven, this room contained a large conference table and ten chairs. There was also a hot-water urn, a matching jar of International Roast, and a collection of toxic-looking dishcloths. I have never seen a less welcoming tearoom.

"Now—you said you wanted to talk to Aris?" Mr. L. remarked, searching the cupboards for a water jug.

"Aris, Alissa and Christine."

"Right. Aris is out on a job, but I told him to re-port in here at ten."

"That's fine."

I was waiting for him to say something—something along the lines of "Hopefully we'll be able to straighten this whole thing out." But he didn't say another word. Having found the jug and a couple of glasses, he arranged them on the table beside my briefcase. Then he gave me a crooked smile and left to find Alissa.

Alissa was the receptionist. She had been named as the co-worker who had allegedly overheard Mr. L. asking Ms. F. if her sex life had improved lately.

Examining her lacquered fingernails, Alissa agreed that Mr. L. had said something to that effect. She sounded bored.

"Has he ever made any other references to her sex life in your hearing?" I asked.

"He might have. I don't listen much when he's not talking to me."

I requested that she describe the relationship between Mr. L. and Ms. F. My reward was an incredulous stare.

"Well . . . he's her boss," she said. "He tells her what to do."

"Anything else?"

A blank look.

"Was there any tension between them?" I asked patiently. "Did she ever cry when he talked to her? Did you ever see him touch her, or make any kind of gestures?"

Alissa's expression didn't change, but her voice held a note of exasperation as she explained that she didn't sit anywhere near Ms. F., so she didn't know anything about it. Personally, she didn't think there had been any sexual harassment. Why should there be? Mr. L. was quite good-looking, for an older guy.

"Then why do you think he asked her if her sex life had improved lately?" I queried.

"Because he was joking around, I dunno." Alissa sighed impatiently. "Guys always ask things like that. They're always asking me things like that."

"Did your boss ever ask you that?"

"No!" Alissa snorted. "Of course not. God, he's like forty or something. And married. I'm talking about *young* guys."

I gave up. Fortunately, Christine was more on

my wavelength. In fact she had a great deal to say, and said it with force and clarity. It was Christine who had advised Ms. F. to contact the Equal Opportunity and Human Rights Board, after Ms. F.'s complaints to company management had received minimal response. (Neither woman would have considered the possibility of approaching a union, even if they had belonged to one.) Christine was a dark and vital young woman of Vietnamese extraction, who was in charge of things like bookkeeping and petty cash. She told me that Mr. L. had indeed referred to Ms. F.'s telephone as her dildo.

"He also called her 'barge-arse,' " Christine said indignantly. "When she told him not to, he said that she should stop jiggling her arse around, and drawing it to everyone's attention." Christine's dark eyes flashed. "She was so humiliated. I found her crying in the toilet."

"Can you tell me about their relationship otherwise?" I asked, and Christine leaned forward in a confiding manner.

"Well this is what I think," she said. "Maria was John's secretary, right? So she knew all about the bust-ups at home. Big bust-ups, because she heard him on the phone. His wife walks out on him, comes back, walks out again, and he's really angry, all the time. But he can't show it, he's got to be nice to all the customers, nice to the senior managers, so he takes it out on his secretary."

"Yes, but—"

"Because Maria walked out on *her* husband, see, so John makes himself feel better by calling her barge-arse. Then when he sees how upset she is, he really gets stuck into her."

"So what you're saying is—"

"That's what the dildo business was all about. He was saying she spent too much time on the phone when she should have been working, and asked her if she was practicing giving blow jobs with her dildo substitute." A hint of distaste must have entered my gaze, because Christine went on with renewed energy. "He wasn't trying to come on to her, it was nasty, you know? The more upset she got, the more he did it. Like with that dildo he put in her drawer. It frightened her—she's a good Catholic."

"But you never saw the sex toy yourself?"

"No. I was on holiday. Maria told me about it, though. John said he knew nothing about it— acted all innocent—and she threw it away. But then he made a big thing of it, told everyone she'd found it in her drawer, so everyone was joking about it—saying it was from an unknown admirer."

"What about your own relationship with him?"

"*Me?*" Christine's eyes flashed again. "If he tried anything with me, I'd kick him in the *balls!*"

Christine had a lot more to say on the subject of her manager's psychological makeup; by the time she had finished, my next witness had been cooling his heels by the door for at least ten minutes. Aris was the illiterate male co-worker I referred to previously—the one who, according to Ms. F., had been the recipient of Mr. L.'s prurient observations. Gruff, awkward and monosyllabic, he was in his late forties, though he looked older. He was also small and wiry and wearing a pair of overalls emblazoned on the back with the company's logo. He kept rubbing his jaw as I talked to him.

So cautious was he—so reluctant to speak or

even meet my eye—that I was fully expecting him
to deny Ms. F.'s claims, if only because he was
afraid of being sacked. To my surprise, though, he
supported them fully. He agreed that Mr. L. had
indeed remarked, in Ms. F.'s hearing, that she wasn't
the sort of woman that anyone would want on top.

"Did he say anything else?" I queried.

Aris studied his boots, and mumbled something
about not listening.

"Did he say that 'she'd need two men, one for
each buttock'?"

A muttered reply.

"I'm sorry?" I leaned forward. "What was that?"

"He said 'butt-cheek,' not buttock."

It was like pulling teeth. Afterwards, I felt quite
exhausted, but satisfied—because by then I had
enough to move on with.

I said as much to Mr. L. on my way out. Not that
he tried to pump me or anything. He didn't even
approach me, as I half expected he would; like a
man with a clear conscience, he behaved as if my
movements were of no concern to him. But remembering the curt tone of his correspondence, I
decided that I might get a better response if I
spoke to him in person, rather than sending him a
report of my findings.

So I knocked on his office door, and asked if I
might talk to him for a moment.

Of course I gave him my usual spiel about ob-
jectivity, resolving a problem, both parties being
given the opportunity to express their feelings and
concerns, et cetera, et cetera. He listened in silence, nodding occasionally. Then I hit him with
the fact that every witness named by Ms. F. had

supported her side of the story. Had he no witnesses of his own, who might help to rebut these claims?

He gave a great sigh, and ran his hands through his hair. "You know," he said, "this is so wrong. This is outrageous." And he shook his head. "You're going to think I'm a nutter, but this is all . . . God, you know, this is all Christine's doing. I don't like to use the word conspiracy, but—call it office politics. She wants my job."

I raised my eyebrows.

"It's true, I swear. If she gets my job, she's promised Maria a promotion, and that's where all this has come from. I know it sounds insane. I know you're not going to believe me, but I'll go down saying it, because I won't admit to something I didn't do." For the first time he sounded upset; he put his fists on the table, side by side.

"But what about Aris? Aris agrees—"

"Of course he does! Because I was joking with him. I admit the jokes were off-color. But I didn't know that Maria was *listening*, my God, I'd never have said anything like that to her face. Is it my fault that she was hanging round outside my office, eavesdropping?"

I studied him. He had such a pleasant, open look. Such a wounded, outraged expression. As for his interpretation . . . well, it wasn't completely off the wall.

"So you're saying that any offense you may have caused was unintentional?" I asked.

"Totally."

"Snapping her bra strap?"

"I didn't do that."

"What about the sex toy?"

"I had nothing to do with that. Nothing."

"Calling her telephone a dildo substitute?"

"I never said that." He spoke firmly. "If Christine told you I said that, she's . . . that is, she must have misheard. I *never said that.*"

The diplomatic backtrack. God, he was convincing.

Then I remembered Matt. Work had made me forget him, for a moment, but suddenly it all came flooding back in a poisonous tide. Matt was intelligent and attractive too, and look what *he* was doing.

"All right." I stood up. "Well, if that's your position, perhaps you'd like to set it down in writing?"

"What's the point? No one's going to believe me. *You* don't believe me, do you?"

"It's not a matter of what I believe." I wittered on for a while about how the Board doesn't take sides, and how misunderstandings often arise that can be settled quite easily, and how equal employment opportunity issues are addressed in certain available training courses . . . that kind of thing. Then I shook his hand. But as I was moving out the door, he said in a tentative voice: "I mean, have you actually seen her?"

"Seen who?"

"Maria." His eyes were pained under a corrugated brow. "There's no reason for me to . . . well, she's not exactly a pin-up girl. Maybe an older guy would be interested—I don't know. I don't think anyone is, at the moment." He spread his hands again. "Maybe that's part of the problem. You know?"

There it was. The classic "why would I harass a dog like that?" followed by the traditional "it's sour grapes because she can't get a root." I'd been waiting for something along those lines.

Dirty bugger.

I was so angry when I got back to the office. All the way from Penrith I'd been thinking about Matt and Mr. L., and the unplumbed depths of male deceit. I'd been wondering why I hadn't got off my butt and *made an effort*, instead of behaving like a victim and wandering about in a daze all the time. It was motherhood, I decided. Motherhood had made me fatalistic. I had done everything I could for Jonah when he was a baby, and it had made no difference at all. He had still cried and cried and cried. In the end, I had realized that the western tradition of endlessly searching for answers to problems wasn't helping me, it was just making me more frantic. What I had to do was *surrender to the suffering*. Be Zen. Accept the karma. Let go. Realize that there are some things you just can't beat—like the inequalities between mother and father, for instance. It all comes down to breastfeeding. Matt couldn't breastfeed (for obvious reasons) and I couldn't express enough milk every day for a night feed. Just didn't have it in me. So I had to keep waking up at night, and Nature triumphed. It almost always does, with kids—though try telling that to some of the policy people at work.

However.

When I reached my desk I immediately called Miriam, only to discover that she'd taken a sick day. A sick day! This was almost unprecedented; was she really ill? There were fifteen calls on her answering machine at home, and I left another one. I didn't have Giles's number. The number for Miriam's mum was in the family address book, which I hadn't brought to work. Neither Ronnie nor Vicki (another mutual friend) knew anything about where else she could be. Feeling a little uneasy, I had to give up on Miriam and call Stuart instead.

Stuart, like Paul, is an old friend from university. In fact I met him through Paul. Like me, he loathes Paul's wife; our main shared interest, these days, is Kerry-bashing—though I don't actually see much of him any more. Perhaps it's just as well. He works for Comcare, sussing out people who've been claiming workers' compensation for non-existent injuries, and it's made him very cynical. He's even dropped a few sour remarks about single mothers, lately. God knows, life can be depressing enough without Stuart destroying your few remaining illusions about sickness benefits and the welfare state. That's why I tend to ration my conversations with him.

This time, however, I needed to pick his brain. I needed to ask him about private detectives.

"You use them, don't you?" I asked. "I remember you telling me."

"Yeah, we use 'em. All the time. Why? What's up?"

I wasn't going to tell him the truth. He wasn't a close enough friend. For a moment I toyed with the idea of confiding that Paul was concerned about Kerry—that he thought she was having an affair. Then I discarded the notion. Too far-fetched. Whoever would want to have an affair with Kerry?

"I've got a friend called Mandy." (Mandy the Wholefood Mother.) "Her husband's run off with a man." (I wish.) "She's trying to find him."

"He's disappeared?"

"That's what she says."

"Then he's a missing person."

"No, no. He's around. He keeps calling her. She just wants to know where he is, and what he's doing."

"Why?"

"*I* don't know. Don't ask me. I just promised I'd find her the name of a good private detective. You know one, don't you?"

He did. He knew several. James McRae, he said, did a bit of marital infidelity work. He was good. So was Jerry Vosilla, but he'd turned down a few jobs, lately, citing health problems as the reason. Hettwer Marcel was good, also. "But they're expensive, Helen. They're not cheap. Does your friend realize that?"

"How much do they cost?"

He told me. Forty an hour, he said.

Ow.

"I'd go for Jim McRae," Stuart went on. "He's reliable. Ex-cop. Do you want his number? If you don't think she's serious, don't give her his number, because I don't want to muck him about. He gets enough of that as it is."

"Where does he live?"

"I don't know. His company operates out of Rose Hill."

"Give me the number. I'll see what she says. She might not be able to afford it."

"Tell her all she has to do is strain her back, and she'll be set for life," Stuart said bitchily. But before he could launch into another one of his diatribes against fraudulent back injuries someone knocked on my office door, and I had to hang up.

It was Jean, telling me that a busload of people had arrived for my two o'clock conference.

"Bugger," I said. "I haven't had a chance to eat my lunch."

"Well they're here. It's conference room two, isn't it?"

"Yeah. Has Cindy set it up yet?"

"Far as I know."

"Could you ask her to get them settled, Jean, and I'll be three minutes? Three."

"Okay."

Fortunately, I'm used to stuffing down half my weight in ham sandwich during whatever brief interval I can grab between peeling an apple for Emily (she hates the skin) and making a cheese-slice-and-fish-finger boat for Jonah. I reckon I could polish off a three-course meal in seven minutes, given half the chance. And I get plenty of practice at work too, because never a lunchtime passes, at the office, without my having to bolt out and pay a bill, or buy more nappies, or go to the bank, or extract a refund from Medicare. So it wasn't much of an effort to consume one peanut butter roll and one fruit jelly dessert in the time that it took me to call Jim McRae. (I'd brought my own lunch, to save money; I can only really afford one lunch date per week.) Unfortunately, Jim wasn't available—out trailing adulterous husbands, no doubt. I had to leave a message on his message-bank, informing him that I was a friend of Stuart's and needed advice. Nothing too specific. I gave him my name and work number, then remembered that I wouldn't be at work the next day, and gave him my home number as well. All this time, mind you, I was folding a bread roll into my mouth, and spooning up two-fruits in apricot jelly. You can't say that I'm not versatile.

Of course the minute I put the receiver down, I regretted making the call. Sitting there, I had a major panic attack: sweaty palms, hot flushes, the lot. What the hell did I think I was doing? I couldn't afford a private detective. If I couldn't afford a café meal more than once a week, then I certainly couldn't afford a private detective. It would cost me hundreds—perhaps even thousands—of dollars. And for what? So I could prove something that I didn't want to know in the first place?

I thought: This is what comes of losing your temper. This is what comes of letting the job (and its attendant sleazebags) get to you. But I couldn't do much to remedy the situation, because there were a lot of highly stressed people waiting for me in conference room two. I had to rush off and make sure that they didn't start fighting each other before I even got there. I didn't have time to fret about private detectives.

I didn't have time to do anything except my job until well after six, when the conference finally ended. Not a bad result, actually—a pregnancy discrimination case, settled by conciliation with a $2000 payment and a written statement of apology. Personally, I'd take a straightforward pregnancy discrimination case over a sexual harassment case any day, because there isn't quite the same level of humiliation or resentment in pregnancy discrimination. There aren't quite as many nasty undercurrents. But that's just my opinion. I know that Bebe, one of the other complaints officers, really gets off on sexual discrimination cases because the settlements tend to be heftier. It's my feeling that she

enjoys wresting $25,000 out of a blue-chip corpo-
ration every once in a while because she used to
work at the Redfern Legal Center when she first
left school.

Each to his own, I guess.

I'd warned Matt that I might be late, so I didn't
panic unduly when I got back to my office and saw
the time. Ten past six. That gave me fifteen minutes until the next train—plenty of time to call Jim
McRae and cancel. I was half-expecting to get his
message-bank again. I certainly didn't expect him
to answer the phone himself.

"Jim McRae," he said quietly.

"Oh. Hello." Help! "That's—that's Jim McRae,
is it?"

Aagh. What an idiot.

"Yes. Can I help you?"

"Look, I'm sorry about this, I—um—I left a
message earlier. I'm a friend of Stuart Klein."

"Helen Muzzatti?"

"That's it. That's me. Um . . . look, I've made a
mistake. I've changed my mind. I'm sorry, I'm
such a dodo. I'm sorry."

"That's all right." He had a great voice, very
deep and calm. He sounded more like a psychiatrist than a private detective.

"Okay, well . . . thanks for calling back. I mean—
no, you didn't call back, did you? Ha ha." Oh my
God, my God, could I have sounded any more stupid? "Don't listen to me, I'm in a complete state at
the moment—"

"I did call you back, Helen."

"Beg pardon?"

"I did call you back. You said after five-thirty I
could reach you at home, so I called that number."

"Oh."

"I didn't leave a message. I didn't know if I should, in the circumstances."

"No. Right." I felt as if I'd suddenly drifted into a John Le Carré novel. "Thanks."

"But if you change your mind, I'm always available."

"Thanks."

"Goodbye."

He hung up. I hung up. Then I stood for a moment with my hand on the phone and my mind in a spin, before I suddenly remembered the time. Six-thirteen. I thought: If only I had a mobile, I could call Miriam on the train. But mobiles cost money, and office mobiles are in great demand.

I knew it would mean rushing, but I dialled her number anyway. Twenty-one messages; she still wasn't answering. It suddenly occurred to me— what if she was lying dead in her bathroom? "Jesus," I murmured. Should I call the police, just in case? Should I send someone over there?

Not until I got home, perhaps. Not until I'd had a meal and a hot shower.

I'd made enough stupid phone calls for one day.

I was a nervous wreck by the time I got home. To begin with, I was worried about Miriam. Furthermore, as the train sat becalmed for ten minutes somewhere between St. Peters and Sydenham, I had the leisure to realize that if Matt had been at home all day, he would have had plenty of time to call the Girl With Purple Hair. For all I knew, he might have *arranged a meeting*. It was with this happy thought foremost in my mind that I finally walked in the front door, and was greeted by a high-pitched yowl that I identified as Jonah's.

I checked my watch. Ten past seven.

"Hello!" I called, chucking my briefcase onto an unoccupied chair. Emily came tearing out of the kitchen to greet me. She wasn't wearing her pajamas, I noticed.

"Hello, Mummy!"

"Hello, darling."

"Jonah made a mess."

"Did he?"

"He got the green cordial and it fell over and it made a mess."

"Oh dear." Sure enough, I found Matthew wiping fluorescent green liquid off the kitchen floor. Jonah had been strapped into his highchair; hence his all-too-obvious misery. Something was boiling on the stove.

"Hello," I said, looking down at my husband.

"Hi." He spoke through gritted teeth.

"M-u-um!" keened Jonah. "Mu-hu-humm-ee!"

"Shut up, Jonah." Matt was in a dangerous mood. Sensing this, I refrained from pointing out that he was using the dishcloth to wipe the floor. But when I looked at the benchtop near the stove, and saw two plastic plates laid out there, each sporting a piece of rolled ham speared with a toothpick, I couldn't contain myself.

"Haven't they had their *dinner* yet?"

"No. They haven't."

I surveyed my children, noting their stained T-shirts. "Or their baths?" I said.

"No."

For fuck's sake.

"*Mu-u-mm-ee!*"

"Be *quiet*, Jonah!" I could hardly think. "So is the food nearly ready, or what?"

"Oh, fuck." He leapt to his feet, lunging for the stove, and turned off the gas.

"*Matt.*" How the hell many times did I have to tell him? "*Not in front of the children.*"

"Yeah, yeah," he muttered.

"I'll dish up. You get the mop and bucket." What had he been doing all afternoon, for God's sake? They were supposed to be in bed by seven-thirty. As he stomped off to fetch the mop and bucket, I drained the vegetables. Frozen, of course. Peas, corn and—what? And toasted muffins, by the look of it. Emily was asking for a drink.

"Wait a minute. Just wait."

"Mummee-ee . . ."

"It's okay, Jonah. Nobody's mad." I wasn't surprised to find Jonah in a state. He must have been starving. His highchair tray was still covered in muck from his last meal.

"You had a call," said Matt, from the doorway. He was listing slightly, dragged to one side by the weight of a full bucket. "Some bloke. He wouldn't leave his name."

"Mmm." No comment from me about that. "Matthew, could you please wipe down the high-chair?" (Since it wasn't done hours ago.) "Are they supposed to be eating muffins, with this?"

"Yes."

"What happened to the spaghetti?"

"They ate it for lunch."

"Wasn't there some rice in there? I think I'll warm up some rice, instead. *Matt!*" I couldn't believe my eyes; he was wiping Jonah's highchair tray with the same dishcloth. "Don't use *that*, it's been on the *floor!*"

Whump! He hurled the dishcloth in my general direction. He might have been aiming for the sink, but it nearly hit me in the face.

"Tell you what," he barked. "Since I'm so useless, why don't you do it yourself? Eh?"

And he walked out.

Can you believe that? He walked out. I'd just come home from work, and he promptly walked out of the house, leaving *me* to do everything that he should have done already.

Needless to say, you can't vent your rage in these situations. Not when your kids are there. Staring at you. Nervously.

I took a deep breath.

"Okay. Emily, why don't you help Mummy, and get out your special knife and fork, and then you can tell me what you did today. Okay? I'm dying to hear all about it. Jonah, you'll get your drink as soon as I clean all that yukky stuff away. No, you have to stay in your highchair. You can get out after you've finished your dinner. And if you're a good boy, you can have a biscuit afterwards. A chocolate biscuit."

"And me!" yelped Emily.

"And you. Both of you."

I was seething. God, I was *enraged*. But I plastered on my mummy smile and rushed around punching microwave buttons, wiping surfaces, pouring juice, cutting ham into car shapes (did he really think that Jonah was going to eat an ordinary piece of ham?), until the kids were each settled in front of a steaming plate, bibs around their necks and mugs positioned well away from the nearest table edge. Then, having reminded them both about the promised chocolate biscuit, I hastened into my bedroom, rummaging through my briefcase as I did so.

Luckily, I'd kept the number.

"Jim McRae." Once again, he answered the phone himself.

"Mr. McRae?" I had to clear my throat. "It's Helen Muzzatti. I'm sorry to bother you at this time of night . . ."

"What's up, Helen?"

"I—look, I'm definitely going ahead with this. I'm sorry about what I said before, but I've made up my mind now." Glancing over my shoulder, I checked that the door was shut. Yes. I lowered my voice. "Definitely, this time. I won't muck you about any more. I'm sorry."

A pause at the other end of the line.

"What seems to be the problem?" he said at last.

"It's my husband. I'm not sure, but I think he might be . . . you know . . ." Suddenly I heard the far-off jangling of keys in the front door. "Oh God. There he is. Can I talk to you tomorrow? I'm home all day tomorrow. Only it'll have to be after twelve, because he doesn't leave for work until—"

"Tell you what," Jim interrupted, calmly. "Why don't we meet somewhere? I can give you a rundown of the fee schedule, you can explain your problem, and if you want to go ahead—if you feel it's the right thing to do—then we can work something out. Only, if you're going to be changing your mind again, then it might be a good idea if you made some sort of payment up front—"

"Yes, yes." I could hear heavy footsteps in the

hall. "But I've got two kids, you see, two little kids. If I take them anywhere they're bound to play up."

"Where do you live?"

"Dulwich Hill."

Another pause. "Well, that's okay," he finally observed. "I've got someone to see in Bondi, tomorrow, so I can drop in. What's the address?"

With some misgivings, I gave it to him. Matt's voice was rumbling away in the kitchen. "If you get here after two, will you please come around the back?" I requested. "Because my little boy goes to sleep around two, and he's in the front room, and if you ring the doorbell he'll wake up, and it'll be hard to get him down again."

"No problem."

"Okay, well—thanks. Thanks so much."

"No problem."

I checked my watch as I replaced the receiver. Matt had been out for just over twenty minutes.

When I opened the bedroom door he was standing there, right in front of me, and I nearly died of shock.

"Jesus!" I exclaimed.

"What were you doing?"

"Nothing." I saw that he was carrying a two-liter container of milk. "Did you go to the shop at the end of the road?"

"Yeah." He took a deep breath. "Look, I'll come clean, I forgot to buy the milk today, so I went and got it—"

"What's the expiry date?" I interjected. The shop at the end of the road was notoriously untrustworthy. We both looked, and saw that the milk was supposed to be used by tomorrow.

"For fuck's sake!" he exploded.

"It's no use going to that shop. I never go there—"

"Well I'm going back there now."

"Matt, there's no point. Matt!" I followed him to the door. "It expires *tomorrow*, not today. You should have checked the date—"

"Oh yeah, right. My fault again." He swung around to face me. "You stuff up yourself, occasionally, do you know that? Do you realize you left Jonah all by himself in the highchair? That's not recommended, in case you haven't read the sticker on the back."

I gasped. I snorted. I rolled my eyes.

"Puh-*lease*," I said.

"Who were you calling?"

"What?"

"Who were you calling? Just then?"

I blinked, and gaped at him.

"Uh—well—Miriam."

"Miriam?"

"Yes! Miriam!" I was getting flustered. "What's that got to do with anything?"

He turned on his heel. "I'll get some more milk," he declared, and pulled open the front door.

"Matt! That isn't particularly helpful, at this stage! The kids have to be washed, they have to be put to bed, the dinner needs to be cooked—*Matt!*"

"I'll be back in five minutes."

He wasn't, naturally. He was back in fifteen. By that time I'd got the kids into the bath; Matt took over the drying, dressing and bedtime procedures as I threw a meal together for us. (Pasta with tinned sauce and iceberg lettuce. Yummy.) Feeling justified in doing so, I started eating without him.

I hadn't even changed out of my suit and good blouse, but I didn't care. All I did was kick my shoes off.

He finally joined me at eight-fifteen. Slouched into the kitchen, dropped into a chair. He looked exhausted.

"Sorry," he said.

A noncommittal noise from me.

"It was a tough day. You caught me at a bad time." He rubbed his hand across his face, as the silence lengthened. "But it's no good criticizing me all the time, you know?" he went on at last. "I'm doing the best I can."

Mmmm.

"It's not like you don't forget things occasionally," he pointed out. "Like my birthday, for instance."

"I'm not even going to—"

"Okay, okay. Okay." He backpedalled, raising his hands. "I'm sorry I mentioned it. I'm sorry."

"That was so unbelievably uncalled for."

"Sometimes I lose my temper."

"Tell me about it."

"I'm *sorry*, okay? I guess I'm just not perfect. Like some people."

I didn't answer that. If I had, I would have done something really feeble, like bursting into tears.

"I did get a new bottle of milk, though," he said, indicating the bottle in question. "It expires next Sunday."

"Good."

I stared down at my pasta, slumped over it, one hand supporting my head. Matt got up. He fetched his own plate, a fork, the parmesan cheese. He sat down again.

"I was gunna suggest we have takeaway," he remarked. "Pizza, or something. You didn't have to do this."

I thought: I did though, didn't I? The way I do just about everything around here.

But I didn't say it.

"The builders came," he offered.

"Oh good."

"They said they'd be coming again tomorrow."

"I'll believe it when I see it."

"Yeah."

Another long silence. Matthew has a weird (but endearing) way of using his fork; he holds it like a screwdriver, and kind of mashes everything up with it. I was watching him do this when he suddenly said: "What's the matter, Helen?"

I looked up. His expression was taut and wary.

I felt a tightening in my chest.

"What's the *matter*?" I repeated.

"Is something wrong?" The tone was almost accusing—I didn't like it at all. The blood rushed to my cheeks. I had to force the words out.

"Well, you tell me, Matt. *Is* something wrong?"

"Eh?"

"You're the one throwing things around and storming out of the house, not me!"

"Yeah, but—"

"What's up with *you*? That's what I want to know!"

Without even trying, I was suddenly teetering on the edge of a precipice. I was staring into a vacuum, holding my breath. Had I . . . ? Would he . . . ?

The question hadn't *quite* been asked. Not quite. I still didn't have the guts.

"Nothing," he replied tonelessly. "Nothing's up with me." He was poking at his pasta, his eyes downcast. "I'm tired, that's all. Tough day. You know what it's like."

None better.

So that was that. All that emoting, all that carry-on, and I still don't know.

Is he a coward or is he an innocent man?

Chapter Six

Wednesday

My cold was ten times worse this morning. I practically forgot about it yesterday, because my sore throat disappeared some time during my interview with Christine, and nothing took its place until last night—when I came down with another ferocious headache. But that was after my argument with Matt. That was when the air was practically throbbing with tension, and the pressure of unshed tears was making my nose run. Naturally, I assumed that my headache was a consequence of the unfortunate atmosphere. So I took a Panadol Forte and passed out for the night, hoping that an eight-hour sleep might solve the problem.

Needless to say, I was disappointed. I woke up with clogged sinuses and a wet cough—the type described as productive in medical literature provided by the local baby clinic. I couldn't chew my toast without gasping for breath. I couldn't measure out Jonah's milk without stopping every thirty seconds to blow my nose or expel crap from my lungs. Matt took one look at me on his way to the toilet and said glumly: "That cold's worse, isn't it"

I refrained from making a sarcastic comment about the bleeding obvious. Instead I just nodded.

"Bloody hell," he groaned, and retreated into the bathroom. Nothing like a bit of sympathetic support from your hubby, I always say.

Fortunately, it was Wednesday morning. Matt goes to work at twelve on Wednesday mornings. So I asked him to please take the kids to the pool while I struggled with a bit of housework; it would be better, I said, if they were kept out of my way as much as possible. Then I waited, nursing a faint hope that he might actually offer to stay home and look after the kids, so that I could retire to bed with a hot-water bottle.

But he didn't, of course. He never does. When you work for ABC, you can't risk giving anyone the excuse to sack you.

"Just an hour in the pool," I growled, resigned to the inevitable. "You'll be back in plenty of time."

"Where are the swimming clothes?"

"In the top right-hand drawer of their dresser." Will you tell me why he can't remember that? When I must have told him about a million times before? "Use the old towels on the *bottom* shelf, please, and don't forget Emily's goggles."

He muttered something.

"Pardon?"

"Nothing," he said. "Hey, kids! Who wants to go for a swim?"

"Me! Me!"

"Oh, I don't think you want to go, do you?" he joked. "Not Emily Muzzatti. She doesn't even *like* swimming."

"I do! I do!"

"No, she'd rather stay here and help Mummy clean the toilet."

"No, no!" Emily cried, and followed him around the house as he collected articles of swimwear, begging him to bring the blow-up dinosaur flotation ring.

"Only if I'm allowed to use it," he replied, stuffing a drawstring beach bag with towels.

"Don't be silly, Daddy!" Emily protested. "You wouldn't fit!"

"Yes I would."

"No you wouldn't! You're too big."

"I am not. Jonah's bigger than me."

"No he isn't!"

"Yes he is, look." And Matthew swung Jonah up onto his shoulders. Jonah began to giggle and crow, and kick his pudgy feet. Matt ordered him to duck his head on the way out.

"Say goodbye to Mummy, you two."

"Bye, Mummy!"

"Bye, Mummy!"

"Bye, guys! Have a good swim!"

They all looked so sweet, filing out the front door: Emily wearing her floaties, Jonah clutching Matt's head like a baby koala, and Matt himself burdened with the purple plastic dinosaur, the Mickey Mouse beach bag, the dangling octopus goggles, the cluster of undersized, fluorescent shower shoes. Normally, I'd be glorying in the fact that they were mine, mine, *mine*. But not today. Today I watched them go with cold fear in my heart.

Then I flopped down on a kitchen chair and castigated myself. Here was I, worried about my husband's fidelity, and all I seemed to be able to do was mope and moan and nag. Did I really believe that this was going to improve matters? If he was actually having an affair, it would only make things worse! Yet somehow I couldn't help myself. My resentment—my anger—kept bubbling to the surface. Even though he was being Mister Perfect, taking the kids to the pool, remembering the shower shoes . . . my eyes filled with tears when I considered those shower shoes. What *right* did I have to complain about Matt, when he had remembered the shower shoes?

It was my cold, I decided. My cold was making me miserable. Not to mention the filthy kitchen, which I would have to clean before everyone else came home. Yesterday's green cordial spillage had not been properly expunged, and now the floor was sticky. There were streaks and splatters all over the cupboard doors. Dirty dishes and cutlery were piled high on the draining board; the stove was greasy; the table was covered with crumbs. Through the window over the sink I could see a grey sky, and a flutter of black tarpaulin. The drains still smelled.

I got up slowly, deeply depressed by the thought of having to clean a kitchen that I hated with all my heart and soul while still burdened by a lurking sense of dread. It's a horrible kitchen, by the way. Dates from about 1973, to judge from its orange tiles and wood-grain laminex. Even the handles on the cupboard doors are putrid. Everything's full of cracks and holes, so I can't keep the ants out no matter what I do. (Which isn't very much, with Jonah around. Baits are out of the question.) You can scrub the vinyl floor until you're blue in the face, and it will still look just as dirty. There's a huge scorch-mark on one of the benchtops. As for the oven, I don't even want to go there. Literally. It hadn't been cleaned for twenty-odd years when we moved in, and I'm still chipping black stuff off its sides, like a coal miner.

One day I'm going to have a nice white kitchen with a stainless-steel dishwasher. I'm going to have a built-in microwave cupboard and a rangehood with an extractor pipe up through the ceiling. One day those builders are going to *finish the job*, and I won't be looking out the kitchen window onto a junkyard piled high with lumber and lengths of rusty pipe and chipped blocks of old concrete. After all, they've got to finish that bedroom one of these days, haven't they? They can't keep pouring the foundations forever. And once the bedroom's done, they'll be able to tackle the kitchen, and I'll be happy.

That is, if I still have a husband by then.

I groaned at the prospect of having to sell up and get divorced before the builders had finished their renovations. What kind of a price would we get, in that eventuality? About enough for a down payment on a caravan in a trailer park, that's how much.

No, no, I thought, madly sloshing water about. No, that won't happen. It *won't*. This is crazy. I should just—just . . .

What? Turn a blind eye?

Out of the question. I had made arrangements with Jim McRae, and those arrangements were set in stone. There was no way on earth that I could change my mind, not again. Feeling the pressure of yet more tears, I whipped off my rubber gloves and grabbed a couple of chocolate biscuits, which

I consumed in about three seconds flat. I would have eaten more, if there had been more to eat. That's the trouble with kids. Wherever there are kids, there are also chocolate biscuits and cartons half-full of rice custard and bits of leftover mashed potato and all kinds of other nursery food that you always crave when you're feeling down. No wonder I've put on so much weight in the last four years. Unfortunately, I'm not one of those people who go off their food when they're under stress. On the contrary, I eat like a pig, because I'm pathetically weak when it comes to sugar-laden food groups. My only strategy for weight loss is to keep out of the way of temptation—and how am I supposed to do that when I'm surrounded by Honey Jumbles and paddle-pops? Especially when they're distributed around a kitchen like this one. It's the sort of kitchen that would send anyone groping for comfort food. I mean, you can clean the whole room, from the kickboards to the cabinet-tops, and it won't look much better. What's more, as soon as the family surges in, you'll end up back where you started. Within half an hour there'll be more crumbs on the floor, more greasy marks all over the refrigerator, more dirty dishes piled high in the sink. Talk about a woman's work is never done.

It's heartbreaking.

It's also unavoidable, however—the murky underbelly of every family's life—so I took a swig of cold coffee and set to work once more, buoyed somewhat by a rousing, kick-ass song from Alanis Morissette which I'd put on the stereo. (Nothing like Alanis Morissette to get you feeling both empowered and victimized simultaneously.) After I finished the kitchen I even had a stab at the living room, where the kids had dumped most of their toys. Putting away toys is a very time-consuming occupation. It's not just a matter of tossing them in a toybox—not when a kid reaches Emily's age. By the time a kid turns four, he or she generally has a squillion toys, all of microscopic proportions, which someone has to keep track of. So every doll's shoe, every Lego block, every miniature plastic giraffe has its own box or bag or drawer, in order that it can be easily found when a child wants it (urgently). And that means endless sorting through tangled piles of discarded toys, making certain that the giraffe goes into the small animals drawer, the Lego goes into the Lego box, the shoe goes into the tin full of dolls' clothes . . .

And don't even talk to me about the doll's house. That's a whole second kitchen I have to clean.

"Mummy!" Emily burst through the door just as I'd finished untangling a knot composed of plastic pearl necklaces, toy parachute strings and frayed hair ribbons. She was followed by Matthew, who was carrying Jonah under one arm and a bundle of wet towels under the other. "Mummy, look what I've got!"

I looked. It was a lollipop.

"Wow," I said.

"Look. I bited it."

"You bit it. Don't do that, Emily, you'll break your teeth. You're supposed to suck it."

"No, I didn't! I didn't break my teeth! Look!"

"All right, all right." I wasn't going to argue. Instead I turned to Matt. "You smell of bath gel. Did you have a shower there? That was smart."

He shrugged. "I didn't want to go to work smelling of chlorine."

"What about the kids?"

"They came in with me."

"Oh good."

I was pleasantly surprised. A shower at the pool meant no baths in the evening. But before I could express my appreciation, Matt disappeared into the bedroom to change. He emerged looking very sleek and deadly in black jeans, a white shirt and a pair of sunglasses.

Dressing up for Her?

"I'm running late," he said, all grim around the mouth. He headed for the front door, jangling his keys. "See you tonight."

"You're not late. You're fine. You'll—"

Bang! The door shut. No kiss, no nothing.

My eyes began to smart.

"Mummy," said Emily. It's hard to ponder your problems when there are kids around. (Which is one of their many attractions, I suppose.) "Mummy, Jonah dropped his lollipop, and he put it in his mouth again."

"Never mind."

"But it's dirty now. He'll get sick."

"No he won't. I just washed the floor in the kitchen."

"But he dropped it in the lounge room. He got hairs on it."

"What hairs? From where?"

"From there."

The Persian rug, needless to say. Our only Persian rug—the only decent thing in the living room, apart from the TV and stereo system. Why couldn't he have dropped it on the scuffed leather sofa? Or the grubby chintz armchair covered in baby puke? Or the second-hand sixties coffee table?

Ah, well. What did it matter, when my marriage was on the skids?

"Never mind," I said, just as Jonah hurled himself at me, complaining that he had hairs in his mouth. "Don't spit on the carpet, Jonah, stop it."

"It's yukky, Mummy, yuk! Get it out!"

"Say please."

"Please."

And then the builders arrived.

I'm not much good at craft. Not like Mandy the Wholefood Mother. At our playgroup, she does basic origami and marbling and potato stamps while I'm fumbling around trying to stick one piece of playdough onto another. She keeps on resurrecting these strange, ancestral pursuits like dried-apple dolls and cotton-reel knitting, while my only contribution to the children's entertainment has been Rorschach ink-blot butterflies. Early this year, she even had a project going where every child in the group drew a house, and each house was stuck onto a big piece of paper (in a sort of streetscape) and then Mandy arranged to have the streetscape reproduced by a muralist friend of hers on the wall of the church hall where playgroup is held. I mean, will you please tell me how this woman finds the *time*? Let alone the energy. Needless to say, her own kids are absolute founts of creativity; Jesse even draws his own designs onto his T-shirts.

As for Lisa, while she couldn't draw an elephant

182   *Catherine Jinks*

to save her life, she has a creative mind when it comes to *conceptualizing*. If Liam wants fake tablets to fill up an old pill-box, Lisa will suggest cutting up a drinking straw. If Brice wants a drum, Lisa will burst a blown-up balloon and fasten one of the broken pieces over the end of an empty coffee tin with a rubber band.

As for me, I'm the sort of person who dreads *Play School*. On the one hand, it's great to dump the kids in front of the TV for half an hour, while you hang out the washing. On the other hand, by exposing the kids to *Play School*, you also risk exposing them to a segment about creating a slippery dip from a toilet roll, a milk carton and piece of string. I can't count the number of times that Emily has come running up to me, after an episode of *Play School*, and asked me to make a mobile phone or a spaceship. It's something I can't do even when I've seen the program—especially since I don't happen to have a bottomless supply of egg cartons, pipe cleaners, cotton reels, plastic lids and cardboard boxes sitting around the house. I mean, I've already got a storage problem. Despite valiant efforts, I really can't keep every single paddle-pop stick that walks through the door.

I once asked Mandy the Wholefood Mother about this—knowing that she was a craft expert—but she wasn't very helpful. Apparently, she won't *allow* paddle-pop sticks through the door, because they're usually attached to paddle-pops. Similarly, her kids are denied access to plastic drinking straws (because they're not biodegradable), the plastic net bags that onions often come in (because she grows her own onions) and the tiny, plastic tables that you sometimes get holding up the lids of pizza boxes. "I believe in allowing children a lot of space for creativity," she explained, in an earnest fashion, "but not at the expense of the environment."

Isn't it always the way? You're damned if you do and damned if you don't. No sooner do I start stocking up on empty little mini-Nutella tubs and plastic ice-cream containers than it turns out I'm ecologically irresponsible. For God's sake, it's recycling, isn't it? In a manner of speaking.

Anyhow, what I'm trying to say is that I'm a bit of a wash-out when it comes to craft. And that's an especially big problem on days when we're all stuck inside. If I could whip up a dinosaur cave out of papier-mâché, or a finger puppet out of an old rubber glove, there wouldn't be nearly as much whining and moaning on days like today. We had to stay at home this afternoon, you see, because I was waiting for Jim McRae to show up. And that meant we hit the inevitable moment when every toy had been rejected, every healthful snack had been consumed, and every drop of enjoyment had been wrung from watching the brick-layers at work in the garden. To distract Jonah from his desire to actually get in and *help* the bricklayers, using his own toy trowel and unrivalled expertise, I had to break out my copy of *Fun Crafts for Little Fingers*. This, in turn, meant raiding my personal supply of cotton-wool balls and typing paper, so that we could make (or attempt to make) a clutch of fluffy little chicks, as well as the three nests to put them in. I tell you, it wasn't a job for the faint-hearted. Jonah, being a perfectionist, gets enraged very easily—and Emily can be rather patronizing when her chicks' mouths (or flowers' petals, or boats' sails) turn out better than mine.

I could hear the builders snickering as she kindly offered to cut out my little paper diamonds "the right way." "It's a bit hard," she generously informed me. "But you can color them in, okay?"

"Okay. Thanks, Emily."

I don't like playing to an audience. It's hard enough pulling off a convincing mummy act in front of the kids; it's doubly hard when you know that someone else is listening. Not that Mike and his mob spend all their time with their ears glued to cracks in the walls. Mostly they're hammering away with their radio turned on. But sometimes they need to use the toilet, or to borrow an old towel. Sometimes they take a break, and sit drinking bottles of water under the kitchen window. That's when they always manage to overhear me explaining to Emily why poos are brown, or what rainbows are for. (They've got to be for something; Emily's convinced of it.) Sometimes I don't realize that Mike's been eavesdropping until a frantic search for a lost plastic spade suddenly ends when he sticks his head through the kitchen door and waves the missing item under my nose, informing me that it was sitting in the clothes basket—which has been left by the Hills Hoist, in case I was wondering.

These days it's got to the point where I feel uncomfortable hanging my underclothes on the line. But what can I do? It's silly to use the dryer just for my underclothes. And really, there's nothing objectionable about Mike or his mates. They're cheerful and friendly, they work hard (when they finally get here) and they always remember to wipe their big, dirty Blundstones on the mat before they come in. Perhaps their taste in radio stations leaves a lot to be desired, but even there I can't fault them entirely, because they hardly ever listen to whatever program they select. They just seem to like a bit of background music as they haul bags of dry cement around in the broiling sun—and who can blame them?

Mike's a nice bloke. He's slow but he's careful, never taking short cuts or making guesses. I generally see him standing around in khaki shorts and a mortar-smeared T-shirt, peering intently at a truss or rivet over the top of his coffee cup, his tool-belt heavy with screwdrivers and tape measures and nails lined up like bullets in a bandolier. He doesn't say much. Nick, on the other hand, likes to talk. He's a hairy little guy who'd be quite happy discussing health insurance or his son's asthma or the fish-markets with me all day long, if Mike would let him. Lars is very young; you can hear his laugh punctuating Nick's monologues, occasionally, and he'll sometimes sing along with the radio when he's by himself. Yusef hardly ever shows up. I don't know much about Yusef. Nick once told me that Yusef has a daughter with Crohn's disease. (Don't ask me how we got on to the subject.)

Anyway, there I was, surrounded by little cotton-wool balls studded with paper beaks, and there were Nick and Mike, mucking around with sand-stock bricks and spirit levels right on the back step, and next thing you know, Jim McRae arrived. He timed it pretty well, actually, because I'd just put Jonah to sleep. Thank God bricklaying isn't a very noisy pursuit, or I never would have managed it; as it was, I had to give Jonah a bottle of warm milk. You'll probably shriek when you hear that. You'll probably say, "Don't you know how bad milk is for his teeth, before bedtime?" Well, the answer is: yes, I do know how bad milk is for his teeth before bedtime. And I also know that if Jonah ends up with dentures, it will be *all my fault*. But frankly, there comes a time when you just don't give a shit—and this was one of those times.

I mean, I had a cold. How could I pat him off to dreamland? Every cough would have woken him up again.

So Jonah was in bed asleep, looking like an angel with his arms flung out and his eyelashes making feathery half-moons on his flushed cheeks. (If you're ever cross with your kids, just look at them when they're sleeping; it puts you right every time.) As for Emily, she was still raring to go, flipping eagerly through *Fun Crafts for Little Fingers*, stopping every so often to raise big, pleading eyes and ask if we could do the steam train . . . the glove-puppets . . . maybe the Egyptian princess costume?

"No, sweetie," I replied, appalled at the complexity of some of the instructions. (*For molding, you need to make paper pulp.*) "We don't want to do anything without Jonah, do we? He'd be really cross." I was trying to persuade her that we should take a break from craft, and perhaps do a puzzle, when someone tapped at the kitchen door. Expecting it to be Mike, I said, "Come in!," my voice sounding snubbed and hoarse. Then I stared in confusion as a totally strange man entered the room.

"Helen?"

"Yes?" I blinked. He was very well dressed, for a builder.

"You told me to come around the back," he offered, and suddenly I recognized his voice. "So I wouldn't wake the baby."

"Oh!" I leapt to my feet. "Yes, of course. Sorry. I wasn't thinking. I was just—I was miles away. Sorry."

"That's okay."

"Um—right. Yes." I tried to think. Where would we talk? The builders were outside. Emily was inside. "Emily, I'm going to put a video on. What about *The Little Mermaid*?"

"No! I want to do a puzzle!"

"You can do a puzzle *and* watch *The Little Mermaid*."

"Will you help me?"

"Not just now."

"Please?" The Magic Word. I was impressed.

"Mummy's got to do something for a while, Emily," I explained, "so why don't I put on *The Little Mermaid*, and you can have some chocolate ice-cream? How about that?"

"Yay!"

"But you'll have to be careful, because I don't want you spilling it all over the rug."

Another bribe. I'm hopeless. But at least it did the trick; in fact Emily was so excited about my unprecedented offer of ice-cream in the middle of the afternoon that she didn't really notice Jim McRae. If she spared him even a passing thought, she must have assumed that he was another builder—because we've had a lot of unfamiliar men passing in and out, over the last few months, and they've all been builders (or architects or plumbers or that kind of thing). She sat herself down in front of the TV without much fuss, and I was able to leave her there for half an hour.

But then I was faced with the problem of where I would take Jim. We couldn't talk in the living

room. We couldn't talk in the kitchen or the enclosed verandah, because Mike and Nick were
bound to overhear. Jonah was sleeping in the kids'
room, so we couldn't talk in there; we couldn't
even talk out the front, near his window, or we'd
probably wake him up.

"It's either the bathroom or our bedroom," I
whispered, wiping my nose. (We were standing in
the hall, and Jonah was too close for comfort.)
"I'm sorry. It's just these bloody builders—I didn't
think they'd be coming today. They *never* show up,
normally."

"It's okay," murmured Jim. His appearance was
a bit of a disappointment. He had such a nice
voice that I'd been expecting someone big and impressive, with possibly a bloodhound's face, all
wise and craggy under a thatch of salt-and-pepper
hair, or perhaps something a bit more along the
lines of Sherlock Holmes, sharp and finely drawn.
But Jim was nothing like that. He was quite young,
for a start. (Maybe even—horror of horrors—
younger than me?) He was also quite short, and his
face was instantly forgettable: fair-skinned, clean-
shaven, with full cheeks and small features. His
eyes were brown. His hair was brown. He looked
like—I don't know, a chemist or something. An accountant. Mister Bland. He certainly didn't look
like an ex-copper.

When I offered him coffee he shook his head.

"No, thanks," he replied.

"Tea? Something cold?"

"I'm fine, thanks."

"Okay, well . . ." I had to take him into the bedroom. It was a nightmare, but what choice did I
have? And of course the bedroom looked like a *tip*,

what with the pile of dirty laundry in the corner,
and the scattering of used tissues on the floor, and
the junk draped over every bedpost and door-
handle: scarves, handbags, broken blind cords,
one of Emily's shell necklaces . . . Thank God I'd
made the bed, is all I can say. But then we had to
sit on the *edge* of the bed (as if I wasn't feeling embarrassed enough) while Jim McRae's bland, brown
gaze flitted from wedding photo to anti-histamine
tablets, from mangy slipper to discarded credit
card receipt, from the stain above the door to the
tear in the doona.

My heart was in my throat; it was like visiting a
psychiatrist or a gynecologist. He just waited, the
way a gynecologist does when you try to explain
why your period's bugging you. Personally, if I
were a private detective, I'd make more of an effort. I'd try to put people at their ease, instead of
watching them like a customs and immigration officer at Sydney airport.

I had to take a deep breath before I spoke, as if
I was diving off a cliff into the sea.

"Well, like I said, I've got this problem with my
husband. I think he might be involved with someone, but I don't know. So I want to find out."

He nodded gravely. He didn't ask if I had discussed the matter with my husband. Maybe he didn't
want to know all the sordid details. Maybe he'd been
the recipient of too many tortuous, hysterical con-
fidences regarding other people's marital difficul-
ties.

"I think it might be the Girl With Purple Hair," I
went on, "but I'm not sure. It might be nothing. A
friend of mine saw them together, but this friend
has a very suspicious mind, because she investigates

bank frauds. And I don't want to ask Matt myself because . . . well, because I just don't want to." It was
none of Jim's business why I didn't want to. In fact
I began to feel quite cross; Jim's silence was getting
on my nerves. His equanimity was almost insulting. What right did he have to sit there with a shut-
tered face, while I was pouring my guts out? It was
offensive. It was *creepy*. I thought to myself: two can
play at that game, Mister Bland. I'm an investigator
myself, in a manner of speaking.

So I shut up and waited, taking the opportunity
to clear my clogged sinuses as I did so. After a brief
pause, Jim said: "Who's the girl with purple hair?"

"I don't know. She might be Josephine Cleary."
I described what Miriam had seen, and my subsequent investigation into Matt's most recent phone
calls. I gave him Josephine Cleary's address and
phone number, which he wrote down in a little blue
book. The little blue book really got to me; I almost
started to giggle as I explained about Megan Molesdale. Then the doorbell rang, and I lost all desire
to laugh.

"Oh, for Chrissake!" I hissed. "Who the hell
could that be?"

"You're not expecting anyone?"

"No! Jesus! It's probably those bloody Mormons
again—they're always waking Jonah up!"

But I was wrong. When I went to the door, and
opened it, I was confronted by two men in suits
who introduced themselves, not as bearers of the
Word of God, but as Cliff Staines and Austin Kneipp,
from the Pacific Commercial Bank. They presented
me with their cards. *Cliff Staines, Manager, Fraud and
Non-Lending Loss Administration*, said one. *Austin
Kneipp, Manager, Investigations*, said the other.

"Are you Helen Muzzatti?" asked Cliff, who was the older of the two. He had grey hair, a red face and a big gut. Austin was darker and slimmer, but a good deal balder.

I stared at them in confusion.

"Yes," I replied faintly. "What—what's up?"

"We're sorry to bother you," said Cliff, "but we're looking for Miriam Coutts. We were hoping you might know where she is."

"Miriam?"

"Coutts. You know her, don't you?"

"Well, yes. She lives in Pyrmont."

Austin expelled air sharply through his nose, and Cliff made a wry face. "Not any more, she doesn't," he rejoined.

I couldn't imagine what he meant by that. And I didn't have time to ask, because at that moment I heard a thin wail, and knew that Jonah had been roused by the doorbell.

"Oh shit!" I exclaimed, and they both looked quite startled. "You've woken my son!"

"Oh," said Cliff. "Sorry . . ."

"You'd better go in. Just go in." I shooed them through the door like chickens. "Maybe he'll go back to sleep again, if we're all very quiet."

Obediently, they tiptoed down the hall, their shoulders tensing with every creak of the floorboards. Jim McRae was still sitting on the edge of my bed; when we passed the bedroom door he looked up, and raised his eyebrows.

Austin paused.

"Hello," he mumbled.

Jim nodded.

"Mr. Muzzatti, is it?" said Cliff, who was bringing up the rear.

"No, I—no." It suddenly occurred to me that introducing Jim as a private detective would entail far too much embarrassing explanation. "He's just a friend," I explained.

"Oh."

Too late I realized that a male friend sitting on a marital bed in the middle of the day was bound to cause speculation of a titillating type. But I couldn't change my story at that stage. Anyway, I looked like death. My nose was running. My eyes were bloodshot. I was clasping a damp handkerchief. Why would anyone have wanted to take me to bed in the middle of the afternoon?

"In here," I said, waving all my big, unwelcome visitors into the living room. "This is Emily."

"Hello, Emily."

"Hello, Emily."

Emily spluttered "hello" through a mouthful of ice-cream, her gaze never leaving the television screen.

I closed the living room door behind Jim, who had quietly followed us down the hallway.

"So what's this about Miriam?" I inquired, my ear cocked for telltale noises issuing from the kids' bedroom. "I've been trying to reach her. I was getting worried, as a matter of fact." Not so worried, however, that I'd hauled myself off my big, fat arse and visited her house. Or phoned her mum. Or even called the police. God, I was hopeless. She could have been lying dead in her kitchen, since Monday afternoon, and what had I done about it? Nothing.

I looked from Cliff to Austin, and back again. "Is something wrong?" I demanded faintly, with a sinking heart.

Cliff cleared his throat. He adjusted his jacket

and smoothed his tie over his ample belly. "Uh-hem," he said. "Can you tell me when you last saw her, Mrs. Muzzatti?"

"Why? What's wrong? Is she hurt?" A terrible thought struck me. "Is she *missing?* Oh my God."

Cliff raised his eyebrows. "As a matter of fact, she *is* missing—"

"Oh my God!"

"So if you can tell me when you last saw her—"

"On Monday," I gasped. "No—I mean, I *spoke* to her on Monday. I *saw* her on Friday. On Monday, I phoned her at the office."

"Ah." Cliff exchanged glances with Austin, just as it occurred to me: these guys weren't policemen. What were two bank managers doing, investigating Miriam's disappearance? "Did the police send you?" I gabbled, between coughs. "What do they think? Have you spoken to Miriam's boyfriend? His name's Giles." I tried to think of his second name. God, what *was* it? "It's Norwegian, I think. Hang on—"

"Giles Gunnerson," Cliff supplied.

"That's it!" So they *had* spoken to him. "What does Giles say?"

Again the two bankers exchanged a quick look. "We haven't been able to question Mr. Gunnerson," Cliff confessed. "The fact is, Mr. Gunnerson seems to have disappeared too. All indications are that he and Ms. Coutts went away together."

I blinked. In that case, why all the fuss? "Then what's the problem?" I queried. "If they're both missing, they're probably in Queensland, or something. Hamilton Island."

Cliff shook his head.

"The Blue Mountains, maybe."

"They took a plane to Los Angeles on Tuesday night," Austin revealed. "We haven't yet been able to trace their movements after they arrived."

Wait a minute, I thought. *Trace* their *movements*? "What are you talking about?" I was getting frightened. "What have they done?"

Cliff hesitated, as if he was reluctant to spill the beans. It was Austin who responded.

"They've stolen some money," he said.

My jaw dropped.

"From our employer," Austin continued. "Approximately seventeen point—"

"Ah-*hem*." Cliff cleared his throat again, this time with all the force and volume of a Hell's Angel revving his engine. Either Austin was speaking out of turn, or I wasn't supposed to know all the details.

"At the moment we're trying to establish their present whereabouts," Cliff went on. "We've searched Ms. Coutts's house, we're going through her files—she's burned a lot of them—"

"That's impossible," I squeaked.

"Well, maybe not burned them," Cliff conceded. "Got rid of them. Shredded them, maybe."

"No—I mean, she wouldn't have stolen anything. Not Miriam."

Silence from the two bankers. Jim McRae's face was a complete blank.

"You must have made a mistake." I sat down. A red hermit crab was dancing and singing on the screen not two meters away; I found it hard to concentrate. "It must have been someone else, not Miriam. Miriam couldn't possibly have done that."

"Why not?" Cliff asked. He was still standing. So were Austin and Jim. Three men in shirts and ties,

making my living room look small. Looming over
me. Outnumbering me.

"Because I know her, that's why not," I said. "I've
known her for years. Look—sit down. Please."

Cliff lowered his considerable bulk onto the
couch, where Austin joined him (at a carefully calculated distance). Jim kind of propped himself
against the arm of the puke-stained easychair.

"So you've had no indication that Miriam's
been planning any kind of fraud?" Austin inquired, his voice very clear and precise.

"No. Of course not." I shook my head, still in a
daze. "It's impossible."

"We've pretty much established that she did it,
Mrs. Muzzatti."

"I can't believe that!"

"It *is* hard to believe." Austin sighed. "I used to
work with her myself. It's been a real shock for us.
All these years she's been chasing down fraud, and
now we find that she's one of the bad guys.
Incredible."

I stared at him, sniffing forlornly. Austin was not
a familiar name; I couldn't recall that Miriam had
ever mentioned him.

"We're pretty sure she's left the country," Cliff
supplied. "It certainly looks that way—plus a lot of
the funds she took seem to have been transferred
to the Cayman Islands."

"Like Christopher Skase, you mean?" I interrupted, and he smiled.

"Sort of."

"It's been going on for at least eighteen months,"
Austin added. "This scam of hers."

"And she's been very smart. Ve-e-ery smart."

"Not smart enough, though. She had to get out in a hurry. She knew we were closing in."

"She left a lot of things lying about. Like her computer."

"That's where we found your name."

"We thought you might have information that we could use."

The two of them suddenly stopped their verbal ping-pong, and fixed their eyes on me. I saw Jim fold his arms in the background. Ariel the mermaid trilled annoyingly on the television screen.

"Well, don't look at me," I protested. "I don't know *anything*."

"Are you sure?" Cliff leaned forward. "We're just searching for indications—anything she might have said about a trip to anywhere . . . ?"

"No."

"Any friends she might have who live overseas?"

I remembered Briony. No. Out of the question.

"No."

"Are you sure?" Austin pressed. "Her mother mentioned someone. Someone she used to live with."

"Mrs. Coutts!" The thought of Miriam's mother hit me like a blow. Poor Mrs. Coutts. She was all alone. She idolized Miriam. "Oh, this is awful! This is terrible!" Tears pricked my eyes, as the truth finally began to sink in. "How could she *do* this?"

"Shh! Mummy! I can't hear!"

"Sorry, Emily."

"Are you sure you don't know anyone that she'd be likely to contact overseas?" Austin was very persistent. "Anyone. No matter how unlikely."

"Well . . . there's Briony. Our friend Briony. But they never really got along."

"Where does Briony live?"

"In Florence. But I don't think—"

"Do you have her address? Her phone number?"

"No. But I can get it. I suppose." I put my hand to my head. If I asked Ronnie to ask Samantha to ask Briony . . . ? Aaagh. "It's hopeless, though. There's no point."

"Nevertheless, it would be very helpful," said Austin. "If you don't mind."

I told him that I didn't mind. What else could I have told him? If I'd been obstructive, they probably would have decided that I was in on it, too. Besides, I was still in shock. I hardly knew what I was saying.

"When you last spoke to her," Cliff said, "did she seem stressed? Was there anything odd about her behavior?"

"Well . . ." I didn't know how to phrase my response. As I cast about for the right words, I caught Jim's eye. It was expressionless. Too expressionless. "We were both a bit stressed," I finally gabbled, "but it had nothing to do with money or anything. It was a personal matter."

"A personal matter," Cliff repeated, almost as if he was taking the piss.

"Yes!" I snapped. "And I'm not going to discuss it because it had nothing to do with this business."

"You're sure of that?"

"Yes!"

Cliff raised his hands in a mock-defensive gesture. "Okay. Okay," he said. "I'm sorry."

"We really are sorry," Austin interjected, obviously intending to soothe my ruffled feelings. "It's not a pleasant job, going around hitting people with something like this. It's a strain for everyone. But since we were passing this way, and we knew you were a friend of hers . . ."

"I just can't believe she'd do it!" I couldn't, either. "She was being so helpful! She never said *one word* . . . there was no *reason* . . ." The depth of Miriam's deceit was only just beginning to hit me. "Eighteen months, did you say? She's been doing it for *eighteen months?*"

"Approximately," said Austin.

"Then—then it must be Giles's fault," I insisted. "Yes, it must be. She's been going out with him for eighteen months—maybe a little more. He's brainwashed her, somehow. Or blackmailed her. Something like that. There's no other explanation."

"Did you ever meet him?" Austin wanted to know.

"Once. He was a prick." I was quite sure of *that*, by now. "Smart, but also a smart-arse. Rich," I added, and gazed at Austin in bewilderment. "He was rich," I stammered. "The house. The car. Why—why—?"

"They weren't his," Austin replied, almost chattily. "We've been looking through his accounts. He was deeply in debt."

"But *she* wasn't!" I exclaimed. "She couldn't have been!"

"She's been giving him money."

"*What?*" I dissolved into a fit of coughing, whereupon Austin leaned over and thumped me on the back.

"I know," he agreed. "It's unbelievable, isn't it? Miriam Coutts. I always admired her, you know— it's tragic. Tragic. What possessed her?"

"Another bad boy," I said hoarsely, having recovered my breath. "She couldn't resist them."

"Pardon?"

"It's been one after the other, ever since I've known her. The stalker. The library book thief. The drug dealer—"

"Really?" I wondered suddenly if Austin was gay. He seemed to be relishing the chance of a good gossip about Miriam's personal life. "But she was always so contemptuous of the people we were dealing with."

"Bankers, you mean?"

"No." He looked startled. "Con men. Scam artists."

"Oh."

"She thought they were scum. She really did. She despised them."

"Only because they were caught," Cliff suddenly observed. "She thought she was pretty hot stuff, that girl."

Girl. I hate it when fat, middle-aged men call grown women "girls." It puts my hackles up. "She was sick of her job," I announced sharply, wiping my nose. "She was sick of bankers. She told me."

"Did she, now?" Cliff drawled.

"She *hated* her boss—what's his name? Vern? She was angry, because he got the job ahead of her. But . . ." But surely that wouldn't account for it? I was pretty disenchanted with my own boss; that didn't mean I was planning to plunder the next payroll. "Could—could he have introduced her to drugs?" I quavered. "Giles, I mean. Is that it?"

Austin shrugged. "You tell me."

"There's no evidence of it," Cliff rumbled.

"Then why? *Why?*"

"Because she saw her chance, and took it," Cliff rejoined. "Simple as that."

"It *can't* be—"

"It is. I've seen her financial records. She was spending up big, she was juggling cards, she was getting to like the high life, and she knew her boyfriend was heading for a fall. So she jumped ship." Cliff shrugged. "It happens."

"She was a label junkie," Austin revealed. "You should have seen her wardrobe. She had a Chanel suit—"

Chanel? That was a shock. Carla Zampatti I could cope with, but Chanel? I tried to remember what her house had looked like, when I'd last visited it two years before. The furniture had been classy, but minimalist. Not much of it, in other words. Concealed lighting. European appliances. An antique bed. *Architectural Digest* on the coffee table. An air of ambition, in other words, but nothing insane. No Mesopotamian sculptures or gilded cornices or two-thousand-dollar French tapestry cushions. Though it hadn't looked like Miriam, exactly (she had employed an interior decorator), it also hadn't looked like someone with a serious case of Rampant Materialism.

Still, a lot could change in two years.

I coughed into my handkerchief, and opened my mouth. But before I could ask for more details, a faint, sinister sound reached my ears. Above the noise of the video, above the clink of Emily's spoon, above the distant scraping of trowels against brick, I could just make out the plaintive cry of a bored toddler.

"Oh, piss," I said.

He hadn't gone to sleep after all. Or had he? If he hadn't, he'd been awfully quiet.

Too quiet.

"Hang on," I moaned, lurching to my feet.

"He's awake after all." The three men looked at me blankly. "My son," I had to explain. "My son's awake after all."

"Oh."

"Oh."

"Hang on a minute." I beat a hasty retreat, leaving the door open behind me. As I trudged down the hall I could hear Cliff—the most avuncular of the three—attempting to converse with my daughter. "Hey, Emily," he said. No reply, of course. It's a waste of time trying to talk to Emily when she's watching television. "Hey, Emily," he repeated, "what are you watching?" As if it wasn't patently obvious. I wondered why they couldn't just sit awkwardly in silence, rather than bothering Emily, who was perfectly content. Then I pushed open the kids' bedroom door, and the sight that greeted me emptied my head of all thoughts but one.

"Oh, my God!" I squawked.

It was appalling. *Beyond* appalling. I almost gagged.

"Oh my *God!*" I wailed. "Jonah! Oh my God, I don't *believe* it!"

His nappy had come off. Maybe he'd taken it off—I don't know. But while I had been coping with traumatic news in the living room, he had been quietly and busily painting the cot, the wall and his sheets with generous daubs of his own feces.

Yes, that's right. Fingerpainting with poo.

"Jonah, Goddamn it!" I yelled, and his bottom lip began to tremble. "That's dirty! *Dirty!* You *know* you shouldn't do that!"

He did, too—he's not stupid.

His face crumpled.

"You've got it in your hair!" I groaned. "God-damn it, Jonah!"

"Oh no," said Emily, from the door. I hadn't noticed the patter of little feet. "Did he do a poo, Mum?"

"Out of the way, Emily."

"Oh no."

"Don't go in there!" I rushed my whimpering son into the bathroom, where I stripped him of his remaining garments and wiped down his wriggling body with a damp facecloth. I didn't know what to do next; my mind was a blank. The facecloth was soiled. His clothes were soiled. His clean nappies were still in the bedroom, with his change table—but it stank in there.

No. Wait. I remembered the travel bag in the kitchen.

"Excuse me," I growled, the heels of my mules slapping against the floor as I marched through the living room with Jonah on my hip. I didn't even look at my visitors; no doubt they were frozen in attitudes of surprise and alarm. "There's been a crisis," I added, leaving them to fend for themselves.

Nick, of course, had heard the commotion. I had to pass him in the garden before I could drop Jonah's dirty clothes into the laundry tub, and despite the forbidding expression on my face, he couldn't resist asking me if everything was all right.

"No," I rejoined. "It's not."

"Something happen to the little feller?" he inquired, over the noise of Jonah's sobs.

"He just undid his nappy and spread poo all over the bedroom."

"Aw no," said Nick. "Aw, that's bad."

"Yes."

"Aw, you naughty boy, eh?" But he could barely suppress a smile. "Naughty boy for your mama."

I couldn't laugh about it—not then. Not with all the mess still to clear up. First, though, I had to slip another nappy on Jonah. And dump him in his highchair with a chocolate-chip cookie, while I filled one of the laundry buckets. What else would I need? A couple of rags. Some disinfectant. Wet wipes?

I could hear the sound of muffled laughter from the garden.

"Can I have a cookie too?" Emily requested.

"In a minute."

"Please?"

"*In a minute*, Emily." Water sloshed over the rim of the bucket that I was carrying. "Can't you see I've got my hands full?"

"Look—ah—we've obviously come at a bad time," Cliff remarked, when I staggered back into the living room. He and Austin were both standing again, nervously adjusting their belts and ties. "Maybe we could just, uh, leave you with what we've got, and if you can think of anything else that might help— like the address of that friend in Florence—give us a call. My number's on the card there."

"Thanks," I muttered.

"You wouldn't be betraying her," said Austin. "She's not played fair by any of us. She's been lying to everyone. It's a police matter now."

"Yeah, yeah. I know." I wasn't really attending. "Emily, you stay in the kitchen, please. Stay and watch Jonah. Tell me if he tries to get out." Plodding down the hall, I could hear heavy footsteps behind me. A foul smell hovered in the air, growing more repugnant as I approached the kids' bedroom. Close on my heels, Cliff and Austin made slightly smothered noises denoting sympathy and dismay.

"Oh dear," said Cliff heartily, from a safe distance. "That's a job and a half."

"Yes," I replied, through my teeth.

"They're little terrors, aren't they? At that age."

"Hmm."

"Well—you've got our details. If there's anything else you want to know, give us a call. Thanks for your help."

"Thanks very much, Mrs. Muzzatti."

"Sorry about waking him up."

"Yes. Sorry about that."

They let themselves out. For the umpteenth time, it crossed my mind that I ought to put a little sign up on the front door, the way shiftworkers do. *Please do not disturb. Baby sleeping.* I bundled all Jonah's sheets into a ball. Happily, his cot is covered in smooth gloss paint, which is easily cleaned, but the walls were more of a problem—semi-gloss, and very pale. It's a dim room, that bedroom (like most of the rooms in this house), but even in the murky light I could make out faint marks after I'd scrubbed madly at Jonah's crude attempts to express himself. How would I ever get rid of the smell if I couldn't get rid of the stains? Some kind of deodorizing spray, or air freshener?

Then the phone rang.

Fuck, I thought. Fuck, fuck, fuck.

"Jim!" I yelled. *"Can you get that?"*

It was cheeky, I suppose, but what else was I supposed to do? Our answering machine had been busted for about two years, and I hadn't been able to organize a message service, or anything. Just hadn't got around to it.

The ringing stopped. I heard Jim McRae's murmur, but not his subsequent footsteps. When he spoke from the threshold, I jumped.

"Someone called Ronnie," he said.

"Oh—ah—tell her I'll call her back."

It's a cordless phone, so Jim was holding the receiver. He lifted it to his ear, just as Emily's piercing protest reached mine.

"Mum-*mmee!*" she cried, thumping up the hallway. "It's *my* turn to answer the phone!"

"She'll call you back," Jim told Ronnie, and signed off. Two seconds later, Emily burst into the room.

"*I* was going to answer it!" Emily wailed.

"I'm sorry, sweetie. Next time."

"But it was my *turn!*"

"I'm going to have to go, Helen," Jim pointed out.

"Right. Yes." There were too many things happening at once. "I'm sorry. The job—"

"You still want it done?"

"Yes. Hang on." We couldn't discuss it there— not in that noxious atmosphere. I rose and went into the hall, shutting the kids' bedroom door behind me and nudging Emily along in front of me. "I just want to find out if this woman—this Cleary woman—is involved with my husband," I murmured. "And I want to find out about *her,* too. Will that cost very much?"

Jim lifted his shoulders. "You'd be looking at a few days' work," he replied softly. "Say—five hundred dollars, to start with?"

"Oh." I swallowed. Five hundred dollars! I could see my dishwasher flying out the window into the Land of Dreams. "Well . . . okay. Whatever you can do for that." I still felt distracted, and didn't realize at first that he was surveying me intently, with a hint of calculation in his eyes. Emily was tugging at my jeans. "What?" I asked her, wiping my nose on my sleeve. "What is it?"

"Can I get my baby?"

"Is it in your room?"

"Yes."

"Well you can't go in. Not yet. It's too dirty."

Emily's bottom lip trembled, but I ignored it. At last I had noticed Jim's close regard. "What's wrong?" I demanded.

"Oh . . . it was just something you said earlier. About your friend." He hesitated. "This Miriam woman—would she be the same one who spotted your husband with the girl? Only you mentioned something about how she investigated bank frauds."

"Did I?" If I had, I'd completely forgotten it. Yet Jim had remembered.

I was impressed.

"It just occurred to me that you should consider the source," he went on. "If this friend of yours is dishonest, then maybe she was lying. About what she saw."

I stared at him in astonishment. The wheels in my head began to grind.

"Why should she do that?" I asked.

"I don't know. You tell me. Is it the sort of thing she would do?"

"No. Not at all." Then again, I would have said the same thing, once, if asked if Miriam was likely to embezzle money from the Pacific Commerical Bank. "There'd be no reason for her to lie," I protested. "I mean, what would be the point?"

He shrugged again. It was the world-weary shrug of someone who was beyond surprise. "Like I said, I don't know. Maybe she doesn't like you. Maybe she never liked you. Maybe she wanted to mess things up for you before she skipped town."

I simply gaped at him. It was too much to absorb all at once. Emily began to whimper.

"I want my baby . . ."

"Look, I don't know the situation," Jim concluded calmly, ignoring her. "I don't want to argue myself out of a job. I just thought you should consider all the possibilities before you pay up." And he waited.

"Oh!" The penny dropped. "You mean now? You want money *now*?"

"I can give you a receipt."

"Will you—will you take a check?"

"Yeah, that's fine. If *you* don't mind." As I gazed at him blankly, he explained: "It'll show up on your statement."

"Oh, that doesn't matter. Matt never looks at the statements. Not the savings account statements. Just the credit card ones." Knowing that my checkbook was in my purse, I headed for the kitchen, with Jim bringing up the rear. Emily trailed after us, still whining. I wasn't thinking straight, or I would have realized that she shouldn't have been with us at all.

When we arrived in the kitchen, we found Nick stooped over the highchair, fiddling with its straps (which are a perpetual source of shame to me, they're so dirty, but how am I supposed to soak them in NapiSan when they're always urgently needed?). He straightened up as soon as we appeared.

"Hello!" he beamed. "I just come in because this little feller was gonna have an accident, eh mate? Weren't you? He was trying to get out."

"Oh dear." Jonah has a tendency to wriggle free of his harness. I could see that he was red-faced and glowering, but interested in Nick's ministrations all the same. He loves builders. "Thanks, Nick. I'm sorry. I should never leave him by himself in this thing, he hates it, but I was just cleaning up in there, and I told Emily to watch him—"

"Yeah, yeah. It's fine. No harm done." With his usual innate courtesy, Nick turned to address Jim. He was always careful that no one should be left out of a conversation. "You got to have eyes in the back of your head, when they're this age. My son, he's been to hospital three times. Never sits still. Always putting things in his mouth."

Jim nodded enigmatically.

"You got kids too?" Nick inquired, not the least disconcerted by Jim's secretive air.

"One daughter," Jim replied, in a measured fashion. "But she's in her teens." (That surprised me. He must be older than he looks, I thought.) "When they reach their teens, you've got a whole new set of problems."

"Oh yeah!" Nick laughed. "I bet." He launched into one of his long family anecdotes while I retreated into the living room, Jonah under one arm and my purse under the other. I had to dump them both on the floor before I could write out a check for Jim. My hands shook while I was doing it. Five hundred dollars would just about clear us out—though I was getting paid the next day, thank God. How would I explain the sudden shortfall to Matt? Perhaps I should take the initiative. Perhaps, before he exploded, I should demand that he explain himself to *me*.

"Um—Jim!" I called, waving my slip of paper. "In here!" But it was Nick who stuck his head into the room.

"Mind if I use the toilet, Mrs. Muzzatti?" he inquired.

"No, no. Go ahead."

"Mummy. Can I have my baby now?"

"*No*." Nick clumped past, scattering smiles and nods. Emily was hanging off my jeans again. Jonah was heading for the video machine, alas. Jim approached me on noiseless feet, like a cat. I couldn't concentrate—there were distractions everywhere.

"Thanks," said Jim, plucking the check from my hand. He spoke in a low voice. "I'll try and keep it quick, but I can't guarantee anything."

"No. Of course not. Jonah, *don't touch that video, please.*"

"Personally, I think the news is going to be good. I think your friend's been putting it over on you for some reason, but we'll see."

"What about the phone calls, though? I don't know this Cleary person. I don't know who she is."

"Right. Sure. Well, we'll find out." Dragging his notebook from his breast pocket, Jim explained quietly that he did most of his work for Comcare and the big insurance companies—hence the fact that he didn't carry receipt books around with him. But Stuart was a mate of his. And he didn't mind the odd little job like this one, just to keep his hand in.

"You don't want any photographs?" he queried, pressing the scribbled receipt into my sweaty palm. I could hear the toilet flushing.

"Oh no. No."

"Good. That's always a lot of work," said Jim. "Can I send you an invoice? In the mail?"

"Well—uh—"

"To your work address, maybe."

"Oh. All right."

"Mummy, look what Jonah's doing!"

"*Jonah, stop it!*"

"I'll call you," said Jim, heading for the front door. I followed him, with many a nervous backward glance. I believe I've mentioned before that Jonah isn't safe to leave—not even for a minute. But I had the same feeling about Jim McRae, for some reason. Perhaps I was slightly afraid that he would take the opportunity to poke around in my bedside cabinet.

"Have you had a good look around?" he suddenly queried, upon reaching the front door. It was as if he'd read my mind. "Checked magazines and things? Pockets? His wallet?"

I rolled my eyes at the closed bathroom door, and put a finger to my lips. I didn't want Nick hearing all my personal problems. "No," I whispered. "Why?"

"It's probably worthwhile." He had lowered his voice. "You never know."

"Okay."

"Might save us a lot of trouble. You got a photograph? Of your husband?" I must have blanched, because he murmured quickly: "So I'll know who to look for?"

"Sure. Yes, of course. I'll—I'll just get one."

I did, from the linen cupboard. Matt at a picnic. Grinning gap-toothed through his stubble, Jonah on his lap. It was the first shot that fell out of the first envelope.

"Right," said Jim. He took it. He studied it. And he was scribbling Matt's work address on the back of it when Nick emerged from the bathroom.

Nick raised his hand to Jim, who nodded and left. At which point Jonah came pounding down the hall, naked except for his nappy. He was dragging a plastic dog on a string.

"Not in there, Jonah. *Not in there*. Not till I've cleaned up."

"I wanna go in."

"No. Wait."

"Nice feller," Nick remarked, following me back into the living room.

"Who? Jonah?"

"No, I mean . . ." He gestured towards the sound of a car engine starting up outside.

"Oh, *Jim*. I guess so. Emily, don't leave that spoon there, you know what I've said about spoons on the rug."

"Is he your brother?" Nick continued. "Your cousin, maybe?"

I blinked. "Who, Jim?" I said. "God, no! Why?"

"Oh, I just thought you look . . . you know." He traced a circle over his face with one finger. "Related."

"Really?" What an appalling thought that was. But perhaps all Anglos looked alike, in Nick's eyes.

"No, no. He's just . . ." Just what? My wits had deserted me. ". . . a friend," I finished. (How lame.) "An old friend."

"What's that?" Jonah suddenly demanded in outraged tones, pointing at the smears of ice-cream in Emily's discarded bowl. He never misses a trick, that boy.

"It's nothing," I said, picking the bowl up. "You watch the mermaid, Jonah. When I finish cleaning all the mess you made, you can get your toys out of the bedroom. No—you leave Nick alone, please. He's busy."

"When the wall's done outside, you can have a look, okay?" said Nick, addressing Jonah with a smile. "When you got your clothes on. Can't come outside with no clothes on."

"That's right," I agreed. God, I was so exhausted. All I wanted to do was sit down and slowly absorb some of the stuff that had been thrown at me since lunchtime. But I couldn't. I was too busy. I had to soak Jonah's sheets, clean his cot, air his room, wash his hair, get him dressed and start his dinner, all the while blowing my nose and beating off Emily's repeated suggestion that I help her with the cotton-wool chicks. "I can't," I kept saying. "I can't, Emily, I've got things to do. I'm busy."

Busy trying to keep my life from shattering into a million tiny fragments. Busy coming to terms with this latest betrayal.

Or was it, in fact, the only one? Was it my husband fucking me over, or my best friend, or both? Talk about nowhere to turn. Talk about losing your faith in human nature. Talk about building your house on sand.

Scrubbing shit off Jonah's T-shirt with a nailbrush,

I remember thinking to myself: Maybe Kerry was right. Maybe we *should* have checked the feng shui of this place before we bought it, after all.

And then the bloody phone rang again.

Chapter Seven

Thursday

Needless to say, I was on the phone for most of yesterday evening. First I called Ronnie, who had been ringing to find out if I would be free for her engagement party. I told her that I would be, and that Jim had been "er . . . one of the builders"; she was as shocked as I had been when she heard about Miriam. Then I called Vicki, Caroline and Lisa, all of whom had either met Miriam or knew about her. Then I called Mrs. Coutts, but no one answered. Then Matt came home, and I blurted out the whole story while he finished the chocolate ice-cream. It was such big news that there was no restraint or awkwardness in our conversation. I had practically forgotten that he'd walked out in a sulk that morning; too much had happened since.

"It's got to be Giles," I said. "Giles's influence. She's always had this terrible problem with lousy men—obviously it's happened again, but this time she's got sucked in, somehow."

"What does he do?" asked Matt. "He's a forensic accountant or something, isn't he?"

"Is he? I thought he was a foreign exchange broker."

"Yeah? God." Matt snorted. "Either way, he'd know how to play the system."

"And so would Miriam. Can you imagine? Can you imagine how much she knows about ripping people off? And if she was working with him—if it was a foreign exchange scam . . ."

"Didn't they tell you?"

"They didn't want to. You can imagine. They probably don't want to spread it around—bad for the bank's reputation."

"Unbelievable," Matt sighed, shaking his head. "Unbelievable."

"Why would she do it?" I was still trying to grasp the extent of Miriam's betrayal. "She was always talking about the sort of people who commit fraud. They're always gamblers, or trying to impress some woman, or slightly loopy—"

"Maybe she was trying to impress some man," said Matt.

"But she couldn't be that stupid."

"How do you know?" Carefully Matt scraped the bottom of the ice-cream bucket. "How do you know there isn't something wrong with her, if she's always had a terrible problem with lousy men?"

"Oh, that's not true!"

"You just said it was. You said she's always had a—"

"Yes, but that doesn't mean she has something wrong with her! That doesn't mean it's her fault!"

Matt shrugged. "Well—I dunno," he remarked. "*I* could never tell what she was thinkin'."

Which was just as well, I decided. Miriam hadn't

been entirely convinced by Matt. She had never really trusted him.

Trusted him. Jesus.

"Maybe she's been thinking like a criminal for too long," I suggested. "Maybe she tried to put herself in their shoes one too many times."

"Maybe."

"Maybe it's a risk that goes with the job. She should have branched out and tried something else for a while. Maybe she became *infected*."

"Maybe she saw how many people got away with it," Matt observed. "Maybe she calculated her chances, and saw how good they were."

"Oh, Matt."

"Well, think about it. You just told me she was really gettin' into the designer labels. Out to dinner all the time. And she had that megabucks mortgage."

"She got a discount on that from the bank."

"Whatever. It still would have been big. And she didn't make that much, did she? It wasn't like she was a top honcho."

"No," I admitted.

"And this Giles was hot shit. Needed a lot of keepin' up with, didn't he? New cars. Mountain bikes. Club Med."

"And his last girlfriend was a model."

"And his last girlfriend was a model. That's what I mean. Maybe Miriam was trying to keep up."

"But he didn't seem like a crook. An arsehole, but not a crook. I mean, he was so *smart*."

"He can't have been that smart, or he wouldn't have got into debt."

"But he must have been, Matt. Miriam said he

was. You know what she's like. She wouldn't have gone out with a drongo."

"How do you know? How do you know what goes on behind closed doors?"

That shut me up. It turned my thoughts down channels that promptly silenced me. We went to bed soon afterwards, and I slept well because I had dosed myself up with anti-histamines and cough medicines. I was drugged, in other words. Very relaxing.

I don't know why people have to use marijuana and heroin when they're stressed out. An anti-histamine and a swig of cough medicine works just as well. In fact I was almost grateful for my cold, because it allowed me to take all that medication, and not lie awake for hours fretting about Miriam and Matt and Jim McRae. (Had I made a big mistake, hiring Jim?)

In the morning, however, my gratitude promptly faded when I had to get out of bed. This was definitely The Worst Day. My virus had a stranglehold on my immune system, which was only just beginning to fight back. This was the day on which I was scheduled to hit rock bottom, before the inevitable long, slow haul back to good health. I knew it. I could feel it. My nose was taking on a reddened, slightly minced appearance, and my cough sounded as if it was coming out of a moose.

But I was due at work. I couldn't miss work. I had a conciliation conference booked for nine-thirty.

And of course it was raining. And of course I nearly walked off without my purse because Jonah was so upset by the fact that *Maisy*, his favorite show, had suddenly disappeared off the morning television line-up. Channel 2 had put on *Oakey-doke* instead, and even I could see that it wasn't an adequate substitute. But as I tried to explain to Jonah, there really wasn't anything we could do about it.

"It'll come back," I assured him, as he sobbed into my chest. Poor darling, he takes things so very much to heart. "And next time we go to the library, we'll look for a *Maisy* video. How about that?"

"Or a *Maisy* book," Emily suggested.

"Yes! That's a good idea!" Gorgeous Emily. She was patting him clumsily on the back. What a blessing that child is. "Cheer up, sweetie—look, it's Thomas on now. Thomas the tank engine. Oh no! Look! He's run off the rails! I think he might be broken!"

"I don't like Thomas."

"Yes, you do, bloke. You love Thomas." Matt began to loosen Jonah's stranglehold, peeling the soft little arms off my neck. He shot me a look which said, as clearly as if he had spoken: Quick! Get out while you can! "What if I make you guys some pancakes, eh?" he offered. "What about that? Yumm*ee.*"

I managed to get away eventually, but I had to run for the train—through the rain, with a streaming cold. By the time I had flung myself into a steam-filled carriage, I was gasping for breath and coughing like a plague victim. I'm sure everyone was sullenly thinking: What a bitch. She's going to infect us all.

But at least it meant that they moved away from me, and I got a bit of space. And a seat, too! So it wasn't *all* bad, this morning. There was a small silver lining on the thundercloud sitting directly over my head.

I was in good time for the conference, which was scheduled to be a shuttle negotiation. A shuttle negotiation is always a lot of work for a Complaints Officer. Basically, the complainant's team sits in one room, the respondent's team sits in another, and I have to scuttle back and forth between them, bearing offers and counter-offers. Shuttle negotiations aren't common. They generally occur when the comparable negotiating capacity of each party is heavily weighted on the side of the respondent—or when the complainant just isn't strong enough to confront his or her nemesis face to face. In this instance, we had a big age gap (twenty-odd years). We also had a business owner versus a humble waitress. And we had a very articulate, very bright and sharp-witted man versus a young girl who was rather inarticulate, rather naive, and not terribly well educated.

I believe that she was doubly confused because this was yet another case of a relationship gone sour on the job. Her boss had overwhelmed her with a flattering and (I would have to say) somewhat obsessive attention, to the point where she had spent one or two nights with him. Then she had begun to regret her involvement. No doubt his groping her at work, and presenting her with various trampy garments to wear in the restaurant, had had something to do with her decision to end the intimate phase of their association. Unfortunately, however, her boss wouldn't leave her alone. He had continued to grope her. He had continued to push her up against kitchen or backstairs walls. He had left salacious drawings in her order-book, written indecent comments about her on the door of the staff toilet, and commented loudly on her personal appearance to some of the restaurant's male patrons. In the end she had been forced to quit.

She had kept two of his lewd drawings, happily; copies of them were tucked away in my file. Photographs had also been taken of the toilet door. And we had one or two witnesses, though not as many as I had anticipated because the patrons singled out as the respondent's confidantes were mostly his friends, who weren't easily pinned down. As for the groping, that had almost invariably taken place when no one else had been around to witness it. The respondent, as I have said, was a very sharp-witted man.

Not sharp-witted enough, though. Despite the high-powered lawyer he had hired, a settlement was reached. The complainant was satisfied. I don't think that the respondent was satisfied, exactly, but he was persuaded to see reason. He was persuaded that the costs associated with a public hearing would be far more detrimental to his business than the payment deemed acceptable to his former employee. It was his position all along that the matter was a personal one—that it was a domestic dispute in which the government had no right to interfere. He was also convinced that the complainant had set out to screw him over, quite deliberately, and that we had all been fooled by the innocent appearance which "that little slut" could assume at will.

I could see why she was afraid of him. In fact it was one of those rare occasions when I could actually sense the threat of stalking—or perhaps even violence—in the air. I almost wondered if he would have attacked her physically if she had been in the room with him.

I rather feared for her safety, to be honest. If I had been in her shoes, I would have taken out an apprehended violence order. Obviously he perceived that she had won the case by extracting money from him, and he wasn't the kind of person who would take kindly to losing, especially to a nineteen-year-old girl.

What a monumental prick, is all I can say.

We broke for lunch. It was agreed that the conference would resume at two o'clock, so I had plenty of time in which to check my messages. One was from Ms. F. One was from Amelia, my co-worker. One was from Ronnie—no doubt she had obtained Briony's address for the good people of the Pacific Commercial Bank Ltd. One was from a complainant called Mr. P. (Interesting case, that one: a man being sexually harassed by his male co-worker, who would goose him, grab his testicles, and simulate masturbation when he walked past. Mr. P., being an admitted homosexual, was an easy target for someone like Mr. H., who strenuously denies that he himself has homosexual leanings. His actions, he insists, were purely the result of malice and bigotry.

(Makes you wonder, though, doesn't it?)

The final message had been left by Jim McRae, at 12:05 p.m. I rang him at once. When he answered, I could tell that he was in a public place—a shopping center, perhaps, to judge from the distant sound of piped music. He had to raise his voice to make himself heard.

"I've got some information!" he said, in a kind of muted bellow.

"Good news?" I asked.

"What's that?"

"Is it good news, or bad?"

"That depends on what you make of it!" There was a noisy pause. "Nothing conclusive," he finally said. "You're in Castlereagh, aren't you?"

"Yes." I gave him the address.

"Well I'm at the Town Hall, under cover, and it's a zoo. I can call you back later this afternoon, and you can risk having the conversation recorded, or I could meet you somewhere for lunch. Twenty minutes, tops."

"What do you mean, I'd risk being recorded?"

"Eh?"

"What do you mean, I'd risk being recorded?"

"For training purposes. In the interests of customer service."

"Oh, we don't do that here. Do we?"

"I was told that you did when I was put on hold, earlier. A little robot said so."

"Really?" I couldn't believe it. We weren't a telecommunications provider, for God's sake. We were dealing with very sensitive material. "Well—well, maybe I should meet you. Where are you now?"

"Town Hall."

"Oh. That's right. Okay, um—can you come over here?"

"To your office?"

"No, I mean to the café next door. There's a café downstairs in the building next to ours. It's called Al Fresco, for some reason."

"Al Fresco. Yeah, I've been there. It's got that collection of old coffee-makers in the window."

"That's the one. In . . . ten minutes, say?"

"Ten minutes."

He signed off. I leapt to my feet at once, gathering up my purse, my umbrella and the office mobile. As I did so, I knocked against a teetering stack of files, which immediately tumbled to the floor. I was on my knees retrieving them, a dangling hairslide bumping against the side of my neck, when there was a tap at the door.

Without waiting for an invitation, the Commissioner stuck her head into the office.

"Oh! Helen." She looked slightly surprised to see me grovelling at her feet, for some reason. God knows, she must be used to it by now. Pretty much everyone grovels to the Commissioner. "Are you all right?"

"Oh yes!" A careless little laugh. "Just picking up some files!" It hardly needed saying. I probably wouldn't have bothered, with anyone else. But I doubt that the Commissioner had picked anything up off the floor for years. At work she has a secretary to do it for her, and at home she has a nanny. That's what I tell myself, when I start to feel envious of her flawless makeup, her exquisite clothes, her gleaming office, her long business lunches and her perfect attendance record. Diane has money to burn, so she can afford support staff. The kind of support staff that *I* could do with.

"Just wanted to say good job on that genital warts case," she smiled. "I forgot to tell you, but I was very impressed with the settlement."

"Oh. Thanks. Thanks very much."

"I'm thinking that you might like to write it up for the annual report," she added. "Would you?"

"Sure. Absolutely."

"Fine. Excellent." She bestowed on me a carefully graded smile, then disappeared as abruptly as she had materialized. You might think: Why didn't she help you with all that mess? If so, you obviously don't know much about organizational power structures.

It didn't take me long to straighten things up, anyway. Within minutes I had tidied my desk, fixed my hair and struggled out into the miserable weather. God, it was a foul day. When I walked through the building's front door, I was hit in the face by a wet slap, as an erratic easterly lashed heavy rain through the canyons of the central business district. The pavements were seething with damp and sullen office workers. Cars swished through puddles on the road, throwing up sprays of dirty water that spattered the ankles of nearby pedestrians. Smelly buses roared and shuddered. Brakes squealed. Walk-signs chattered like machine guns.

But I didn't have far to go, thank God. About four meters. Then I turned into the wide, glossy entrance of the Building Next Door, which is one of those Shangri-La shopping complexes wedged under a fancy-pants office block. Lots of brass and marble. Glass elevator. Small tropical jungle, sculptural water feature, and artistic, suspended light fittings about two stories high. The shops are all really classy (the sort that Miriam's probably been patronizing): a gallery, a perfumery, a jeweler's that isn't a chain store, a clothes shop containing about twenty-five garments and no mannequins.

Al Fresco is a café with attitude, sitting right on the street. Matt and I have eaten lunch there sometimes, though not often, because (a) it's pretty expensive; and (b) it's a little too postmodern. You know—the sort of place where the coffee's been elevated to a religion. And the salt cellars look like components from some kind of NASA filtration device. And the cook can't produce anything as simple as a chip or a sausage without larding it heavily with ironic references. Take the prawn cocktail, for instance. Last time I ate there with Matt, there was prawn cocktail on the menu. I couldn't believe it. Prawn cocktail! With *iceberg lettuce!* Al Fresco isn't the kind of place that usually serves iceberg lettuce. You'd be more likely to find a jar of *Vegemite* on the premises. I pointed it out to Matt in astonishment.

"Must be a misprint," he suggested.

"You mean they were trying to say 'medallions of truffle hindquarters with braised alpaca jus and marinated kumquats'?"

He burst out laughing—and everyone stared. You don't snort and honk in the Al Fresco café.

"Sorry," he muttered, smothering a grin. "Maybe the prawns are stuffed with pheasant livers, or something."

"You'd hope so, for the price."

"Are you going to get them?"

"Shit, yes. Live dangerously—that's my motto."

"*You* said it, sweetheart. Not me."

"Yeah, well." My one and only encounter with food poisoning had resulted from a dish of English scampi. "At least I'll be able to sue. At least these guys will have some money."

"I hope so. I wouldn't want you sticking your head in a toilet for less than fifty thou."

In the end, it turned out that those prawns *didn't* contain pheasant livers. Nor were they a misprint. No—they were an amusing, retro *homage*, with pink sauce and everything. Very nice too, I might add,

though the iceberg lettuce was nothing special. I
mean, it hadn't been pickled or spiced or rolled
around a few scallops, or anything. It was just lying
on the plate. Chopped.

Maybe there was a joke in that somewhere, and
I didn't get it. I'm not really an Al Fresco kind of
girl, I guess—not any more. But even if the chef's
humor escaped us, Matt and I still had a good
laugh.

Those were the days.

I arrived in the café about ten minutes before
Jim did, and ordered myself a mineral water. Then
I perused the menu, looking for something inex-
pensive, before deciding on the pumpkin soup. I
was informing the waiter of this decision when Jim
McRae appeared; without warning, he seemed to
materialize in the seat opposite me. He gave me
quite a shock, I can tell you.

"God!" I exclaimed. "Did you beam down, or
what?"

"Pardon?"

"Nothing. I didn't see you come in." He was
wearing a raincoat, I noticed—a trenchcoat-style
raincoat. Beige and everything. It made him look
quite different, somehow. Seedy.

"A raincoat." I couldn't believe it. "At last you're
wearing a raincoat!"

He blinked at me. "Eh?"

"You know. Like Columbo."

"Oh." For the first time, I saw him grin. "Right,"
he said. "But I only wear a raincoat when it's raining." He turned to the waiter, who was hovering
impatiently. "I'll just have a coffee please. Black."

Black. But of course. No lily-livered milk for Mister
Bland. Suddenly I'd run out of steam. Reaching

my destination, even after such a brief trip, had filled me with a sense of warmth and hilarity which had evaporated quickly in Jim's presence. I don't know what it is about that guy. He has such a squelching effect on me.

"Have you ordered?" he asked.

"Soup," I replied, lowering my voice and glancing warily at the service counter. "You said it wouldn't take long."

"It won't." He dragged his little blue book from an inside pocket of his raincoat, flipped through the pages, read an entry, and returned the book to its original hiding place. "Okay," he said. "Well I had a bit of luck, as it happens. I was in Darlinghurst on another job, and I dropped into that café your friend saw your husband in. To ask about a girl with purple hair. Regular customer, perhaps? Turns out she used to work there. Josephine Cleary."

"You mean that Josephine Cleary—"

"Dyes her hair purple. Though she used to dye it pink."

"Oh."

"I had a bit of a chat with the manager. He's an old acquaintance of mine from my days on the Darlinghurst beat. Reformed alcoholic. Nice bloke. Had to sack Josephine because she was so unreliable." He began to shrug his raincoat off. "Drugs," he added.

I just stared at him. Then his coffee arrived (they're very quick, at the Al Fresco—I'll give them that) and he sipped at it cautiously.

"I got a bit of a description," he finally went on. "Purple hair, fair complexion, tattoos on her left upper arm, no definable track marks, about five foot four, which would translate into . . . let's see, now . . .

around 165 centimeters. Does that sound like your girl?"

I nodded.

"When Dick realized what was going on with her, he got rid of her before she had a chance to start robbing the till. It wasn't hard, because she was always taking sickies. Showing up late. Locking herself in the toilet. He thinks she might have hepatitis."

"Oh my God," I breathed.

"He had an old address—wasn't the one you gave me. She'd been arrested, according to Dick, but he couldn't remember the details. He wasn't interested, at the time. He's been arrested himself." Jim sipped at his coffee again, and carefully placed the cup back onto its saucer. "I could probably find out the details, if you want them."

"I—I don't know." I was still busy absorbing the information; I didn't know what I should actually do with it. "What do you think?"

"Well, it's leverage. If your husband's involved with a junkie—"

"Yes, yes." I put my hand to my forehead. "I see."

"That's all I've got. It was sheer luck. Dick didn't remember seeing your husband in the place, with or without Josephine, but they get a lot of people through there, and not many regulars. He said Josephine comes back every now and then because she knows it bugs him, so he said he'd keep an eye out. I don't know if he will."

"Right."

"When do you think they actually meet? Josephine and your husband?"

"Lunchtime," I answered. "Maybe . . . sometimes he's home late after work. His shift finishes at about half past eight or nine, but he doesn't get home till half past ten or eleven. He reckons it's drinks . . . meetings . . ." I was so reluctant to say all this. It was private stuff. "On Mondays and Thursdays he's got about two hours between dropping the kids at day care and going to work." I looked up suddenly. "You're not going to *follow* him?" I gasped.

Jim studied me with his bland, brown eyes.

"Would that be a problem?" he queried.

"Well . . . no, I . . ."

"Might be the best way to tackle things. Might not be."

"Couldn't you follow *her*, instead?"

"I could. If that's what you'd prefer."

"I would. Very much."

"But if it's not Josephine he's seeing, you'll be wasting your money."

Covering my eyes, I swallowed. It was all too much. "Do what you think," I said shakily.

"Your husband will be easier to track. He hasn't a lot of time to play around with. I can make sure someone's on his tail at those specific periods that you're worried about."

I nodded again. I couldn't speak. Blinking back tears, I stared at the tablecloth.

"Cheer up," said Jim. All at once he leaned forward and squeezed my wrist in a reassuring fashion. "I think you're going to be pleasantly surprised. I think this is all a set-up." He released me. "You heard anything about that friend of yours? Miriam?"

I shook my head. "No," I squeaked.

"Well, like I said, remember the source." Glancing at his watch, he clicked his tongue, and rose to his feet. "I've got to go," he added. "You okay?"

"Oh, yes."

"This is why I do mostly insurance work, these days," he said casually. "Not as stressful as domestic cases, one way or another. I'll get back to you in a couple of days. See what I can dig up in the mean-time."

"Okay."

"Thanks for meeting with me."

He dragged his raincoat back on. He took a last swig of coffee. And then he did something really, really weird.

He picked up my hand, and kissed it.

So now I had even more to worry about. Suddenly, in the midst of all this other chaos, a private detective decided to kiss my hand. He didn't do anything else. He just kissed my hand, turned on his heel, and disappeared into the rain. But it was so *bizarre*. So unexpected and out of character. For a few minutes after he left, I just sat there, gap-ing, until my soup arrived.

I thought: What was that about?

I thought: Uh-oh.

I thought: I must be imagining things.

Needless to say, I burned my mouth on my lunch—which I couldn't seem to finish. I was in a state of complete abstraction, functioning on auto-matic pilot; I ended up paying for Jim's coffee without feeling even a twinge of irritation. On my way back to work I kept bumping into umbrella spokes and traffic-light poles, and finally found myself at my desk without being consciously aware of how I'd got there. I had been too busy ponder-ing, with growing alarm, the possibility that Jim McRae had just made a pass at me.

The usual things went through my head (I've heard them a million times before): Maybe I'm reading too much into this. Maybe it was just a bit of Olde World courtesy, employed by a man with an eccentric streak—or a weird sense of humor. Maybe it was a gesture of genuine respect, and he doesn't realize that it's likely to be misinterpreted. Maybe I've worked on too many sexual harassment cases . . .

Then along came the more uneasy, second thoughts: He walked off before I could say anything. He didn't give me any warning. He surely can't have thought that I'd *welcome* a stupid piece of bravura like that, in the circumstances? For Chrissake, I'm his *client!* He's been entrusted with my personal details—my marital problems, my work address, my home telephone number—and should therefore behave with the professional circumspection of a doctor or a massage therapist. His detachment might have been a bit disconcerting, at first, but it had been reassuring as well. Why had he suddenly blown it all with this ill-judged flourish?

A cold sense of dread began to invade my gut. I had laid myself wide open to this man. I had given him a foothold into my life, and now I didn't even know if his intentions would stand up to close scrutiny. How could I possibly trust him, after that hand-kissing business? How would I know where he was coming from? Suppose he made a habit of hitting on women who approached him with the fear that their husbands were unfaithful? Suppose he was always on the lookout for vulnerable, confused women who couldn't exactly complain to the Equal Opportunity and Human Rights Board,

unless they wanted the fact that they were employ-
ing a private detective to be widely and publicly
known?

Not that I think I could have lodged a formal
complaint with any success. I wasn't sure of what
Jim's intentions had been—not really. After all,
kissing someone's hand wasn't exactly offensive. It
wasn't like pinching bums or exposing genitals.
Some people might argue that it was charming.
Sweet. Funny, even.

And then it occurred to me that Jim McRae
might have been indulging in a little joke. Maybe
he had been kissing my hand *because* I worked for
the Equal Opportunity and Human Rights Board.
Maybe he disliked the whole premise—the whole
concept—and was daring me, consciously or un-
consciously, to make a big thing of his sly little
peck.

Was that possible?

It didn't seem possible. It's often difficult to believe that an ordinary working man, striving to do
his job, improve his prospects and juggle his
schedule, could find the energy to squander that
much attention on a woman he might encounter
at brief intervals while earning his pay. Most men
don't seem to end up lavishing a lot of attention
on their own *wives* (and I can attest to this); what
makes some of them suddenly wrench their thoughts
away from food, football or office politics long
enough to make themselves offensive to some poor
woman they hardly know? I often ask myself this.
I've discussed it with people like Amelia, who will
also look nonplussed. A lot of the policy officers,
who are single, high-powered women with feminist
outlooks, maintain that once men get married,

they don't feel that they *need* to pay attention to
their wives, who have effectively been "conquered."
It's a power thing, say Judy and Trish and Bebe
and Kate. But Amelia and I still have our doubts.
We still nurse the suspicion that women in general
just aren't that important to most men; hence our
unfailing astonishment at the behavior of stalkers
and womanizers and people of that sort. How
could they be bothered? Where do they get the energy, when our own husbands seem to be so utterly
exhausted at the end of every working day that
they can't get off their backsides long enough to
change a lightbulb or put the garbage out?

On the other hand, we might be underempha-
sizing the importance of sex. You tend to do that,
when you become a mother. Sex tends to get side-
lined—first, because of hormones; second, because of sheer fatigue. (I'll never forget the snorts
and rolling eyes of the mothers at Tresillian whenever the subject of sex was raised.) You often forget how prominent a part it plays in some people's
lives—or indeed in your own life at one stage, before you grew so old and weary. When sex is way
down at the bottom of your "Things to do" list,
below "Write to Auntie Beth" and "Visit the op-
tometrist," you find it hard to understand why
someone as neat and calm and competent as Jim
McRae would be secretly stewing over some unre-
solved dilemma or sexual defeat to the point
where he'd be jeopardizing his own business just
to throw you off balance.

I might have been overreacting, of course. My
job was probably causing me to build mountains
out of molehills. But I wondered, in that case,
whether I should have a word with Jim McRae on

the subject of acceptable and professional behavior, lest he was stupid enough to believe that kissing hands, in this context, was appropriate. Was that the answer? A few firm, well-chosen words?

The trouble was, I didn't want to talk to him. I didn't want to see him again. For one thing, raising the subject at all would be acutely embarrassing, and would have an effect on our association just as destabilising as the kiss itself. For another thing, I didn't know if I wanted to employ a man who needed a few firm, well-chosen words to set him on the right path. If he was so badly attuned to the wishes and needs of his clients, was he actually the sort of man I could trust?

I was sitting there, trying to work out whether I should call him again and cancel the job, when my phone rang. I picked up the receiver.

"Hello, Equal Opportunity and Human Rights Board, Helen Muzzatti speaking."

"Hi. It's me."

"Oh."

"I called you earlier, but you weren't there." Matt's voice sounded strangely flat and expressionless. "I wanted to meet you for lunch."

"Oh. I'm sorry. I was out."

"Who with?"

I wasn't about to tell him that, needless to say. "No one you know. A woman from work."

"Uh-huh."

Silence. My neck muscles began to tense. "What is it?" I said. "Is anything wrong?" I realized, suddenly, that there was a lot of background noise at the other end of the line. "Where are you? At your office?"

"I just wanted to have a talk."

"A talk?" Now I was really worried. "What about?"

"Things." He made a funny, strangled noise. "Not over the phone, though. It doesn't matter. I'll see you tonight, and we'll talk then."

"Matt—"

"I can't talk now. It's not a good time. I'll see you later."

"Wait!"

"Helen, I told you. We *can't talk now*."

"About what?"

"Things."

"What things?"

"I'll tell you later. At home. In private."

"Why? What's wrong?"

"I'll tell you later."

That's all I could get out of him. He hung up, and I was petrified. Matt had never behaved like this before. Not once had the soap-opera phrase "We have to talk" ever passed his lips. It was out of character. It was a danger signal. I thought: He's going to do it. He's going to walk through the front door tonight and tell me that he's in love with someone else. That he needs time to think. That he has to move out.

That he wants a divorce?

It was too much. Suddenly, for the first time, my fears seemed terribly real. I could feel the full weight of the dark shadow that had been creeping across my sunny horizons.

I tried to call him back, but he wasn't at work. He had gone out for lunch, I was told. So I left a message, put my head down on the desk, and cried.

It was Cindy who found me there, sobbing amongst the Post-it notes and lime-green complaint files. She's one of the younger administrative assistants, a nice little thing from Jannali, who has fluffy brown hair and a sweet voice and favors barrettes, lockets, jabots, and shirtmaker dresses with narrow belts. I don't know quite what she makes of her job, or some of the people she works with. When one of our policy officers, a fervent lesbian separatist, was hospitalized with meningococcal meningitis (she got better, fortunately), Cindy visited her with a copy of the *Women's Weekly*, a manicure set and a pair of fluffy pink slippers.

"Oh. Um—your complainant is waiting for you in conference room three," she said, hesitating on the threshold.

I made an incoherent noise.

"Are you all right?" she asked.

"Yes. Yes." I straightened, and rubbed my hands across my face. "PMS."

"Oh."

"Thanks, Cindy."

She moved a tissue box from Amelia's desk to mine, and I thanked her again before blowing my nose vigorously.

"I think—maybe you should do your makeup again, before you go in," Cindy suggested. Thank God she wasn't one of the assertive and opinionated policy officers, who would have been far more intrusively helpful, raising the subject of stress leave, sympathizing with my plight as a working mother, or offering me some kind of strengthening herbal compound. All I wanted was to be left alone for a minute.

"Yes," I told Cindy. "I'll do that. Thanks."

She departed apologetically, and I checked the hand-mirror in my purse. As expected, I looked like a disaster area. So I went to the ladies' room to freshen up.

The rest of the afternoon was a nightmare. It felt as if a leaden ball was sitting in my stomach; I could hardly concentrate on what I was supposed to be doing. I was all right during the conference, when people were talking and required answers. But as soon as it finished, I was left with enough time to contemplate the full extent of the damage being done to my life. Miriam had pulled a major rug out from under me. Jim McRae was a possible threat, with his seedy hand-kissing habits. My husband was almost certainly an adulterer, unless he had something even worse that he wanted to tell me. That he was a serial killer, perhaps? That he had been diagnosed with some terrible disease?

Everywhere I turned, there was a horrible source of anxiety to be faced.

I tried to phone Matt again at work, but he insisted that it was a bad time—that he couldn't talk. "I'm due on the desk in thirty seconds," he said. "We'll talk later." And since I found it impossible to make any other phone calls, or write reports, or even open mail because of the condition to which I'd been reduced, I decided to leave work early. That was at four o'clock. No one objected; in fact I got the impression that Cindy might have discussed my tearful episode with some of the other staff, because I was aware of a distinctly sympathetic air about the place as I made my way to the foyer. Kate asked me if everything was all right. Bebe reminded me not to leave my umbrella behind. Even Jean raised a quizzical eyebrow at me when I asked her to take messages, as if to say: "Life sucks, but what can you do?"

Luckily, the Commissioner wasn't around. While she's *theoretically* sympathetic to female employees with family problems, I've always had my doubts about her real views on the matter. She might have two kids of her own, but she also has a nanny—and almost no imagination. Plus, she probably doesn't give a hoot what her husband does with his time. From what I can see, that marriage is more like a company merger than anything else.

Basically, after the grovelling episode, I didn't want her thinking I was unstable.

I caught the 4:15 train to Marrickville. On the way, I wondered if I had ever felt worse, and decided that I had on only three occasions: when my grandmother died, when Jonah stopped breathing for a short time after he was born, and when my first boyfriend dumped me by showing up with my (former) best friend at my very own birthday party. (Even now, I still can't listen to that song, "It's My Party and I'll Cry If I Want To.") Desperately I racked my brain for something positive about my existence, and concluded that I was very lucky really because my kids were fine, my job was okay, and my health was good. Not great, exactly—my nose was still dripping like a leaky tap, and my sinuses were full of sludge—but good. No high blood pressure. No kidney disease. No lumps in the breast. Nothing like that.

It was something to cling to, anyway. Something to keep me from dissolving while I picked the kids up from day care and took them home. At home, the breakfast dishes were sitting in the kitchen sink, unwashed. The builders' wheelbarrow, parked out side the laundry door, was full of water. The wash on the clothes horse was still wet. Every room in the place was dim and dispiriting.

I boiled some noodles and vegetables for the kids. I put on a cassette of fairytales while I fed them. I admired the drawings that they'd done at day care, peeled off their clothes and hurried them into the bath. I got them out, dried them, dressed them, cleaned their teeth, drew the curtains in their bedroom. I read them *Where the Wild Things Are.* I sang them "Old McDonald Had a Farm," and kissed them goodnight. I sang them one more song. I gave them each one more kiss. I said "goodnight" and "I love you." I left the room, then came back again when Jonah dropped his teddy bear. And when Emily had to go to the toilet. And when Jonah heard a car alarm.

I couldn't bring myself to think about Jim McRae, or whether I should ring him, or what I should say when I did. It was all too difficult. Instead I ate a piece of buttered toast, a cheese stick, a shortbread biscuit, a Ritz cracker, a couple of dried apricots, a muesli bar and a small tub of yogurt. Between bites, I would trudge into the living room, stare out the window onto the street, and return again to the kitchen. I was waiting for Matthew. I couldn't settle.

Outside, darkness fell. The streetlights flickered on. Cars pulled into driveways. Inside, the clock ticked and the plumbing grumbled. Eight-thirty—I checked the TV guide. (Nothing.) Nine o'clock—I went into our bedroom and rifled through his underwear drawer, his sock drawer, his shirts and jumpers, the pockets of his pants and jackets. (Nothing.) Nine-thirty—I did the same with his toiletries bag, his fancy shaving kit, his backpack, his guitar case, his box full of old computer disks and audio equipment and drumsticks and sheet music, his scrapbook of gig reviews, his collection of *Q* and *Rolling Stone* (U.S. edition) and the odd, very ancient, very dog-eared copy of *Hustler*. (Nothing.)

By ten-thirty, he still wasn't home. I called his number at work, and got his voice mail. By ten forty-five, I was beginning to lose it. I was muttering to myself and pacing the floor. It was unspeakably cruel and insulting that he should threaten a momentous "talk," then fail to get home early—or even get home at all. What the hell was going on? Was he with Her? Had he been in an accident? If there was a problem at work, why hadn't he called me?

I didn't know what to do. The nearest hospital was Royal Prince Alfred. The nearest police station was up the road, more or less. What was the usual procedure in these circumstances? Phone the hospital? Phone the police? Was there some kind of traffic accident hotline? Or should I wait until someone else found his wallet or his registration, and phoned me with the news?

Then it occurred to me that, before I jumped to the worst possible conclusion, I ought to eliminate all the alternatives first. Maybe I wasn't thinking straight. Maybe I shouldn't have drunk two glasses of red wine with my buttered toast and muesli bar. Whatever the reason, I was filled with a sudden, urgent desire to call Josephine Cleary. To punch in her number and see what happened.

I did it, too. It was ten to eleven at night, but I punched in her number all the same. I figured that a party animal like Josephine wouldn't be tucked up in bed at eleven o'clock at night—unless my husband was tucked up with her. I figured that I wouldn't be waking anybody unless I called after twelve. And I was right, as it happened, because my old mate Paul answered the phone. Paul of the rough voice and bored, un-tutored manner.

"Yeah?" he said.

"Is Jo there?"

"Nah. She's out. Can I take a message?" From his distracted tone and the screams in the background, I deduced that he was busy watching something like *Re-Animator* on video. Unless he was disembowelling someone himself.

"What about Matt?" I asked, in a voice that wobbled. "Is *he* there?"

"Nope."

A pause. I didn't want to labor the point, in case he became suspicious, but I couldn't tell if the name "Matt" meant anything to him or not. Fearing that it might, I took a deep breath and continued.

"Okay. Well . . . actually, Jo was supposed to meet me, but I can't remember where. Do *you* know? It was a club or a restaurant, I think."

"Sorry, I dunno. Sandra might. *Hey! Sandra!*"

Sandra? That was a new name. With Paul's phone pressed to something massive and muffling—like his chest—I could hear very little of the ensuing conversation between him and Sandra. It didn't matter, though. I got what I wanted.

"Sandra says she's gone to the Siam Thai in Newtown," Paul finally informed me. "Who is this, by the way?"

"It's Helen."

"Helen?"

"You don't know me," I said, and hung up.

So Josephine was at the Siam Thai. She was a

drug addict who couldn't get it together enough
to hold down a waitress's job, yet she was frequent-
ing exotic restaurants. I can't remember the last
time I ate at a Thai restaurant. I can't remember
the last time I had Thai takeaway. But I do remember the Siam, because Matt and I went there once,
long ago, for an intimate birthday dinner. That
was after I'd given Matt a new set of cymbals for his
birthday present, and he'd had to wipe his tears
away. There had been no fretted screens or crim-
son curtains at the Siam Thai, but only a smattering
of bamboo, lots of black lacquer, linen tablecloths,
silk orchids, and comfortable chairs. We had consumed pad thai and quail and ginger chicken and
minced pork salad and a great deal of wine. Matt
had worn his leather jacket, and his hair had fallen
over his face as he kissed the tips of my fingers,
one after the other . . .

Suddenly I felt the strongest urge to take a pair
of scissors to that leather jacket, which my husband still cherished. It also crossed my mind that I
could easily burn his *Q* magazines, or slash up his
drum kit, or do something really, really insulting
to his shoes. I've read about women going mad
with a kitchen knife or a can of spray paint. In the
past, I've assumed that such women resemble
Briony, in that they lack a well-developed means of
controlling their impulses, while at the same time
possessing an exaggeratedly melodramatic understanding of their own life story.

Now I'm not so sure. Now I realize that a few
glasses of wine, a tiring day at the office and an
acute state of nervous tension—brought on by
anxiety and fear—can lead even a sensible law
graduate to contemplate savage acts of vandalism.

I was suddenly angry, with an anger that was more frantic than focused. I wanted to kick something. To smash something. Josephine's face, perhaps? I had always maintained, when contemplating other cases of adultery, that a wife should never primarily blame the mistress in these circumstances. It is not the mistress, after all, who has betrayed the wife—unless she happens to be a friend. But logic hadn't long survived the fury of my feelings. I would happily have smashed Josephine Cleary's head against the wall, had she been available. It gave me some relief to picture myself doing exactly that—much as I'd visualized cracking Jonah's head open when he was a tiny baby. Oh yes, I used to entertain such monstrous thoughts. I told you that I was a bad mother. Though I've always claimed, in my defense, that if I hadn't found relief in imagining acts of violence against my helpless darling—against my precious boy whom I love so much even though he's so like me—then I might actually have been driven to throw him across the room (something that I've never done and never will do, in case you're wondering). I once met a mother at Tresillian who confessed, with tears in her eyes, that she sometimes had to put her baby down and step outside because of her overwhelming desire to hurl him off her second-floor balcony. It happens. I'm not the only one. And if it eases the pressure of endless crying to indulge in a few grisly mental images, what's the harm in that? As long as they stay in your head where they belong.

So I conjured up a vivid daydream of seizing a handful of purple hair and driving the attached head into a slate floor—one, two, three, four times. Then I imagined throwing a pot of spaghetti bolognese at Matt, before bashing him over the skull with his own bass drum. Then, because I still felt as one does during a particularly bad bout of PMS (the only time, in the normal course of existence, when I have the courage to snap at someone who takes up too much room on a train seat or throws a cigarette butt into a flowerbed), I picked up the phone book and did a feverish search for the number of the Siam Thai restaurant.

I found it in the *White Pages*. It was there in bold face; it positively leapt out at me, hitting me straight in the eye. Eight digits that formed a mocking little tune when I keyed them in.

As I waited for someone to answer my call, I considered summoning a cab and going to confront my purple-haired enemy, before dismissing the idea. It was nearly eleven. I couldn't leave the kids. I couldn't ring someone like Lisa, and ask her to sit for me. I couldn't wake up the kids and drag them down King Street into a huge marital spat that would probably end up taking place on a public footpath. Perhaps some mothers would have done it, but not me. Not with my upbringing.

Suddenly I heard a thickly accented voice pronounce the name of the Siam Thai, and ask how I might be helped. I replied that I wanted to talk to one of the restaurant's patrons. A customer. One of the people eating there tonight.

"It's an emergency," I insisted.

"Yes?"

"She has purple hair. Her name is Jo Cleary. *Jo Cleary.*"

"Yes?"

"Would you mind if I spoke to her? Very quickly?"

"She's here? She's eating here?"

"I think so. She has purple hair."

"I'll go see. Wait, please."

Clunk. I could hear the faint strains of Asian music. A distant buzz of voices. Staring at the dusty southeastern corner of my bedroom, with our cheap, old-fashioned wardrobe huddled dimly against it, I imagined all the warmth and light and cooking smells on the other end of the line. Trendy couples finishing their coffee. Groups of friends trying to divide up various bills in an equitable fashion (always a doomed attempt). Empty bottles of wine. Bloated stomachs.

"Hello?"

I sat up straight. It was a female voice. Young. My heart took off.

"Hello?" she repeated, more impatiently. "Who is it?"

"Is that Josephine?"

"Yes. Who's this?" Her voice, to my surprise, was pitched quite high. It lacked both range and sinew.

"Is Matt there?" I asked. Each word was like a chip of stone.

A pause. The longer it stretched out, the more she condemned herself. I held my breath.

"Who is this?" she said again, but with quite a different emphasis and far more depth of tone.

"You know damn well who," I replied.

"What?"

"Is he there?"

"What?"

"*Is Matt there?*"

"Matt who? Matt Muzzatti?"

"Is he there?"

"No, of course not." It was almost a whine. "Who is this? Do I know you?"

"I'm his wife. His *wife*, okay?"

"Oh." She sounded nonplussed. "Are you looking for him or something?"

"You're bloody right I'm looking for him!"

"Well he's not here."

"Where is he, then?"

"What do you mean, where is he? How should I know? What is this?" Her voice cracked on a plaintive, petulant note. "How come you're ringing me here?"

"Don't give me that bullshit," I said hoarsely. My diction was unsteady—my hands were shaking—but I plowed on. "Don't even try it. I know you've been seeing him."

"So?" Anger flared on the other end of the line. I couldn't believe the gall of the girl. "Why shouldn't I?"

"*Why shouldn't you?* Why, you—you little *shit!*"

"Hey, fuck you!"

"Fuck you, too!"

"He's my father, okay? I've got a *right* to see him! And if you don't like it, you can go fuck yourself!"

Click.

She hung up on me.

Chapter Eight

The first day of the rest of my life

She wouldn't talk to me again. I rang back (after recovering a little from the shock) but she wouldn't come to the phone. So I was left sitting there in the dark, my head reeling and my mouth hanging open. Her father? My husband? Her father?

What insanity was this?

"No," I said aloud. It was a lie. Some sort of excuse. Surely Matt wasn't even old enough to be her father? He was forty-one. Forty-one minus—what? Twenty? Twenty-two?

Well, maybe he *was* old enough—but only just.

Suddenly I heard the noise of an engine. A jolt of adrenaline went through me before I realized that it wasn't the sound of our car; it had a deeper, more rhythmic pitch. But it seemed to be growing louder. It was throbbing away right outside our house.

I got up and went into the living room. Twitching one of the former owner's lace curtains aside (we can't afford new ones, yet), I peered out at the rain-lashed street. I saw glowing windows. I saw puddles of watery light pooling under the street lamps. I saw a taxi pulling away from the curb, its rooftop sign dimmed, its interior empty except for its shadowy driver.

Though I craned and strained, I could see no one else. There was no one walking up the front path. Why should there be? Matthew had taken our car to work. He didn't need to hire a taxi.

Then I heard the hinges squeaking on the screen door out back.

He had gone down the side of the house and around to the kitchen, because he didn't want to wake the kids. He was soaking wet. His hair was plastered to his forehead, his white shirt was almost transparent, his faded jeans were scattered with darker patches on the knees and around the ankles. He wiped his nose with the back of his damp wrist, staggering slightly.

"I'm not screwin' around," he blurted out. "I thought you were."

But my attention was focused on another matter of interest.

"Is Josephine Cleary your daughter?" I demanded.

"Yes."

There it was. The truth at last.

"Shit, Matthew!"

"I'm sorry."

"I thought you were having an affair!"

"I know."

"How do you know?"

"I just ran into that bloke you hired. That detective."

"You *did?*"

"He was tailing me, Helen. Jesus, how *could* you?"

We both of us paused, gasping for breath. I don't know what my face looked like, but Matt's looked tortured. His nose was red. His eyes were bloodshot. He kept sniffing and blinking, as rivulets of water trickled down from his hair.

"You'd better get a towel," I said automatically.

"Fuck the towel! Jesus, Helen! Goddamn it!" And all at once he burst into tears.

Well, he'd been drinking. I worked that out when I approached him, and put my arms around his wet, shaking shoulders; I could smell the smoke and the beer. I said: "Where have you been?"

"I've been . . ." He sniffed. Swallowed. "I've been out with Ray."

"Getting pissed?"

"What do *you* think? I . . ." His voice cracked on another sob. "Goddamn, I thought . . . God, Helen!"

My own eyes filled with tears. I pulled away. "Miriam saw you!" I cried. "Kissing Josephine! What was I *supposed* to think?"

He mumbled something that I couldn't hear.

"What?"

"You could've asked me," he repeated.

"And you'd have told me what? That she was your daughter? Then why didn't you? Why wait until now?"

"Oh Christ." He broke away from me. He dragged out a kitchen chair and cast himself into it, covering his face with his hands. He looked so big, hunched in that little chair, but he kept snuffling and gulping and wiping his eyes.

I sat down next to him.

I waited.

"You'd better tell me," I said at last. "Who's her mother?"

"You don't know her," Matt replied. He gave a deep, shuddering sigh and leaned back, his arms dangling. "Her name's Megan Molesdale. We used to hang out when I first came to Sydney."

"Oh." *That* was a blow I hadn't anticipated. It left me breathless.

"I didn't even know," he went on, despairingly. "She never told me. She disappeared—went to Indonesia—must have come back, but I never saw her again. Not until . . ." He made a weary gesture.

"So you . . ."

"She was okay. She was a bit of a flake. We were drunk when we did it the first time, then we got together once or twice after that. I dunno. I dunno why she didn't tell me." He scratched his head furiously with both hands. "She should have told me!"

"Well at least you know now," I said, in a tone that was astonishingly tranquil. Inside, though, there was magma oozing from my heart. All this, and he had never dropped so much as a hint. He had cut me off.

"She must have hated me," Matthew suddenly announced. "She must have, because she made Jo think that this Cleary bloke she married was her father. Jo's father. Then when the marriage broke up, she got the shits with Cleary, and didn't want Jo seeing him. She told Jo the truth, then, but she wouldn't tell the poor kid who her real father was. Can you believe it? No wonder she's so fucked up."

"Who? You mean Josephine?"

"Oh yeah." Another deep sigh, as his head fell back. "Oh yeah."

For a while he stared at the ceiling. The clock ticked. Rain thrummed against our roof. Finally I had to prompt him.

"Go on," I said.

"Well, shit. She's a fuckin' junkie, you know? My own daughter. She's turned tricks, she's done B and Es, you name it. She left home when she was fifteen, she was on the streets for over a year—"

"How old is she now?"

"Nineteen. She just turned nineteen."

I scratched my wrist thoughtfully. No comment.

"A few months ago, she suddenly realized—I dunno, maybe someone told her—she suddenly realized that she could legally find out who her father was. It's on the birth certificate, right? So she tracked me down, got hold of me. We met."

He threw himself forward and covered his face again.

"God, Matthew."

"I felt so bad," he squeaked.

"Why didn't you tell me?"

"I don't know!" he wailed. "I was so . . . it was so hard! I felt so bad! Everything was so tough for you, and now this. A stepdaughter? A fuckin' *junkie*? You didn't deserve it."

"But I was going to have to find out sooner or later."

"Yeah, but it was always such a bad time. We were all getting gastro, and then your sister was in hospital, and then they had to pull those floorboards up—"

"But Matt, this was *important*! Really important!"

"But you were losin' it, Helen! Do you think I can't tell? Your nerves were shot. And you were always mad at me . . . I felt so useless . . ."

"Well Jesus, Matt, I mean—"

"Fuck it, I *am* useless! I'm fuckin' useless! Breaking the mower, and everything—fuck, I thought you'd given up on me! I thought you were involved with that detective!"

"What?"

"I saw you with him. I saw him kiss your hand."

Talk about a leveller. Talk about out of the blue. I nearly choked.

"You're not, are you?" he whispered, lifting his face. "You're not foolin' around with that guy?"

The tone of his voice was heartbreaking. My tears began to flow.

"Of course not!" I whimpered.

"Then why did he kiss your hand?"

"I don't *know*!" Sob, sob. "He just did it!" More sobs. "It freaked me out, it totally freaked me out!"

"Oh, darlin'."

He got out of his chair, kneeled down, and put his arms around me. They were still damp. His hair was still damp. His shoulder was damp under my cheek.

"I didn't know what to do!" I cried, then quickly lowered my voice as I remembered the kids. "I didn't know what to do. I thought if Miriam was wrong, then you'd never find out—you'd never know that I was even wondering . . ."

"But he was following me around! He was *trailing* me!"

"I'm sorry . . ."

"When I saw him, I nearly decked him. I was off

my skull. Jesus, I just spent two hours talking about
the guy, and he suddenly shows up in the bar!"

"What do you mean?" I was deriving some comfort from Matt's body heat, and the rumble of his
voice as it reverberated through the bones of his
chest into my ear. But I had to raise my head. I had
to lift my eyes so I could look at his face. "Do you
mean tonight?" I sniffed. "You were talking about
him tonight? With Ray?"

"Of course I was. I just told you—I thought you
were foolin' around. I was goin' bloody spare."

"Because you saw him kiss my hand?"

"And other things."

"Wait a minute." I had to get something
straight. "You saw me at the Al Fresco? You were
there at lunchtime?"

"That's right."

"How—how did you know where to find me?"

"I didn't. I wasn't looking for you there. I was
heading for your office. I always pass that place,
when I head for your office." Close up, I could see
every crow's-foot and cavernous pore and broken
capillary on his face, but it didn't matter. On the
contrary, it made me feel good. Like me, he was
human. Like me, he had suffered. Like me, he had
skin problems and pouches under his eyes. "I was
walkin' by," he added, "and I looked in, because—
well, you know. The prawn cocktail."

"But why were you coming to see me?" I wanted
to know. "Why didn't you warn me?"

"Well, think about it," he said. Then, as I stared
at him blankly, he climbed to his feet again (knees
cracking) and collapsed back into his chair. "I've
been out of my mind," he growled. "Goin' spare.

All these phone calls. You've been makin' 'em and gettin' 'em and I didn't know what to think. Some guy calls up—won't leave his name. You shut yourself in the bedroom and jump a foot when I come in."

"Oh, but—"

"And then this morning!" he exclaimed, before my frantic gestures made him clap a hand over his mouth. (The kids! Of course!) "This morning I got the mail," he said quietly. "What was I supposed to think about that?"

"About what?"

"Didn't you see?"

"See what?" I was genuinely bewildered.

"It was here on the table." He looked around, his forehead puckering. "I'm sure I left it here. That postcard—and the stuff from the real estate agent. Wasn't it here?"

I shook my head.

"Then where . . . ?" He rose. He cast about for the missing items. "Hang on a second," he muttered, and disappeared into the living room. I listened to him shuffling through magazines, his footsteps heavy and deliberate. I was getting a headache.

Then he came back, looking embarrassed.

"I put 'em in me bag," he muttered. "I was gunna talk about 'em at lunchtime."

Matt's bag is a kind of floppy, brown suede facsimile of a briefcase. A briefcase but not a briefcase, if you follow me. It perfectly suits Matt, who's a corporate cog but not a corporate cog.

From its scuffed and battered depths he produced a postcard and some papers. The papers had been sent by a local real estate agent. There was a letter, addressed to me, explaining that I had requested the enclosed details about rental accommodation in the area. There was also a collection of listings: units for rent, houses for rent, townhouses for rent. It took me a moment to recall that I had, indeed, asked for this material. So much had happened since.

"Oh. Right," I said.

"So what the hell was that all about?"

"Oh . . ." I put the papers on the table. "It was . . . I was in a bit of a panic. I thought that if you were going to . . . you know . . ." I could hardly force the words out. "If you were going to leave, we might have to sell the house."

"For Chrissake, Helen."

"I freaked. What do you expect?"

"And that? What's that?"

The postcard depicted Sydney Opera House on the front. On the back, I recognized Miriam's handwriting, and my heart skipped a beat. *Helen— please don't be angry*, it said. *Will call. Lots and lots of love, x x x ♡*

The postmark was a local one. The date was Tuesday.

"Who sent this, if it wasn't some bloke?" Matt inquired.

"Miriam, of course." I spoke dully. "Didn't you recognize the writing?" I wondered if I should be passing this piece of correspondence on to the people at the Pacific Commercial Bank, then dismissed the idea. Miriam's message had obviously been mailed at Sydney airport, or somewhere close by. It offered no clues as to Miriam's whereabouts. "Maybe she didn't sign it because she was trying to cover her tracks. In case someone was monitoring my post, or something." I could no longer guess

what Miriam's motives might have been. I didn't
know what was going on inside her head, any
more. "I wonder why she sent it?"

We both fell silent. After a while, Matt got up
and filled the electric kettle.

"What will you do if she does call?" he asked quietly.

"I don't know." Frankly, I had other things on
my mind.

"At least she seems to care what you think about
her," Matt remarked. "I guess that's something."

"I guess." The postcard went on the table. "Are
you making tea?"

"Do you want some?"

"I'd love some."

Down came the mugs—his and mine. Out came
the sugar bowl. The milk. The tea bags. I watched
Matt as he performed those familiar tasks, fumbling a little over actions that should have been
smooth and fluid. His hands shook. He dropped a
teaspoon.

The beer, I thought, is getting in his way.

"So you thought this postcard was from Jim
McRae?" I eventually queried.

Matt grunted.

"Why, though? You hadn't even seen Jim when
the post came . . ."

"Nick turned up this morning about ten." Matt
folded his arms and propped his hip against a cupboard, waiting for the water to boil. He confessed
that Nick had appeared at the house, briefly, to pick
up some equipment. "Something about an inside
job at Marrickville. Under cover," Matt continued.
"But he had to stop for a yak, and he told me about
your visitor yesterday. Your friend Jim." Matt low-

ered his eyes. "I didn't even know you *had* a friend called Jim," he added.

"Oh, Matt." I was truly sorry. "It was the first thing that came into my head. I couldn't tell Nick that he was a private detective—can you imagine?" Even as I spoke, I could feel the hot blood rushing to my cheeks. "Anyway, what business is it of Nick's, for God's sake?"

"He was just shootin' his mouth off. Said he felt sorry for you yesterday, with people traipsing in and out. Him and Mike and the guys from the bank and "your friend Jim." I think he was more interested in the guys from the bank than anyone else. Maybe he's worried that we're defaulting on the renovation loan, or something."

"But how did he know that they were *from* a bank? It's not like they went out back and introduced themselves!"

Matt shrugged. "Well, you've said it before," he pointed out. "They hear things, those builders."

"Bloody stickybeaks!"

"Should I have a word with 'em?"

"No, no." I was too tired to maintain the rage. "Don't piss them off. We can't afford to do that."

"They're not gunna sabotage the work, Helen."

"I know. But I have to live with them. I couldn't do it, if there was an atmosphere. Here—let me do that. You're spilling it everywhere."

"Sorry."

"It's all right."

"I'm a little bit rooted."

"I know."

"That's why I caught the cab home. I didn't know if I could drive."

"Sit down, Matt."

He sat down, and I gave him his tea. Then I sat down opposite him. He was drying off, I noticed; his chest hair was no longer visible through the fabric of his shirt.

"So what happened tonight, exactly?" Despite my fatigue, I knew that everything would have to be thrashed out before we went to bed. While the kids were still asleep. "You went to a bar with Ray, and Jim followed you there?"

"I freaked," Matthew admitted, not looking at me. "First Nick mentions this Jim character, then I get the mail, then I see you with a bloke who's all over you, and then when I ring you, all I get is a lie about lunch with some *woman*—"

"Sorry."

"—so I completely lose it, I can't even face going home without a drink, and Ray comes with me, and we talk, and next thing I know there's your friend the hand-kisser, hangin' around near the loos."

"I can't believe you saw him."

"I saw him, all right."

"But Stuart said he was good. He can't be very good if you saw him."

"I guess he didn't know I'd recognize him. Neither of you saw me at lunchtime."

"That's true." All the same, I wasn't impressed. "So then what happened? Nothing bad, I hope."

"Oh, I nailed him." Matt began to scratch at the tabletop with his fingernail. "I lost it, a bit."

"Oh, Matt."

"I didn't hit him, don't worry." He flashed me a dark and complicated look, which I ignored. "He didn't get hurt."

"It's you I'm worried about. You can get arrested for brawling in pubs."

"Well I didn't. I didn't brawl. I told him to leave my wife alone, or else."

"You're kidding!"

A giggle escaped him. "It was the beer talkin'," he observed, and I eyed him doubtfully. This was the side of Matt that I wasn't very familiar with—the tattooed, pub-crawling, pig-shooting side—and it made me anxious.

"He used to be a copper, Matt."

"He's still smaller than I am."

"So what did he say?"

"He told me who he was, and why he was there." Matt fixed me with another intent look over the rim of his teacup. "He said you should probably call him."

"Mmph."

"Don't you want to call him?"

"Not particularly." I sipped my tea and cleared my throat, avoiding my husband's eye. "I think he's a bit of a creep. He was all right at first, but then that hand-kissing business . . . I don't know."

"Do you want me to call him?"

"Please," I said, before adding: "If you can be civil."

"I can be civil."

"Just tell him that we don't need his services any more."

"I'll do that," Matt agreed softly. "And I'll tell him that we never did."

We never did. I gazed at Matt, sitting there in his clammy clothes, and realized suddenly that he was, indeed, mine. That slick black hair, curling damply

at the ends; those big, bony hands with their reddened knuckles and hairy wrists; that lopsided,
gap-toothed grin—all mine. Those tattoos were
mine, as was the history behind them. I still had
first dibs on his spicy pork chops, his old flan-
nelette pajamas, his encyclopedic knowledge of
popular music, his first-class driving skills, his stories about culling kamikaze roosters, his effortless
ability to make the kids laugh—his past ten years,
in fact. And his immediate future? It too belonged
to me.

Well, perhaps not entirely to me.

"So what's the deal with Josephine?" I asked,
and he groaned.

"I dunno." He shook his head. "God, Helen, I
just—I'm so sorry."

"Is she working? Is she still an addict? Does she
need help? What do we have to do?"

"Nothing." He set his cup down. "I mean, you
don't have to do anything. It's my problem."

"If it's your problem, Matt, then it's my problem
too."

"No," he said firmly, shaking his head. "No,
see—that's the thing. I didn't want you to have to
cope with this girl. This girl . . ." He faltered, lost
for words. "She's trouble," he finished.

"How?"

"Oh . . ." More furious head-scratching. "Look,
she reckons she's gettin' it together—she's got a
job in a tobacco shop, some bloke she's livin'
with—but I dunno. I dunno." Tentatively, Matt
tried to express his feelings on the subject of his
daughter's character. Jo worried him, he said. Her
mother was a head case; there was no doubt about
that. A bit scatty, a bit paranoid. Given to unrea-

sonable and somewhat obsessive behavior. At the
same time, though, you could see why she'd pretty
much given up on Josephine.

"Jo's robbed her. Jo's attacked her. I mean, they
must set each other off, big time. Megan might
have fucked the poor kid over, once or twice, but
not . . . I mean, not deliberately." Though Matt has
never been much good at articulating his perception of social contracts or personal relationships, I
could see what he was getting at. "It's just the way
she sees the world," Matt went on, his brow fur-
rowed. "It's all a pitched battle for her, you know?
She should never have had a kid. And Jo—she's a
bloody terror with Megan."

"Which doesn't necessarily mean she'll be a terror with you," I pointed out.

"N-n-o-o . . ." Matt sounded unconvinced. "But
she's got it all worked out, Hel. She reckons I owe
her. Well, I guess I do, in a way. She wants money.
She wants support—"

"How much money?" I wish I hadn't jumped on
that, because Matt winced, and looked away.

"Coupla hundred. So far," he replied. "I told
her she ought to go to rehab, and she wants me to
pay for that. I had a word with Megan about it, but
she jumped down my throat. No help there."

"Oh, Matty." All at once I felt so sorry for him.
No wonder he'd been on edge. It sounded like a
nightmare.

It also sounded ominous. Very, very ominous. I
pictured guilt trips, ugly relapses, emotional
labyrinths. I pictured financial crises. I pictured
midnight phone calls, bedraggled waifs on the
doorstep, and frantic visits to police stations. But I
had to be careful about what I said.

"So . . . what do you want to do?" I inquired cautiously, and he took a deep breath.

"Well, first off, she's not comin' here."

"Really? But—"

"Nah." Another firm shake of the head. "Not yet. Not until I'm good and sure she's not gunna come back and strip the place when we're out, some time. It could happen."

"Oh, Matt," I said sadly. "You think so?"

"It happened to Megan. You can't be too careful. Not with junkies. I used to live with one."

"But some of them sort themselves out, don't they?"

"I guess." His tone wasn't confident. "Anyway, she's not really interested in you. Or the kids. She's interested in what she needs, and she reckons she needs me."

I could imagine. Big, gentle, genial Matt, with his rackety past and respectable job, his troubled conscience, his easy and expansive charm, his good credit rating, his newfound sense of responsibility (engendered and nurtured by two small offspring) . . . oh yes, he was a perfect father figure. Reasonably reliable but not overly uptight. Responsive but not controlling.

What more could a needy teenaged troublemaker want?

"Um . . . I think you should try to help her, Matt," I declared. "I think you're right about that."

"Yeah." He sounded resigned.

"You can't just walk away."

"No."

"The thing is, though . . ." Dear oh dear, I didn't want to come across as aggressive, cold-hearted and territorial. I could understand his position.

Nevertheless, there was a point that had to be made. "She sounds like she's going to want a piece of you, sweetie," I plowed on. "And fair enough, because she is your daughter. Only, if her mother's like she is, and Jo's got all these problems—"

"Yeah."

"—she might want a big piece, is what I'm saying."

"I know."

"If she's got a great big hole inside her that needs filling, well fine. I'd be willing to make an effort myself, as long as it *can* be filled. You know what I mean? As long as it's not one of those black-hole situations."

"Absolutely. You're absolutely right."

"Because you can't pour all your energy into a vacuum. You can't. You've got two other kids—and me. We all need our fair share. That's the bottom line, Matt. Sometimes the noisiest kid gets the most attention, and I don't want that happening here."

"Shit, no."

It suddenly occurred to me: would I have been better off if Josephine *had* been a brief, aberrant fling? As a long-lost daughter, she not only had rights—she had a lifelong and justifiable claim. The thought of what might lie ahead made me feel dismayed and exhausted. There would be a big shift, no doubt about that. An upheaval. I hadn't yet got my brain around the implications . . . the possibilities . . .

But then Matt got up, and pulled me to my feet, and wrapped his arms around me. I could feel his mouth on my hair.

"Thank God," he murmured. "Thank God for you."

"I'm sorry about the detective."

"It was my fault."

"I should have come out and asked, but I was so scared. Because of what happened to Jenny. When *she* came out and asked, her husband just walked away—"

"Oh Hel, I'd never do that. Don't you know me? Don't you know I'd never do that?"

"I guess. But it's not you, it's me. I don't know what's happened to me. I'm falling apart. All I do is snap and moan. I can't seem to get it together . . ."

"Are you kidding? Hel, you're the one who *holds* it together."

I thought about that. I thought about that as he rocked me to and fro. (God, it felt good.) I thought about the unpaid bills, the piles of dirty laundry, the unanswered letters, the shambles in the garden, the mad dashes for the train, the toy-strewn floors, the forgotten birthdays, the filthy car, the endless stream of sugar-laden bribes, and I had to disagree.

"No," I said. "That's the thing. I don't hold it together. Everything's a mess."

"No."

"Yes." I looked up at him. "I try, but I can't. In fact I shouldn't even have to. I need help, Matt. Do you know what I'm saying? I need more help."

He swallowed, and opened his mouth. Hesitated. Then he uttered a sharp sigh, and his shoulders sagged.

"Yeah," he said.

"We've got to work something out."

"I know."

"You were trying to lighten the load with Jo, and

I appreciate that. You've got a lot on your plate. You've got a full-time job. Those lousy shifts. But if you could just—just . . ." I took a deep breath, and grasped the nettle. "Baby, if you could just put your own underpants in the laundry basket, without me asking . . . well, that would mean a lot."

It was an anxious moment. I didn't know if I had overstepped the line, with Matt still reeling from the brand new burden of a long-lost daughter. In my opinion, blokes tend to think you're being petty-minded when you keep harping on about underpants and garbage bins and toilet bowls. They hate it, they really do. And after all, what had I expected when I married Matt? He had fucking tattoos, for God's sake.

But he smiled. He smiled for the first time in—oh God, in ages. Days.

"Deal," he said. "Dawn of a new era. Underpants in the basket, or they get hung on the front door."

And he gave me a rib-cracking, spine-warping hug.

So there you have it: a happy ending. *Major* bonus. *Total* relief. A testament to my own good sense in marrying Matthew, when everyone else seemed to think that I was making a big mistake. It just goes to show that you can't judge a guy by his tatoos or his missing tooth.

Let's not forget, however, that life goes on—and on, and on. Roofs leak. Toilet-training hits a snag. Long-lost daughters break up with their boyfriends, get thrown onto the street, and need a place to stay. I should have seen it coming, of course, and I was lucky—very lucky—that Josephine's domestic tribulations coincided with the complete gutting of our kitchen. We couldn't have put her up even if we'd wanted to, because the kids and I were living with my parents for a couple of weeks while Matt imposed upon his old mate Ray (who has a sofa-bed in his front room). Thank God I didn't have to put my foot down. Thank God Matt didn't have to make a choice. We were saved from that, at least, though not from the crisis that ensued. Phone calls were made, counsellors consulted, relatives appealed to. A cousin of Matt's, living in Punchbowl, nobly bowed to family pressure and allowed Josephine to occupy a spare room while Matt thrashed things out with Megan. I must say, I was impressed by the way Matt's family stepped in. Some of them—the male ones—came all the way down to Sydney for a Muzzatti problem-solving conference, which took place in our disordered living room. I was touched, I really was. Especially when I saw the way Matt's brother Ben played with Jonah, and the way all those big, bright, noisy Italian boys transformed our dingy, half-finished house into a warm, comfortable, cheery place. With the Muzzattis knocking around in it, our house assumed the smiling, well-worn air of a proper family home, with a banging screen door and nice cooking smells and everything. They do that, those boys. Like Matt, they have an *aura*. It made me realize how obsessive I've become about our house, which really isn't so bad.

It also made me realize that I ought to be making more of an effort with the Muzzatti clan. They might live far away, but that doesn't mean I should be leaving them out of my equations. Now that

Jonah's older, we can visit them sometimes. On the weekend. And it will cheer us all up, I'm sure.

As for Megan—well, to her credit, she came to the party. Megan split the cost of a bond with us. So Josephine found herself a share house, and Megan agreed to an armed truce with Matt, and the two of them cautiously agreed that, while Matt may have been something of a feckless, self-absorbed fuck-up twenty years ago, Megan had perhaps been a little unfair to him since.

But it's not as if we've all buried the hatchet. You won't see Jo and Megan cozying up to us at any relaxed, suburban barbecues in the very near future. You won't see Jo babysitting her little half-brother and half-sister, or Megan busily making coffee mug sets for my birthday. Owing to the fact that Jo's prospects still look pretty dicey, there's a lot of tension in the air. It's like living on top of an earthquake fault; you never know when the tattered shreds of Jo's stitched-together existence might suddenly blow apart. I haven't even met her yet—not in the formal sense—so I've really no idea what she's like as a person. (Matt's not much good at descriptive character sketches.) To me, she's still a kind of cipher: a fleshless family skeleton that's suddenly fallen out of the closet. And I certainly haven't told the kids about her. I don't think there's any point, until we're sure that she won't drop out of our lives as abruptly as she dropped into them. Anyway, I'm not convinced that she'd be a very good role model. I can just imagine what my mum would say, if I allowed Emily and Jonah to become infatuated with a heroin addict. (I know, don't tell me—I'm beginning to *sound* like my mum.) As a matter of fact, I haven't told my parents about Josephine yet, either. It'll confirm all their worst fears about Matthew, so I'm putting off the dreaded moment for as long as possible. There are just so many things that a person can cope with at one time, and I've got enough on my plate at the moment.

Like Miriam, for example. Miriam hasn't called me so far—I'm not really expecting her to—but she did transfer a large sum of money to her mother's current account, to ensure that poor Mrs. Coutts didn't get stuck with Miriam's mortgage payments. It was weird. Various interested parties are still trying to trace the source of that transfer, but no one's located Miriam yet. So I still receive calls from the Pacific Commercial Bank, and occasionally from the police, whenever some flummoxed investigator wants to ask a question about the contents of Miriam's case files, or something. And when that happens I get worked up all over again, because I haven't properly recovered from Miriam's about-face. I don't know if I ever will. God, it was a shock, that business. I'll never forgive her for deceiving me with such *flair;* it's made me doubt my own insight and intelligence. For all I know, she might even have poked around in my purse one day and stolen my credit card details.

Nevertheless, despite all my misgivings, I was still worrying about her for a while, there. I couldn't help it. I asked myself: Has she settled down in Brazil or Thailand or somewhere like that, to live her dream of Paris clothes and marble bathrooms? Or is she being sucked into some drug cartel vortex, some intimate hell of regret and despair, abandoned by Giles and perpetually glancing over her shoulder? It was hard to imagine the fastidious Miriam in that sort of mess, but you know me—the eternal pessimist. I fretted and fumed, in equal proportion. And then one day I had lunch with Ronnie, and my fears were laid to rest.

It was one of those typical, pre-wedding get-togethers, scheduled for the purpose of discussing bridesmaids' dresses and honeymoon plans. Veronica and I met in the usual subterranean coffee shop, sat at our usual table, and ordered our usual microwaved croissants. As we pored over fabric samples, however, I couldn't help basking in the fact that, while in many ways this meeting was similar to our last, there was at least one glaring difference. This time I wasn't eaten up with dread and suspicion. This time I could confront Ronnie's wedding with equanimity.

This time I was a happy person.

"Oh!" Ronnie exclaimed, after we had settled on the coffee-colored silk under the embroidered beige gauze, "I almost forgot! God! You'll never guess!"

"What?" I could sense a Briony story heading my way. "Don't tell me—what's she done now?"

"Who?"

"Briony!"

"Oh—well, yes, it *is* about Briony, but you'll never guess who she saw!"

"Who? Briony?"

"*Yes!*" Veronica leaned back, eyes wide, as if she wanted a good, panoramic view of my reaction. "Samantha got an e-mail from her the other day, and apparently she's dumped the Argentinian, and she's back on the yachts with some ancient American millionaire. In Spain."

"She never could stay away from yachts."

"Yes, but guess who Briony ran into, when she was in Majorca?"

I tried. "Michael Jackson?"

"Miriam Coutts!"

"What?" I gasped.

"Miriam Coutts. Briony saw her drinking on some balcony. They saw each other, as a matter of fact, but Miriam pretended not to recognize Briony. And Briony—well, she was a bit confused. She's heard about Miriam, you see. Samantha e-mailed her."

"Didn't she go to the police?"

"Who—you mean Briony? Are you kidding?" Veronica snorted into her orange juice. "As a matter of fact, Samantha wants to know who *she* should talk to about it. She asked me to ask you for a phone number. A police contact."

I hesitated. It took me a minute or so to make up my mind, because sometimes I wonder if living in close proximity to the chaos of my life finally tipped Miriam over the edge. Did she look at the culmination of all my hopes and ambitions and think: So much for the Great Australian Dream—I think I'll take the High Road, thanks very much, and bugger the consequences? I can't help feeling guilty about the fact that she took off without warning. *Without warning.* How could I have called her my friend, and failed to see what was on her mind? How could she have called *me* her friend, and deceived me so completely? There was a terrible failure, somewhere, and I'm sure I had something to do with it.

So I was reluctant to play a part in her arrest, despite the fact that I was still uncertain about her motives in reporting to me her glimpse of Matt in the Oxford Street coffee shop. On the whole, I think that she was tying up loose ends. Sorting out all the nagging problems in her life before disappearing into the wild blue yonder. She wanted me to know the truth about *something*, even if it couldn't be about her own criminal behavior.

The trouble is, I also can't help believing that she found a certain satisfaction in doing it—in screwing up my life before she totally screwed up hers. In demonstrating to me that my man was as imperfect as her own was. Schaden-freude, in other words.

"I dunno," I sighed. "I guess you should tell Samantha to contact the bank. The Pacific Commercial Bank. Ask for a guy called Cliff Staines."

Ronnie wrote this down as I sat there, feeling as if I'd finally turned a corner. It was tough, but I'd done it. I had distanced myself from Miriam and the code of concealment that she seems to have been living by. If only I had been able to grasp what was going on inside her head, as well! It disturbs me to think that I might have missed some screamingly obvious signs (through blatant self-absorption?) and that I still can't be sure if she had my interests at heart or not. It's troubling, being left up in the air.

Fortunately, I'm not up in the air when it comes to my old friend Jim McRae. Jim McRae has turned out to be a prime scuzzbag. First of all, he had the cheek to call me after Matt had asked him to please piss off. He maintained that he was checking to make sure that this decision to give him the heave-ho was genuinely my wish, or whether Matt had strong-armed me into making it. After I had

assured him, very firmly, that he was no longer required, he sent me a little note with his invoice (*A
great pleasure working with you. If you are ever again in
difficulty, do not hesitate to call*), followed by a rather
gooey Christmas card. All of which wasn't conclusive, by any means. Taken in isolation, not one of
these attempts to communicate could be described
as suspicious. Two weeks ago, however, I received a
typed letter from Jim, at my work address, alerting
me to the fact that he possessed some information
which I might care to hear, if I was willing to meet
with him at a time and place of my choosing.

This, as you may imagine, was a most unwelcome blast from the past. And before I told Matt
about it (knowing that he would absolutely hit the
roof, when he heard), I rang Stuart. Remember
Stuart? The guy who recommended Jim? I rang
him and asked if this Jim McRae bloke was really
on the level.

"What do you mean?" Stuart asked, perplexed.
"What's he done?"

"Have you had much to do with him, Stuart? Do
you know what his background is? Why did he
leave the police force, anyway?"

"*Helen.* What's he *done?*"

"He kind of . . . well, he won't leave me alone.
That's all. It's creepy."

Silence on the other end of the line.

"I don't know if he's touting for more business
or what. I don't know what to think." A pause.
"Stuart? Are you there?"

"I'm here." He sounded grumpy. "All right, I'll
see what I can do."

"Thanks, Stuart."

"I mean, *I'm* not a private detective. I can't promise anything. But I'll ask around."

So he did. And he found out that Jim McRae had left the police force after an incident involving a policewoman. "I couldn't get any details, really," Stuart apologized. "You know what they're like. But I found out he was moved off the marital infidelity stuff by his former agency, after he had an affair with a client."

"Ah."

"Sorry, Helen. Nobody told *me*, as usual. I'm *right* out of the loop."

"In other words, he's a bit of a sleaze?"

"Could be. Looks like it." Stuart snorted. "Funny you haven't run into him yourself, working where you are."

"Yeah. Well thanks, Stuart."

"I'm sorry. It wasn't my fault. If anybody ever bothered to communicate with anyone, around here, I might know what the bloody score was."

I told him it didn't matter. And it didn't, really, because all I had to do was send Jim McRae a strongly worded letter, on a piece of office stationery, warning him of the consequences that he might experience if he continued to harass me in such a manner. Harshly put, perhaps, but these things are best nipped in the bud. Especially when you know exactly where you stand. That had been my concern, you see—I'd been afraid that I was overreacting. It was *such* a relief to discover that I wasn't having paranoid delusions. About Matt, yes, but not about Jim. My instincts about Jim McRae had been spot-on.

Anyway, the letter worked. Jim McRae dropped

out of sight, instead of lurking in the background like an evil smell. What's more, my kitchen's been done. Yes! It's all finished, and it's *beautiful*! Microwave shelf, Whirlpool dishwasher, stainless steel rangehood . . . the list goes on and on. I can sit there and bask in the gleam of it, the way other people bask in the sun. The back garden still looks like a dump (or should I say a Waste Management Facility?), but the extra bedroom's great—or will be, when it's painted—and who cares that it's yet another space to strew toys all over? That's what I tell myself: who cares? Who cares that Lisa's kids had chickenpox, last week, so mine will probably come down with it too? Who cares that Lisa and Simon have just paid off their mortgage, and are talking about buying an *investment property* on the north coast? Who cares that Paul and Kerry are also talking real estate, at the moment? (I guess Kerry's current abode isn't palatial enough for her; not enough bathrooms, perhaps?) Who cares that Ronnie's decided to spend a year overseas, travelling with Phil, after they get married? Who cares that Mandy the Wholefood Mother is five months pregnant? Yes, that's right—pregnant. She's heading for her fourth child now. How does she do it? How the hell does she cope? Do you know that woman uses cloth nappies, for God's sake? Is she *trying* to make me feel inadequate? Is that her bloody purpose in life?

But I won't let it get to me. I have to count my blessings, not cry for the moon. Until recently, I wouldn't lie in bed congratulating myself because I'd got a stain out of the good, damask tablecloth. No—I'd think about Matt's curious perception deficiency when it comes to things like dirty glasses

or discarded shoes. I would think about the back
garden, and the front gate (falling off), and the
stains on the couch, and the new stove (which has
a faulty element), and the old hot water system,
and the overdue bills, and the state of my hands
(latest score: six Band-Aids), and Emily's diarrhea,
and the fact that I'm eight months overdue for a
Pap smear, and I would wonder why everyone
else's life seemed to be so much more organized,
glamorous, or aesthetically pleasing.

Since the business with Josephine, however, I've
discovered an entirely new perspective on things—
a perspective which has only been strengthened by
my twenty-year high school reunion.

I went to the reunion because Matt was safely at
my side. Without Matt, I wouldn't have gone. He's
a bit of a trophy, after all, and I was still glorying in
the fact that I had managed to keep him. I had
photographs of the kids, of course (it was an
evening event, with no kids allowed), but snap-
shots of my offspring aren't something that I like
to wave boastfully around. Don't ask me why. Other
people do, and I always cringe when they start
blathering on about accelerated learning programs and swimming certificates and computer lit-
eracy as if they're boasting about Porsches and
beach cottages and harbor views. There's something about the whole process that makes me uneasy.

Anyway, I went. I wore my Lisa Ho cream silk
chiffon (which was beginning to stretch a little at
the seams, but who cares?), my Italian slingbacks,
my mother-of-pearl evening shawl and my gold

earrings. I looked okay. Matt wore black pants, a dark grey shirt and his wedding ring, and looked devastatingly gorgeous. We hired a professional babysitter—I won't even tell you how much she cost—and drove to a hotel at Milson's Point, where we had a lot of trouble finding a place to park.

The reunion committee had hired a convention room from seven-thirty until one; there were drinks, canapés, and a modest dance floor. Everyone was given a name tag. The venue was fitted out in your typical corporate-hotel fashion, so blandly and correctly that I can hardly remember a thing about it. (Shades of veal and cinnamon? Curtains hiding the walls?) Hotel staff in black and white circulated with trays of spring rolls, marinated prawns, miniature quiches, satay sticks. Music played continually, but no one paid it the slightest attention at first.

We were all too busy talking.

School reunions are curious things. You suddenly feel young, but at the same time incredibly old. You converse with people so easily, falling back into ancient habits, yet at the same time you're aware that you have almost nothing in common with them any more. I recognized and remembered almost every schoolmate there, because I went to a girls' school; no one had gone bald or grown a beard. Nevertheless, many of them had changed enormously, in attitude as well as appearance. It was difficult to reconcile the bitch-queens of old with the dazed and worn-looking part-time physiotherapists who came up to me with tremulous smiles on their faces, saying: "Do you remember on the train, when we used to flirt with the guys

from Grammar?" Many of the former cliques and
divisions seemed to have evaporated into thin air.
Uneasy truces had somehow blossomed into noisy
expressions of delight: screams, laughs, embraces. A
teenaged stunner had metamorphosed into a
pudgy, middle-aged mother of six. A notorious flirt,
now twice divorced, had turned up unaccompanied,
white and jittery and angular, chain-smoking on
the terrace outside.

Yet the ghosts of the past still exerted some control
over the present. The awkward outcast remained,
to some degree, an awkward outcast, despite her
hugely successful career in the public service. The
noisy, joyous, opinionated leader was still the center of attention, as dishevelled and sharp-witted as
she ever was. The bony artist was now a bony graphic
designer. The childhood sweethearts had now been
married for nineteen (nineteen!) years. My old
friend Caroline was wearing the same sort of stuff
she wore on that memorable hen's night when I
first met Matt.

I had braced myself for the success stories, and
there were several. There was a woman who, in
partnership with her husband, had made a colos-
sal amount of money from computers, and now
owned a villa in the south of France as well as a
waterfront penthouse in Sydney. There was a TV
anchorwoman whose name had been linked (in
publications such as *Who Weekly*) with a well-known
Australian actor. There was a neurosurgeon. An
opera singer. A hot-shot corporate lawyer who'd
been mentioned on the news.

I'd been fairly close to the lawyer and the opera
singer at school. The lawyer, whose name is Tracy,
was then a tall, pale, sarcastic girl with a rather

sickly constitution. She's still tall and pale, but her health's a lot better, and her attitude is one of quizzical resignation. The opera singer, Sally, has the same fluting voice and bouncy hair that she once did, but she's put on weight (she has a *fabulous* cleavage) and seems a lot wilder than she was. I found myself talking to them both, and to my old mate Deborah—who was a teacher before she decided to follow in her mother's footsteps and raise three strapping children for a wealthy man on the North Shore—and I was astonished, absolutely astonished, at what they had to say.

First of all, they informed me that I hadn't changed a bit. Not one little bit. When I replied that I had gone up four dress sizes since last we met, there were groans all round. "Only four, you lucky bitch?" Sally chirruped. "I should be so lucky!"

"It's the kids that do it to you," said Deborah. "Five kilos for each kid—that's my experience."

"But I don't have kids!" Sally objected. "At least, not little ones. I've got a full-grown child helping to pay the rent, but I don't think he'd really work as a father."

"Do you want kids?" asked Tracy, standing in a poignantly familiar attitude, her long legs crossed awkwardly at the knee.

"I don't know. Probably." Sally's expression was rather blank. "But I'd want a place to put them in first. A decent home. Not to mention a reliable other half."

"Adam and I are on IVF," Tracy revealed, and there was a sympathetic murmur.

"For how long?" I inquired.

"A year. I get so sick from those hormone injections."

"Really?"

"Oh yeah. It's terrible." She went on to reveal that she'd had two miscarriages. Deborah had also suffered a miscarriage. Their lives began to take shape in my head: Tracy was all set up in a Coogee house, with a sympathetic husband and a nursery fitted out with Laura Ashley drapes and Lamaze soft toys, calmly and patiently waiting as she pursued her high-profile international cases. Sally, who was being poorly paid for her romantic roles, yearned for a decent little flat of her own, and perhaps a decent man to put in it, though she seemed to be making do with a series of very sexy, if somewhat rackety, theatrical types. Deborah had survived a nasty bout of postnatal depression after her third child (now three) was born, and couldn't praise her husband enough because he didn't let the pressures of his business overwhelm him to the detriment of his family.

"But I can't believe you're working," she said to me, shaking her head. "I can't believe you manage it. I'm in awe."

"So am I," Sally agreed.

"I've only got two kids, Deb," I pointed out. "You've got three."

"If I had *one*, it'd still be too much for me," Sally declared. "I babysit my nephews, and I'm a *wreck*. A wreck! I have to go to bed for a whole day, afterwards."

"Do you find it difficult, Helen?" Tracy asked, then smiled. "Silly question, I suppose."

"Actually, work is the least of my problems," I admitted. "Work's a piece of piss. Moving everything else around to accommodate it—that's the problem."

"I don't know how *we're* going to do it," Tracy said thoughtfully. "I'll have to keep working, because of the mortgage, but I'm not sure how."

"Where do you live, Trace?" Sally wanted to know.

"Coogee."

"Oh, Coogee." A sigh. "God, I'd love a house in Coogee." Sally glanced at Deborah. "Or Pymble. Or Dulwich Hill. Or *anywhere*. You lucky things."

"Be fair, Sal." By this time I'd learned her boyfriend's name. He was an extremely attractive stage actor who had recently bagged a small part in a big-budget movie. "You've got Ian Braidwood on tap," I said. "You can't have every-fucking-thing, you cow."

"Says you," Deborah interrupted, and turned to Tracy. "Have you seen her husband? What's his name—Matthew? He is such a hunk."

"Really?" Tracy cast about. "Where?"

"Over there."

"Oh yes. I see. Mmmm . . . nice."

She wasn't envious, however. Appreciative, but not envious. That's what I noticed about all of them. They felt that they had achieved something. I could tell that just from the tone of their voices when they talked about the important things in their lives. What's more, they felt that *I* had achieved something. They said as much. It didn't matter to Deb that I used disposable nappies instead of cloth ones; she still called me "supermum." It didn't matter to Sally that my house was dim and narrow, with a broken front gate; she still viewed it as an unattainable prize. As for Tracy, she sighed gently over my photographs of Emily and

Jonah. "They're gorgeous," she said. "You must be so proud of them."

"I am," I replied. And it's true. I know that I bitch and moan (a mother's got to vent, as Lisa would say), but I'm proud of my kids, and the fact that I raised them. They're an achievement. So is my job, and my house, and the state of my marriage. I've been lucky, of course, but I've also worked hard. I've cooked and cleaned and sewn and budgeted and planned and laundered and bluffed and negotiated my way to this vantage point. It might have been a messy road, but it's actually led somewhere. When I stop and reflect on my life as a whole, it occurs to me that I've pretty much got where I wanted to go. I guess I've just lost sight of the forest for the trees, on occasion. (Mind you, some of those trees have been pretty damned big.) All things considered, I'm not such a hopeless, disorganized slob after all. Okay, so I let the kids watch too much TV. Okay, so I can't get rid of certain stains on the couch. Well none of us is perfect, right? Except perhaps Mandy the Wholefood Mother. And even she resorted to plastic surgery, at one stage.

I was telling Deborah about this particular nose job when the music was bumped up a few notches, and colored lights began to flash. Clearly certain members of the reunion committee were determined that some of us should hit the dance floor. At first, I was annoyed at this presumption. I still wanted to tell Tracy about Ms. F. (Her case was conciliated, by the way; she received $8,000 and an apology, while Mr. L. received training in all the relevant equal employment opportunity issues.) I

also wanted to tell Sally about Miriam, because
they'd met a few times, many years ago. But Matt,
bless his heart, was in a frisky mood. Since I can
never drink much alcohol without throwing up, I
had agreed to fill the role of designated driver—
and Matt, in consequence, had taken full advan-
tage of the freely circulating drinks tray.

"Come on," he said, attacking me suddenly
from the rear. I felt his arms creep around my
waist and his chin drop onto my shoulder. "Come
on, let's dance."

"Oh, no."

"Come *on.*"

"Go on," said Deborah, with a smile.

"I'm not going out there," I protested. "No one
else is."

"Then you can be the first," said Deborah.

"No—*you* can be the first," I rejoined. "Where's
Sean? He was here a minute ago."

But Deb withdrew, laughing, into the crowd,
and Matt began to hustle me towards the empty
parquet square under the mirror ball. I'll say this
for him: he's never afraid to get up and make a
fool of himself when properly lubricated. He can't
dance for nuts, mind you. Neither of us can. He
tends to throw his arms about dementedly while
bouncing on the spot with bent knees. My style is
much more restrained—a sort of muted twist—unless he takes it into his head to spin me a bit.
That's what he did as "Let's Do the Time Warp
Again" blasted out of the nearby sound system.
Chugga-CHUGGA-chugga-CHUGGA-chugga went the
music. Bounce-bounce-BOUNCE went Matt. Then
he seized both my hands, pumping my arms back

and forth like someone playing choo-choo trains, before dropping one of them and using the other as a sort of pivot to whirl me around and around as if I was a figure skater.

This move normally has the effect of making me so dizzy that I crash into his chest—a result that he always appreciates.

"Christ," he said. The rough texture of Band-Aid had finally communicated itself, via the nerve endings in his fingers, through the alcoholic fog enveloping his brain. "What the hell have you done to your hand *now?*"

Still reeling a little, I gazed down at my right forefinger and thumb.

"I burned myself on the pizza pan," I replied.

"God help us."

"The other's a paper cut. And that's just where my skin's cracking up again."

"Poor baby."

"Battle scars," I declared. "They're battle scars. Nothing to be ashamed of."

"No, no. 'Course not."

"They're like stretch marks, aren't they? They're badges of honor."

"Absolutely."

"You admire them, don't you? You look at them and think: This is My Woman. She has shed blood for me."

"That's right."

Which is total crap, needless to say, but what would life be without these little illusions?

Then a new song started.

Matt immediately launched into a really tragic piece of choreography which was heavily reliant on pelvis and elbows. His gap-toothed grin was a challenge. He was practically daring me to leave the floor.

I didn't, you know. I stayed. I put up with his highly individual interpretation of the moonwalk, and was rewarded with one of his nice, smoochy variations on the two-step when he got too tired to do anything else.

Swings and roundabouts, I suppose. Give and take. A negotiated settlement.

You just have to get used to it when you're in for the long haul.